EASY TO KILL

WILLIAM STRICKLIN

CITIOFBOOKS, INC.
3736 Eubank NE Suite A1
Albuquerque, NM 87111-3579
www.citiofbooks.com
Hotline: 1 (877) 389-2759
Fax: 1 (505) 930-7244

Ordering Information:
Quantity sales. Special discounts are available on quantity purchases by corporations, associations, and others. For details, contact the publisher at the address above.

Printed in the United States of America.
ISBN-13:   Paperback   979-8-90124-112-7
                 eBook   979-8-90124-114-1
                 Hardback   979-8-90124-113-4

Library of Congress Control Number:

THE VANDERBILT HOME ON FIFTH AVENUE

To society snobs of the day, such as the Astor family, the Vanderbilts were still "new money". When an infamous "list of 400" was circulated by Mrs. Astor (aided by social arbiter Ward McAllister), identifying the people who could be counted as members of New York's "Fashionable Society" amongst the vastly increasing rich families of the Gilded Age, the Vanderbilts were deliberately left off the list. Mrs. Astor did not receive an invitation to the Vanderbilt ball. Nor did her daughter Carrie Astor, who had been excitedly preparing her costume and dancing skills for weeks. When all their friends received invitations except for them, Mrs. Astor was going to have to do some groveling. Festivities kicked off at the stroke of ten, as some 1200 New York socialites arrived in carriages. Police reportedly had to hold back gathering crowds outside the home to witness the party of the century unfolding and catch a glimpse of society's "It girls" in their outrageous costumes.

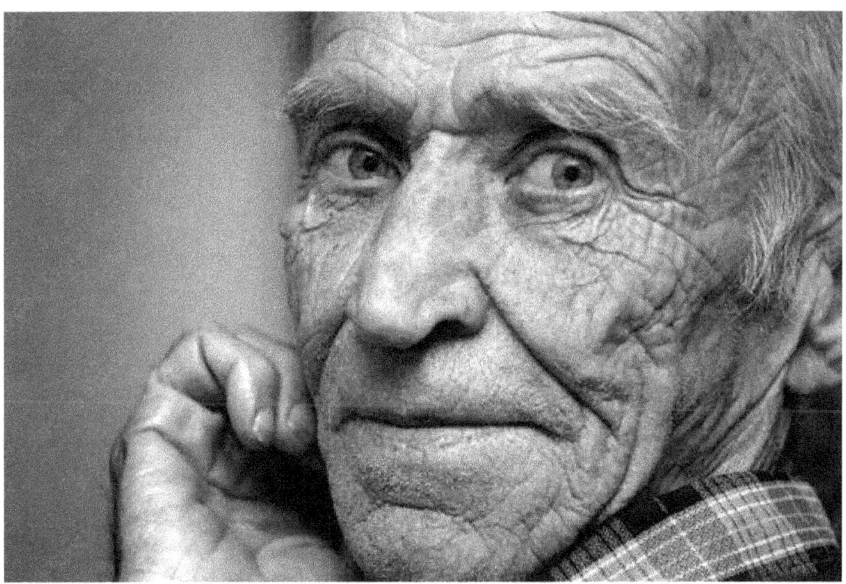

Our heroine, Mary Eliska Girl Detective, is a well-to-do young lady whose grandfather Albert Stricklin is a newspaper publisher in Piedmont, California, who supports her as a reporter for his paper The Piedmont Star, aware that she likes to dabble in detective work. Flying in her airplane and driving her jalopy "Calamity Jane", Mary Eliska joins with her three best friends: nieces Jacqueline Gray ("Jax") and Marlow Ray, and nephew news photographer Liam McAdam to solve the occasional case out of curiosity and sometimes to earn money separately from her family. Mary Eliska Girl Detective gives life to my daughter born sixty-two years ago, March 10, 1963, whose life was cut short in Clifton Springs New York September 12, 1963. She has charming manners, oscillates between tomboyishness and a feminine ideal. She knows law and manifests moral righteousness. Often she wears enviable dresses. Mary Eliska's detective stories and unsolved mysteries I have re-written from the public domain tales by Carolyn Keene (always a pseudonym), Anna Katharine Green, Mildred Augustine Wirt Benson, Frances

Crane, Hulburt Footner and anonymous writers about Penny Parker, Mary Louise, Nancy Drew, and others. There's evil lurking among the wealthy people in their mansions. Mary Eliska Girl Detective gets on the trail of a lad named Nick, a wellborn gent who is pretty slick at black-mailing people who're old and sick. If they don't come through, they pop off quick. Well, anyway, after being captured by the arch villain and his social registrite accomplices, Mary Eliska Girl Detective and her secretary Jax escape with the help of two gentlemanly gunmen, take refuge with genial recluse, Betsy Pryor, and set a trap for Nick. Mary Eliska Girl Detective to the rescue!

CONTENTS

ꝹEDICATED TO MY OHANA

This publication is dedicated to the ohana of the writer William A. Stricklin. As a student of the Hawaiian language in the 1960's the writer learned that "ohana" means family, and it extends beyond blood relatives to include friends, neighbors, and the community. The concept emphasizes a sense of belonging and mutual support, where "family means nobody gets left behind". It also has a literal meaning connected to the taro plant, referring to the shoot ('oha) which is cut and replanted to grow new plants, symbolizing regeneration and new generations.

- Family: This is the most common translation, and it includes the nuclear and extended family, close friends, and community.
- Belonging and support: All members of the 'ohana are connected through mutual care and support, regardless of blood ties.
- The taro plant: The word "ohana" comes from the Hawaiian word for the taro plant. The 'oha is a shoot from the taro plant that is cut off and planted to grow a new plant. The suffix "-ana" is associated with regeneration. Sh
- A "hanai" son or daughter refers to a child who was brought up by a person or family who is not their biological parent through the Hawaiian traditional practice of informal adoption or fostering. The word hanai itself means to raise or adopt with a bond of love that is considered as strong as a biological connection.

The Writer's ohana includes, most prominently: My dear wife Dr. Rebecca Robbins, Born August 8, 1955. She is my best friend, my confidante, my muse and my dearest love. My wife Rebecca's brother Dr. William Calvin Robbins MD Born January 7, 1957 his wife Susan Robbins Born August 16, 1955; and Rebecca's sister Nyla Robbins. My brother Robert Curtis Stricklin Born April 18, 1943. (My brother's wife is Elizabeth)

My daughter Dr. Martha Christine Stricklin Heppard M.D., Born

October 25, 1960

My hanai son Sean Hall, Born January 23, 1966; his son Blaise, Born December 20, 2009.

My son John Robert Stricklin, Born February 18,1966. His wife

Name: Deanna Louise Hoffinger Born October 8, 1971

Ten living grandchildren:

Name: Ka'io Martin, my daughter Sarah's daughter, Born June 21, 1976.

Name: Aaron Shegrud, my son Bill's son, Born: December 4, 1981,

Name: James Freudenberg-Pu, born September 17, 1988

Name: John William Stricklin-Pu, Born December 18, 1987

Fiancé Name: Victoria Katherine Rustom DOB March 3, 1992

Name: Patrick Lee Heppard, Born March 15, 1990

Name: Matthew Glenn Heppard, Born March 15, 1990

Name: Daniel Heppard, Born February 7, 1993. Married to

Margaret Katherine "Maggie" Heppard Born May 26, 1993

Name: Marlow Ray Stricklin, Born June 9, 2008.

Name: Jacqueline "Jax" Gray Stricklin, Born: October 17, 2009

Name: Liam McAdams Stricklin, Born: October 17, 2009

Twelve living great grandchildren:

Name: Kekoa Hanapi (Kamuela's son Born February 19, 2006

with wife Mapuana Hanapi Dudoit a respected Kumu (teacher)

who is dedicated to preserving and teaching the Hawaiian culture)

Name: Kamuela Hanapi: May 2, 2025, to girlfriend:

Noelani Piliati-Yagin

Name: Christine Hanapi (Kamuela's daughter Born March 28, 2007

with wife Mapuana Hanapi Dudoit

Name: Kiana Martin, Born August 9, 1994

(Ka'io's daughter who became the mother of Kamawaokele on June 20,

2022)

Name: Kaimana (Ka'io's son) Born December 28, 2002.

Name: Melanie Kreutz (Ka'io's daughter) Born September 25, 2007.

Name: Varun Heppard (Patrick and Aarathi's son) Born September 2, 2025.

Name: Landon Heppard (Matthew's son) born October 13, 2024.

Name: Kaai Martin (Ka'io's son) Born April 6, 2009.

Name: Rell Huali Grace Freudenberg-Pu, born December 11 2013

(daughter of James and Mikyla)

Name: Faith Freudenberg-Pu, born August 24 2018 (daughter of James and Mikyla)

Name: Teava Matthew Freudenberg-pu, born July 28, 2023.

(son of James Freudenberg-Pu and his wife Moi from Tahiti)

Name: Nāulu Emma Freudenberg-pu, born April 19, 2025.

(daughter of James and wife Moi from Tahiti)

Names: Two living hanai great granddaughters: Tatiana and Kaimi

Two living great great grandsons:

Name: Kamawaokele (The eyes of the rainforest) Born June 20, 2022

to my grandson Ka'io Martin's daughter Kiana Martin

Name: Kamuela Hanapi, Born: May 2, 2025, recently a

(Kekoa Hanapi and Girlfriend: Noelani Piliati-Yagin)

Extended family members in my ohana include

My co-workers, neighbors and close friends in my ohana include

Name: Morris L. Angell Born September 1945 my Federal co-worker

Name: Anju Shreshtha Born October 1978 my Federal co-worker

Name: Margaret A. "Margy" Silver Born June 1947 our neighbor

Name: Virgil L. Silver Born January 20, 1947, our neighbor

Name: Jeffrey A. Cambra Born 1951, immediate next-door neighbor

PROLOGUE

Like they do at prom, the guests of the 1883 Vanderbilt fancy dress ball each had the opportunity to have their photo taken at the event of the year, or perhaps the century. All of New York's elite society turned up at the Fifth Avenue mega mansion dressed as pirates, goths, animals, gypsies and other inventive and slightly ridiculous get-ups.

Invites had been hand delivered by uniformed servants and the press had been invited beforehand to take exclusive photographs of the decor and build the hype. The Vanderbilts were trying to flex their muscles for New York's high society, particularly Mrs. Alva Vanderbilt, the new ambitious wife of William Kissam Vanderbilt, grandson to Cornelius "Commodore" Vanderbilt, the shipping and railroad mogul who had struck it rich after the Industrial Revolution.

As the gossip stories go, Alva (pictured above) claimed that since Mrs. Astor had never called on the Vanderbilt home on Fifth Avenue to introduce herself formally, she had no address to send an invitation. Mrs. Astor begrudgingly dropped in on the French chateau style mansion that overshadowed all the other luxurious homes on the street and left her visiting card. The following day, the Astor's received their invitation.

N. Sarony
752 BROADWAY N.Y.

707 BROADWAY, N.Y.

Alva Vanderbilt's sister in-law (who is pictured above) showed up as a hornet, the earliest version you'll find of the common kid's bumble bee costume today.

Another guest, Miss Strong fondly known amongst her circle as "Puss", came with a dead stuffed cat on her head and cat tails sewn onto her skirt. Mrs. Cornelius Vanderbilt's dress lit up from a battery-powered torch hidden under her skirt, representing an "Electric Light".

Adebaucherous party it surely was, costing an estimated $6 million in today's money, with roughly a million of that being spent on the champagne alone. It might be worth noting here that in 1973, the Vanderbilts held a family reunion. Not one of the 120 decedents were millionaires at the time. Dinner for the Vanderbilt ball wasn't served until 2am by an army of servants and dancing continued until sunrise.

CHAPTER ONE

THE MILLIONAIRE RACKET

Mary Eliska Girl Detective drove her own car "Calamity Jane" up to Newport. According to instructions, we left it standing at the front door of the Van Tassel mansion, and made our way by a path around to the rear. This was to avoid coming in contact with the house servants.

In the darkness under the side windows our way was suddenly blocked by an armed guard. The unexpectedness of his appearance almost fetched a scream out of me. In a husky whisper he demanded to know our business. Mary Eliska Girl Detective gave him the password that had been furnished us—"Redwood"—and he drew back. I had the feeling that other men were watching us from the shadows of the shrubbery. Who would want to be rich, I thought, if you had to live in a state of siege like this.

At the back of the mansion, looking over the cliffs toward the sea, there was a wide outdoors room that would have been called a porch in any ordinary house, but at the Van Tassels', we learned, it was dignified with the name of terrace. It was glassed in all around for bad weather, and though now the June night was warm and sweet smelling, all the sliding panels were closed. Here Mr. and Mrs. Van Tassel had arranged to be waiting for us.

I glanced with strong curiosity at the bearers of so famous a name. Neither was very impressive.

Howard Van Tassel was an old man suffering from some form of heart trouble that forced him to keep his mouth always hanging open and to breathe with difficulty. You were always uneasy in his presence because he seemed likely to have a stroke at any moment. His wife had been a beauty. Her faded hair was tricked out in the puffs and whorls and kinks that went out of fashion years ago, and her faded cheeks were bright with rouge. They showed little of the dignity you would expect from people of their position.

But nobody appears to advantage, of course, when he is frightened. Both old people were trembling. Indeed, the whole place seemed to be held in a spell of fear. It infected me in spite of myself, and I kept glancing around at the glass sides of the terrace, half expecting to see a murderous face peering in from the dark.

Of the two, Mrs. Van Tassel had herself better in hand. "You are Mary Eliska Girl Detective, the detective?" she said.

"I prefer to call myself psychologist," said Mary Eliska Girl Detective, with a smile; "but it doesn't matter."

Mrs. Van Tassel stared rudely. She was a stupid sort of woman in all her finery. "And who is this person?" she asked, with a nod in my direction.

"My secretary, Miss Jacqueline "Jax" Gray."

"Can't she wait in the car?"

"She is my principal assistant," said Mary Eliska Girl Detective, politely and firmly. "I depend on her for everything."

Nothing further was said about bouncing me.

Mrs. Van Tassel was so frightened and suspicious, it was difficult to bring her to the point. Several times she seemed about to send us away without telling us why we had been summoned. Finally she blurted out, "My husband has been getting letters demanding large sums of money."

"For how long?" asked Mary Eliska Girl Detective, coolly. By her calm air she sought to put them at their ease.

"The first one came last summer. It asked for twenty five thousand dollars. During the fall and winter there were two more, each demanding forty thousand...."

"These sums were paid?"

Mrs. Van Tassel nodded. "And now a fourth letter has come, demanding fifty thousand dollars." Her voice scaled up hysterically. "This can't go on!"

"Certainly not," said Mary Eliska Girl Detective. "You never should have paid anything!"

"I never wanted to pay," said Mrs. Van Tassel, with a glance at her husband, "but Mr. Van Tassel was afraid."

That shocking old wreck suddenly roused himself. "I have a bad heart condition," he said, whiningly. "My doctor told me a shock would kill me. I would rather pay than live in terror of my life!"

"What good does it do you?" snapped his wife. "You live in terror, anyhow. And the demands are constantly increasing. It's got to stop somewhere." She turned to Mary Eliska Girl Detective. "We are not as rich as people suppose. And our expenses are enormous."

"Did these letters come through the mail?" asked Mary Eliska Girl Detective.

A shudder went through Mrs. Van Tassel's frame, causing her earrings to tinkle. "No," she said, very low. "That is the worst of it. Somehow, a way was found to introduce them into the house. In each case Mr. Van Tassel found them on the desk in his study....Oh, it is awful, not to feel safe even in your own house!"

"Surely," said Mary Eliska Girl Detective, sympathetically. "Have you saved the letters?"

"Only the last one."

"May I see it?"

Mrs. Van Tassel glanced around her with haggard eyes. "I....I am afraid," she stammered. "How do we know who may be spying on us from the outside?"

"There are guards stationed in the grounds," muttered the old man.

"Where did you obtain these guards?" asked Mary Eliska Girl Detective.

"From the —— Detective Agency."

Not wishing to increase their fears, Mary Eliska Girl Detective did not tell them that this protection was little better than none. Such men are nearly always to be bought. I knew it, and it did not make me feel any more comfortable. We were making entirely too good a target sitting there in the brightly lighted terrace.

"Let us go inside," suggested Mary Eliska Girl Detective.

"The servants...." objected the old man.

"We can go in through the French windows," said his wife, "and lock the room door."

The upshot was that we adjourned to a room opening on the terrace that they called the breakfast room. After carefully pulling the curtains shut and locking the door, Mrs. Van Tassel produced a letter from the little bag she carried. It was a brief typewritten letter on a single plain white sheet. Mary Eliska Girl Detective read it, and afterward examined it through the magnifying glass she always carries.

She finally said: "From the style of the type I see that this was written on an Underwood. It was written by one who was not expert in using the typewriter, because the keys were struck with varying degrees of force. The machine has not been used very much, and the ribbon was a new one."

She handed the letter to me to read. It began abruptly, without any form of address:

'Get fifty thousand dollars from the bank in bills: 100s, 50s, 20s, no higher, and keep it in the house until I send you instructions how to hand it to me. If my instructions are not followed out to the letter, or if you try to entrap me in any way, you will suffer the same fate that lately overtook your old friend Kip Havemeyer. He was said to have died of heart disease, but nobody saw him die. When I wish to strike, no locks can keep me out of your house or guards keep me from your side. Remember, old men are easy to kill!'

This was signed, "The Leveler."

I handed the letter back.

"Written by a man accustomed to the forms of good speech," said Mary Eliska Girl Detective. Mr. and Mrs. Van Tassel exchanged a startled glance. "How did Mr. Havemeyer die?"

"He was found dead in his garden," muttered Mr. Van Tassel. "They said heart disease...but he had a terrible look on his face."

"You are prepared then, to hand over the money when a demand is made for it?"

"I wouldn't," said Mrs. Van Tassel, with an ugly look at her husband.

"Certainly I am!" cried the old man, shrilly. "I'm not going to be shocked to death like Havemeyer!"

"If you're going to pay, what can I do for you?" asked Mary Eliska Girl Detective.

"We want you to undertake a quiet investigation," said Mrs. Van Tassel. "Find out where the money goes. It can be marked. Get evidence against this scoundrel so that we can confront him with it, and make him stop!"

"Confront him with it?" echoed Mary Eliska Girl Detective, struck by this phrase.

Mrs. Van Tassel said nothing.

After a little thought my employer said: "I am willing to take the case. But I ought to point out to you that if anything happens, I should not be in as good a position to protect you as the police. The men you have now are worthless. I advise you to consult the police."

Both became wildly agitated. "No! No! No!" they cried together.

"Why not?" asked Mary Eliska Girl Detective.

"Never mind," said Mrs. Van Tassel sharply. "You have your instructions."

Nobody can talk to Mary Eliska Girl Detective like that and get away with it. Her smile was like polished glassware. "I cannot serve you," she said, "unless you furnish me with complete information."

"We have no information."

"You suspect somebody."

"No! No!" they muttered, wretchedly. "It is too terrible!"

"Then you had better let me retire," said Mary Eliska Girl Detective, gently. She was sorry for the old pair, with all their wealth.

Mrs. Van Tassel weakened. "Why not tell her?" she said to her husband. "It's her business to keep her mouth shut."

"All right," he mumbled, turning away his head.

Mrs. Van Tassel put her handkerchief to her lips.

I wondered what was coming. "We have no evidence," she stammered, "but...but we suspect that Nicholas Van Tassel, my husband's nephew, is behind it all."

Mary Eliska Girl Detective was surprised into an exclamation. "Good God! Nicholas Van Tassel! I thought he was the head of the family and the richest of you all.'"

Mrs. Van Tassel shook her head. "He was left a pauper," she murmured.

Some moments passed before we could get a coherent explanation out of her. She finally said: "It is forgotten now, but my husband's father, who was the fourth Nicholas Van Tassel, cut off his eldest son, Nicholas, with six million dollars, and left the bulk of his fortune to my husband. His eldest son had displeased him by marrying an actress. This one, the fifth Nicholas, caused the story to be circulated that his brothers had equalized their shares with him. This was untrue, but it did not seem worthwhile to deny it. Later it was reported that he had made a great fortune in Wall Street, but this was also untrue. As a matter of fact, he spent every cent he possessed and committed suicide."

"Suicide?" said Mary Eliska Girl Detective. "I never heard of it."

"It was supposed to be an accident. When his money was all spent, he and his wife drove their car over a cliff in Switzerland. Nobody outside the family knows it, but the present Nicholas, the sixth of the name, was left nothing but two big houses that were mortgaged to the limit....Yet he is reputed to live at the rate of a million a year. It must come from somewhere."

"Quite! It must come from somewhere!" murmured Mary Eliska Girl Detective.

There was a silence. My employer turned her brilliant eyes on me. Good God! What a case! her expression said. As for me, I was staggered by the prospect.

As we were leaving, Mrs. Van Tassel said, patronizingly—even in her distress of mind she could not overcome the habit of arrogance: "Of course expense is no object. We think you should live here in Newport incognito, and conduct a quiet investigation."

Mary Eliska Girl Detective declined to be patronized. "Sorry," she said, smiling, "but that would be impossible. I have a hundred acquaintances here in Newport. I should be recognized the first time I went out....My arrival must be publicly announced. I can let it be supposed that I am here for the social season. My friend, Mrs. Lysaght, will sponsor me."

Mrs. Van Tassel ran up her aristocratic eyebrows at the notion of a mere detective (as she thought) crashing the exclusive gates of Newport. She had a lot to learn. She was not accustomed to having her wishes opposed, and for a moment the two pairs of eyes contended; Mrs. Van Tassel's haughty, Mary Eliska Girl Detective's smiling. It was the haughty eyes that bolted first.

"Oh, very well," said Mrs. Van Tassel, with assumed indifference. "You may communicate with me here by telephone at any time. I will see to it that there can be no listening in at this end."

As Mary Eliska Girl Detective was starting her car, the guard who had stopped us on the way in showed his brutal face at the window beside her.

"Say, sister," he said, with crude insolence, "if you enjoy life, you better steer clear of this burg, see? I happen to know it's damned unhealthy for you."

We drove away with the sound of his ugly chuckle in our ears. Mary Eliska Girl Detective's answer to the threat was to stop in at the central telephone office and summon six of her best men to Newport; the two Criders, Stephens, Morrison, Scarfe, and Benny Abell. We then left a social note at the office of the local newspaper stating that Mary Eliska was the guest of Mrs. George Lysaght at her cottage on Catherine Street, and drove on to that lady's.

My brain was still spinning with what had happened. "It is scarcely worth a hundred and fifty thousand a year to keep that old hulk alive," I remarked.

"Apparently Mrs. Van Tassel agrees with you," replied Mary Eliska Girl Detective, dryly, "but he does not."

CHAPTER TWO

THE HERO OF NEWPORT

There were half a dozen separate conversations going on around Mrs. Lysaght's luncheon table—the usual things that women talk about—clothes, tennis scores, the new play at the Casino, the latest divorce—when Mrs. Beekman Alston was heard to say:

"Nick Van Tassel told me so himself."

The name seemed to lay a spell on all the women present. They stopped talking, and every eye was turned toward the speaker. I looked, too, you may be sure, and pricked up my ears for what might be coming. Mrs. Alston, a very pretty woman, had to submit to a kind of cross examination.

"Where did you see Nick'?"

"At the Chowder Club."

"Was he alone?"

"He was at that moment."

"Do you mean to say he danced with you?"

"We sat out one of the encores."

This was received with open expressions of disbelief by Mrs. Alston's dear friends.

"You're only jealous!" she retorted.

The conversation became general and excited, and within a few minutes I had received more information about the famous Nick than I could possibly remember without a notebook. He could win the men's singles in a walk over if he would stop drinking. He had contributed fifty thousand to the building of the new cup defender. He could always be depended to put his hand in his pocket for sport.

He had bought a trimotored Sikorski seating six.

He had brought a girl nobody knew to the Goadby dance. Mrs. Goadby was furious, but what could she do? Nobody dared say anything to Nick.

A good deal of it I didn't get, because the places and the people referred to were strange to me, but it was clear that their Nick was a very high flyer indeed. There was a lot of talk about a place called "the Dump," which I gathered must be Nick's own house. It was evident that there were gay doings there, and it was equally evident that any woman present would have given her best earrings for an invitation.

Mary Eliska Girl Detective finally cut in with a smile. "What is there about this young man that excites you all so much?"

"Don't you know Nick Van Tassel?" they cried.

"Well, of course I know who he is. Nick the son of Nick, the son of Nick, and so on back almost to the Flood. There has always been a Nick Van Tassel at Newport. I should think it would be an old story."

"There never was a Nick like this Nick," said Evelyn Suydam. "He's unique!"

"How?" asked Mary Eliska Girl Detective. "What is the secret of his fascination for the ladies?"

"The men are just as bad," retorted Evelyn. "Haven't you noticed how they're all wearing the collars of their coats turned up, and their hats bashed in in funny ways? Nick started it because he doesn't give a darn how he looks, and now they're all doing it. If Nick came down Bellevue Avenue walking on his hands, they'd all be following suit the next day."

Nick Van Tassel

"Is he handsome?" asked Mary Eliska Girl Detective.

They went into a huddle over this. The final verdict was, "No, not exactly handsome."

"Clever?"

This was received with a laugh which spoke for itself.

"Ardent?"

"No, not ardent," they admitted with sighs. "Cool as headcheese" one girl said, raising a laugh. "Hardboiled," said another.

"Then what is it?"

"It isn't anything in particular," said Evelyn helplessly. She was a little person, blonde, with a smart tongue and over size, wistful blue eyes. "It's just because he's Nick."

There was a handsome tall girl called Ann Livingston sitting next me, and she said, with a gleam in her dark eyes: "I'll tell you the secret. Nick Van Tassel grins and does just what he damn pleases always. And Newport can take it or leave it."

"And Newport takes it?" said Mary Eliska Girl Detective.

"Of course!"

After the ladies had gone, Mrs. Lysaght, Mary Eliska Girl Detective, and I settled ourselves for a comfortable gossip in our hostess's sitting room on the second floor. You couldn't possibly find anybody better equipped than Mrs. Lysaght to give you the lowdown on Newport. So secure was her position, that when she was left a widow with very little money, she was able to go into business without losing caste.

She was an interior decorator. She had no shop, but merely "consulted" with her clients, and collected fees from both sides.

"I must meet Nick Van Tassel," said Mary Eliska Girl Detective.

Mrs. Lysaght threw up her hands. She is an ample woman, clever and good natured. "My dear, I might as well ask the Prince of Wales to dinner!"

"Surely he would come here."

Mrs. Lysaght, since she has been on her own, has acquired such a reputation for doing the smart and unusual that invitations to her little house are greatly prized. Her own circle is considered one of the most inner in Newport. But she shook her head.

"He wouldn't come," she said. "He won't go anywhere unless the fancy happens to take him. He will tell you so to your face. He's the rudest young man of them all...and the most attractive."

"Mercy!" murmured Mary Eliska Girl Detective, lazily. "We must have him over."

"He's a strange person," Mrs. Lysaght went on.

"Nobody can understand how the respectable run-of-the-mine Van Tassels happened to produce such a one. Van Tassels are noted for their dullness. That's how they've kept their money so long. But Nick...."

She was interrupted by the entrance of the parlor maid, who said, "Mr. Nicholas Van Tassel is calling, madam."

"Well!" drawled Mary Eliska Girl Detective. "Here's a miracle!" But she had a good idea what had brought him, and so had I.

Mrs. Lysaght was stunned for a moment. After thinking it over, she said: "He must have come to see you, Mary Eliska Girl Detective. You are a famous woman, my dear, and your arrival was chronicled in the morning paper. Even the young eagle stoops to give you the once over."

"Let's have him up," said Mary Eliska Girl Detective.

When I heard the heavier tread on the stairs my heart began to beat fast. If what we had heard was true, this was one of the most remarkable criminals of modern times.

Well, I saw a tall, energetic young man with miscellaneous American features, not handsome, it is true, but with an electric quality about him that instantly made you sit up and take notice. He had a bold nose and a compelling glance that caused you to feel a little helpless when it was turned on you. I learned later that he affected most women in the same way. He subdued them in spite of themselves.

"Hello, Leonie!" he said, offhand, and marched up to my employer without waiting for an introduction. "You must be Mary Eliska," he said, with a mixture of boldness and deference that was very flattering. "It's great to meet you. I have followed all your cases. It isn't often that anybody like you comes to roost in the Newport hennery."

"Well!" said Mrs. Lysaght.

"Oh, I wasn't including you, Leonie," he said, with his impudent grin. "You don't fly with these birds; you prey on them!"

Like you! I thought.

As a quite insignificant person he was prepared to overlook me entirely, but Mary Eliska Girl Detective made him acknowledge an introduction. He made a perfunctory bow, and immediately turned away. I should have liked to slap his face, but if I had I should undoubtedly have burst into tears. That was what he did to you.

Apparently he was completely outspoken. Such a person always creates havoc in company. I say apparently because I never doubted but that there were many secrets hidden behind his hard black eyes. He made no bones of the fact that he had come to see my employer, and he devoted himself exclusively to her. Mrs. Lysaght and I had to be content with an occasional half cynical, half flattering remark flung to us like a bone to a dog. Mrs. Lysaght was no better than the other women; she almost fawned on him. As for me, I sat silently fuming, but I had a sinking feeling that if he ever held up a finger to me I should have to go.

"How long are you going to stay?" he asked.

"As long as Leonie will have me."

"Whatever brought you to Newport?"

"Can't I have my little fling?"

"What can a woman like you, who does things, expect to get out of this one ring circus?"

"I'm on my vacation."

"I don't believe it," he said, with his attractive grin. "I'll bet you're after some gilt edged crook that's operating among us without our knowing it."

"Why, of course I am.'" said Mary Eliska Girl Detective, facing him out with a smile.

"Gosh! I wish you'd let me in on it! Don't you need a brisk young operative with a college education'? I'd like to do something for my country, but nobody will give me a chance."

"Well, I'll think it over."

"I may not have much brains, but I know Newport like a book. Forward and backward. If your man is here I'll ferret him out."

This dangerous fencing made me a little breathless. Mrs. Lysaght knew nothing.

"When Leonie puts you out, come and stay at my place," he went on.

"It wouldn't be proper."

"I have a house on Ochre Point that you could have to yourself. I don't use it."

"Why don't you rent it?"

"Well, 'Sans Souci' has never been rented, you see. Newport wouldn't like the idea....Are you fond of flying?"

"I adore it."

"I have a little Moth that can do better than two hundred."

"Half of that would satisfy me."

He stayed for nearly an hour, which I understood as an unprecedented thing. He made believe to fall hard for Mary Eliska Girl Detective. Or perhaps there was something in it. I never knew. Mrs. Lysaght said she had never seen him so struck by anybody.

When he arose to go he said: "Will you and Leonie dine at the Dump tonight? We'll dance afterward, or what you will."

"The Dump?" said Mary Eliska Girl Detective, elevating her eyebrows.

"My farm on the Sakonnet River. Oh, it's got a perfectly good name; Omega Farm—because nothing goes any farther. But Dump suits my style better."

Mary Eliska Girl Detective looked at Mrs. Lysaght. "Of course we'll come," said the latter, highly gratified.

"If I may bring Miss Jacqueline "Jax" Gray," said Mary Eliska Girl

Detective.

"Sure!" he said, without looking at me. "Delighted!...Shall I send a car for you?"

"Thanks, I have my car."

As soon as Mary Eliska Girl Detective and I were alone together my pent up feelings broke out. "I won't go!" I cried, with the tears springing to my eyes. "That young man is unbearable! I don't care how many Van Tassels he's got to his name. Every time he looks at you it's an insult!"

Mary Eliska Girl Detective smiled at me in a way that smoothed my ruffled temper. "Oh, Bella, what do you care, my dear? He's just an interesting specimen for our museum."

"If he's the man we've got to run down, how can we accept his hospitality?" I objected.

"If he's the man, he knows we're after him," said Mary Eliska Girl Detective, serenely. "Because we were followed last night. If he dares us to come to dinner—well, that lets us out, doesn't it?"

"Do I have to go?"

"I may need you tonight, my dear."

CHAPTER THREE

THE DUMP

Dinner at the Dump was a showy affair. About thirty people sat down at the table, and many more came in afterward. Mary Eliska Girl Detective had the seat of honor. It was such a meal as one might dream about. I was soon informed that Nick Van Tassel employed a twenty five thousand a year chef, and that he had a cellar of vintage wines and an acre or so of greenhouses in orchids. All this represented the fastidious and blue blooded side of Nick.

It was an astonishing house. We gathered in a royal salon filled with priceless Louis XIV furnishings, and proceeded down a long corridor across the front to a superb dining room paneled in English oak and hung with rare sporting prints. After this, imagine the shock when I was introduced later to a frontier dance hall of the days of '49. This room represented Nick the rough neck.

Except for the corridor I have spoken of, it occupied the whole of the central block of the house, a wide, low room lined with rough logs in which little crooked windows had been set. There was a bar at one end, and a rude stage at the other, with a gaudy painted curtain and a row of footlights behind leaning tin reflectors. It all made a piquant background for the elegant company of Nick's guests.

Not that all the company was elegant. The best looking and most attractive of the sporting element mixed with the guests; jockeys, airplane mechanics, vaudeville performers, and young pugilists. I saw the aristocratic Mrs. Welch Goadby talking to a horse trainer in a fawn colored topcoat. The smartest people in Newport angled for invitations to the Dump because they thought they saw life there.

Nick Van Tassel naturally was the head and front of the show. He looked princely in evening clothes.

He sat at our table, scornful and good humored. It made me savage every time I looked at him. I could feel my finger nails growing. I wished that I were beautiful so that I could put him in his place.

There was a black face jazz band all rigged out like old time minstrels in striped satin suits and wing collars with points sticking out beyond their ears. Their music was as smooth as egg nog. At intervals girls came out on the stage dressed like soubrettes of the period, and sang exaggerated sentimental songs. The audience guyed them, but they didn't mind. It was part of the comedy. A make believe sheriff acted as master of ceremonies—an immensely tall man with a broad brimmed hat and a pair of six shooters at his waist.

"Childish, isn't it?" drawled Nick to Mary Eliska Girl Detective; "but it seems to amuse them."

And makes an effective blind for your real business, I thought.

"A little too realistic," murmured Mary Eliska Girl Detective, glancing at the guns.

"Property guns," said Nick. "Wooden."

I wondered.

Some friends of Mrs. Lysaght's presently joined us, and Nick drifted away. I watched him moving among the tables with his insolent smile. Everybody made room for him, but he passed on with a wisecrack. He was never at a loss. After a somewhat aimless course around, he went through the door. After a moment or two the tall, handsome Ann Livingston followed him out, and I wondered if this had any significance. At the dinner table they had seemed like good pals, ragging each other unmercifully.

At this moment I happened to catch sight of the face of Evelyn Suydam, the charming little blonde I had met at Mrs. Lysaght's. She was at the next table but one, and I had picked her out as one of the gayest of the gay. But now for a second I surprised her big blue eyes fixed on the door with a desperate look. I pitied her. I could wish no worse fate to a woman than to fall in love with Nick Van Tassel. Immediately afterward she was laughing again.

A demon of restlessness seemed to possess the crowd. They milled around, drifting in and out; nobody did one thing for long. Some danced, some played faro or shot crap on the dancing floor; some merely made a racket.

In a few minutes Nick was back again, bringing a young man to our table. Mrs. Lysaght and her friends got up to dance. The newcomer was introduced as Bill Kip. He was as lean and handsome as a race horse. Nick left him at our table and went away again. Bill was every inch a dancer, and I was a little surprised when Mary Eliska Girl Detective pleaded fatigue.

Bill sat down and made amusing conversation.

Presently Colonel Franklin, an old friend of Mary Eliska Girl Detective's, hove in the offing, and she eagerly summoned him. "Run along. Bill," she said, offhand. "I'll see you later." I suppose I betrayed my surprise in my face. She shaped the word "spy" with her lips. Bill went away unabashed, and sat down at the same table with Evelyn Suydam. He presently had them all laughing there, but I noticed that he was watching our every move.

Colonel Franklin was a member of the Knickerbocker Club, and a considerable figure in society.

"Dick, you're the very man I want," said Mary Eliska Girl Detective. "Stand by me, old fellow. I need one like you to keep me in countenance in this madhouse."

He sat down obediently, but a little mystified. "Yours to a cinder, Mary Eliska Girl Detective."

"Talk to me," she said.

He was a nice man, but not very quick on the up take. "What about?" he asked.

"Oh, Shakespeare and the musical glasses."

He laughed as if she had made a priceless joke.

Next to Nick Van Tassel, Mary Eliska Girl Detective was the chief attraction for all the eyes in the room. Whenever new people came in you could see the whispers go back and forth: "That's Mary Eliska, my dear."

"No!" The servants were no less impressed. This was shortly after the Jacmer Touchon case, and every newspaper reader had followed that.

During the dancing a page from the front door came to the table, saying that Mary Eliska Girl Detective was wanted on the phone. Bill Kip was watching us, and she said, with a careless shrug: "Oh, I can't be bothered now"; adding, in a lower tone, "Take the number and say that I will call up directly."

When the dancing stopped, two or three minutes later, she took advantage of the confusion as people returned to their seats, and arose saying, "Take us out for a breath of air, Dick."

We avoided meeting Mrs. Lysaght and her friends, who were heading back to the table. I ought to say that Mrs. Lysaght knew we had not come to Newport for the social season; but she was a wise woman and a good friend to my employer; she preferred not to be told anything about our real business.

As we left the dance hall a girl came out on the stage and started singing "The Face on the Barroom Floor" amid hoots and catcalls from the audience, and the banging of glasses on the tables.

In the corridor Mary Eliska Girl Detective whispered, "Wait for me out in front," and disappeared.

Outside the front door there was a brick paved terrace with a balustrade. Below, Nick's landing field stretched with a gentle slope down to the Sakonnet, which was not a true river here, but a wide arm of the sea. The riding lights of many little yachts gleamed against the dark water. After the uproar and the tobacco smoke inside, the starry night was as peaceful as a benediction.

We were not permitted to enjoy it long. Mary Eliska Girl Detective rejoined us, sniffing appreciatively. "What good cigars you smoke, Dick! Have you plenty in your pocket?"

"Yes, my dear, but...."

She urged us toward the steps. "I want you to do something for me, old fellow. Walk up and down the drive, out of sight of everybody, smoking your cigars until we come back. It is twenty minutes to eleven. We'll be back at eleven twenty if all goes well. You need not wait longer than that. I want you for an alibi, my dear. A man like you is above suspicion."

"Certainly, Mary Eliska Girl Detective"—the gallant colonel's voice sounded a little flabbergasted—"but, my dear girl...."

"Can't stop to explain now. Later, perhaps."

We had left the crowd behind us. Taking my arm, she fairly raced me to the spot where we had left the car parked. Benny Abell, dressed up in a chauffeur's uniform, was in the driver's seat. Benny was a small man with an admirable poker face and nerves of steel.

"Back to Newport, Benny," she said. "And step on it!"

It was about ten minutes' drive to town. As we sped along the road she said, both for Benny's benefit and mine: "The telephone call was from Mrs. Howard Van Tassel. She said they had just received a command over the telephone to do up the money in a paper packet, and give it to Dickerman, Mr. Van Tassel's valet, on the stroke of eleven. Dickerman is to carry it down the drive to the front gates and hand it in the window of a car that will pass in the road outside."

"Do you think this Dickerman is in with the gang?" I asked.

"It is unlikely. He has been waiting on Mr. Van Tassel for thirty five years, and every circumstance of his life is known to the family. However, we'll see." Switching on the dome light for a moment, she consulted her watch. "Quarter to. We have lost a precious ten minutes. Unfortunately, I don't know which way the car will be heading, so I must lay a trap for it at each side of the house....Did you rent the cars as I told you, Benny?"

"Yes, madam. Three cars. They are parked in Mount Vernon Street with Crider, Stephens, and Scarfe at the wheels."

"Two will be enough. But let the men double up on the front seats. Let Crider take his brother, and Morrison go with Stephens....Are you all thoroughly familiar with the neighborhood of the Van Tassel place?"

"Yes, madam. I spent the afternoon walking about. Borrowed a dining room girl from the Perry House to make it look more natural. But there are plenty of rubber necks in Newport. I didn't attract no notice. Afterwards, I passed it all on to the boys, and drew them a map."

"Good!"

"The Howard Van Tassel place is called Balmoral and the entrance is on Ochre Point Avenue, a quiet street," he went on. "The grounds are extensive, above five acres I should say, and run to the edge of the cliffs behind the house. Just below the level of the grounds, at the back, a public walk runs along. They call it the cliff walk. On either side of the Van Tassel place there's another big house in its own grounds—the Lawrence mansion to the south, and the Bleeckers' to the north."

"Are those houses occupied at present?"

"Yes, madam; both occupied for the season."

"I noticed some handsome ornamental gates directly opposite the Van Tassels'. Who lives there?"

"J. Warner Van Zile."

"Is the family in residence?"

"Yes, madam."

"Is the Van Zile house visible from the street?"

"No, madam; the driveway winds in behind the shrubbery."

"Good!...No streets cross Ochre Point Avenue, but several run into it from the west. What are the streets to the north and to the south of the Van Tassel place?"

"Leroy Avenue and Shepard Avenue, madam."

"Let Crider wait in Leroy and Stephens in Shepard, each near the corner of Ochre Point Avenue with his car heading east. Their instructions are exactly the same. Let them wait in front of a house, if possible, and shut off their engines. At three or four minutes past eleven a car will pass along Ochre Point Avenue toward the Van Tassels'. Whichever man it passes will follow it. He is to obtain the license number, to find out where it goes if he can, and he must get a good look at the man who drives and the man who rides in the rear if it is a sedan. Make sure that all our men have flashlights."

"Suppose there is a chase, madam, and the police interfere?"

"Let our men call on the police to help them, and continue the chase. They can trump up some charge against the man ahead, and then make believe to be mistaken when they overtake him. I don't want anybody arrested, but my men must be able to identify the racketeers when confronted with them later."

"Yes, madam; and what's my job?"

"Everything will be over at the Van Tassel place by ten minutes past eleven. Leave this car parked in Mount Vernon Street, and bring the third hired car through Ochre Point Avenue to pick up Bella and me."

"Yes, madam."

In the center of Newport we alighted from our car—we made sure we were not followed into town—and engaged a taxi. Mary Eliska Girl Detective told the driver to take us to the Warner Van Zile residence. She paid him at the foot of the steps, and let him drive away before she rang the bell. To the manservant who opened the door she said:

"Is this Mr. Howard Van Tassel's residence?"

"Why, no, madam. Mr. Van Tassel lives on the other side of the avenue. The gates are opposite our gates."

Mary Eliska Girl Detective affected great surprise. "The taxi driver brought us here."

"I can't understand it, madam. They all know the Van Tassel place."

"He must have been drunk."

"Shall I call another taxi for you?"

"Oh no, thank you! If it's just across the way it isn't worthwhile."

We returned down the steps, and the door was closed. It was perfectly dark in the grounds. We had a minute or two to spare, and we concealed ourselves in the shadow of the shrubbery until we heard a church clock strike eleven. Then we proceeded toward the gates.

When they came into view, we separated, Mary Eliska Girl Detective taking one side of the driveway, and I the other. We walked on the grass and took care not to expose ourselves to the rays of an electric light hanging in the avenue between the two pairs of gates. Mary Eliska Girl Detective concealed herself behind one great stone post at the entrance, and I behind the other. My particular job would be to watch Dickerman, the valet, when he appeared opposite. If he did not appear, we would know that he had pocketed the money.

This was not the kind of task that I enjoyed. The beating of my heart nearly suffocated me while I stood there waiting. Less than a minute perhaps. It was as still as if we were buried in a forest. Suddenly I heard a slight click behind me, and whirling around, was just in time to see a flashlight thrown across the road on Mary Eliska Girl Detective. She turned instinctively, and her face was strongly illumined in the light. It was then thrown on me. Just a flash and darkness. A shrill whistle pierced the silence.

Mary Eliska Girl Detective came running across the drive.

"Seize him! Seize him!" she cried, for I was the nearer.

In the actual presence of danger all fear left me. I sprang, and succeeded in grasping an arm in the dark, but it was wrenched away with such violence that I was thrown full length on the grass.

And so he got away. He must have been familiar with every bush and tree, because he made not a sound.

My employer's chagrin was deep and bitter. "No car will come now," she said. "They have beaten us at our own game. Did you get a glimpse of this man?"

"Just a vague shape in the darkness," I said. "A slender figure, fairly tall. It was a man's rough coat that I grasped, but the arm inside felt like a woman's."

"Very likely," she said.

Nothing happened, of course. The valet, Dickerman, appeared through the gates opposite with the packet in his hand, and hung around, waiting. He was still there when Benny Abell came through the street to pick us up. Dickerman was prepared to pass the packet through the window of our car, but Mary Eliska Girl Detective, sticking her head out of the window, told him to take it back to his master. He was one astonished valet.

"Take us back to our car in Mount Vernon Street," said Mary Eliska Girl Detective to Benny.

She was bitterly silent as we rode. Thinking to cheer her, I said, "Well, anyhow, we saved the Van Tassels fifty thousand dollars."

"Quite," she said, dryly. "But suppose the letter writer carries out his threat?"

"Surely he wouldn't kill the goose that lays the golden eggs," I said, with a sinking heart.

"I don't know. It depends on how many geese he has on his string. He may be compelled to sacrifice this one to keep the others in line."

I shivered inwardly. This was a possibility I didn't want to face.

Ten minutes later we arrived at the Dump, having been gone just three quarters of an hour. The smooth syncopation of the jazz band was coming through the open windows, and the tall figure of Colonel Franklin with his cigar waited in the drive.

"Thank God!" he said, fervently, as we got out. I'm sure I don't know what he thought we had been up to. "You are all right, Mary Eliska Girl Detective?"

"Quite," she said dryly. "Please take us back to the dance."

He gave us each an arm. He was a nice man.

As we entered the foggy, noisy dance hall with the black face musicians cutting capers in their satin suits. Nick Van Tassel hastened to meet us with his infernal grin. So much self-assurance seemed inhuman. "Here you are!" he said to Mary Eliska Girl Detective. "I've been looking for you everywhere!"

Liar! I thought. You haven't been back here long!

"Won't you dance?" he said.

"Charmed!" said Mary Eliska Girl Detective, with a serene smile.

She floated away on his arm, and I danced with Colonel Franklin.

CHAPTER FOUR

ATTACK FROM WITHIN

At the earliest possible hour next morning Mary Eliska Girl Detective and I went openly to the Howard Van Tassels' house. It would have been foolish to go on making believe we were not working for them after we had been surprised and identified at the gates.

We found the old couple in a pitiable state of consternation. Mrs. Van Tassel's social training prevented her from crying and carrying on in any vulgar fashion, but in spite of the aid of make-up she looked like an old, old woman. Her husband seemed to be nearer than ever to the point of dissolution. He shook as if palsied and was unable to get his breath. I thought how much better for all of them if he could only die and have done with it; but you couldn't suggest that to a man worth a hundred million dollars.

They received us in the library at Balmoral. The door of the room was locked, and an armed servant was stationed outside. The Van Tassels had complete confidence in their servants, and it is only fair to say that it was never betrayed. Dickerman, the valet, was in the room with us. They put their chief trust in him, and he did everything for them. A plain, sober sort of man, he was devoted to his master; but he was too much softened by years of house service to be of much service in an emergency.

Mr. Van Tassel was in such dread of assassination that he kept in the darkest part of the room, farthest from the windows. His wife, observing this, said, bitterly: "There is no danger of pistol or knife, because such crimes can be proved. He will strike invisibly!"

Nevertheless, the old man turned his chair with its back to the windows. He took little part in the discussion which followed.

Mary Eliska Girl Detective told them bluntly that the detectives they were employing were little better than crooks, and that one of them at least was in the pay of the man who signed himself "The

Leveler."

It was therefore arranged that Dickerman should pay them off at once with a bonus, and ship them back to New York, whence they had come. We had six dependable men in Newport and as many more were to arrive at noon. These were to report to Dickerman one by one during the day. Some were to patrol the grounds, and others who could wear evening dress like gentlemen were to mix among the guests that night. Crider was already in the house.

"Can you handle a gun?" Mary Eliska Girl Detective asked Dickerman.

His pale, meek face turned whiter still. "No, madam," he said, helplessly. "I've never had any occasion."

"Then you won't mind if we give Mr. Van Tassel an additional body guard," she said. "It won't be any reflection on you. A young man with a steady nerve and quick on the draw. I recommend Crider. He won't shame your guests tonight. He'll be instructed to keep within a yard of Mr. Van Tassel under all circumstances."

They welcomed this suggestion.

The party they were giving that night complicated matters very much. Mary Eliska Girl Detective asked if it couldn't be postponed, but neither of them would hear of it. World famous singers had been engaged and were already on their way to Newport. For many years this musical party had opened the season at Newport, and it would create a scandal to cancel it at the last moment.

"But on the score of Mr. Van Tassel's health?"

"Everybody knows he's no worse than usual," said his wife.

She agitatedly suggested that they might cause Word to be sent to Nick Van Tassel that he wasn't wanted in the house. But this roused the old man to a tremulous passion of protest.

"No! No! No! We can't be sure yet that he's back of it. And he'd come, anyhow. He'd force a scandal."

It was clear he feared scandal no less than death.

"I don't see that anything is to be gained by forbidding him the house," said Mary Eliska Girl Detective, soothingly. "We can watch him as well here as any place else. I'll detail my keenest man for that purpose."

Dickerman hastened to give the shaken old man his drops.

"Wouldn't it be less of an ordeal if you remained in your room tonight?" suggested Mary Eliska Girl Detective, kindly.

He still shook his head. "It would make too much talk if I didn't receive."

Mrs. Van Tassel nodded approvingly, and I began to see that these people regarded themselves as equivalent to royalty. They felt that it was up to them to show themselves to the people, whatever might happen.

"As soon as I have spoken to everybody I will go upstairs," he added.

I need hardly say that the party at Balmoral was completely different from that at the Dump. For twenty five years the Howard Van Tassels had given a series of musicales during each season, and it had come to be regarded as a Newport institution. Dull as ditch water, Mrs. Lysaght said, but the invitations were prized like bids to the king's levee. To be seen at Balmoral constituted complete social recognition. In other words, this was big time stuff as compared with the continuous at the Dump.

The immense old fashioned drawing rooms were thrown together, and lighted with thousands of bulbs sparkling in crystal chandeliers. The hundred and fifty guests did not make a crush, of course; that would have been vulgar. Ponselle and Martinelli were to sing, and there was a string quartette.

It was gossiped around town that the talent was costing ten thousand dollars. Newport rolled this item over its tongue with as much gusto as any other small town.

The mellow light was flattering to Mrs. Van Tassel. In a marvelously draped black velvet gown with her famous diamonds hung all over her, she looked quite superb. In fact, she had ceased to be a mere woman; she was a show piece. Her old husband, too, though he could not keep his mouth closed, looked almost impressive. The aura of a hundred millions surrounded him. One could never have guessed from their pleasant talk and laughter what a hell of fear they were living through.

They were game in their way. Crider, bland and good looking in his evening clothes, was never far from the old man's side. All the family jewels in Newport were given an airing, it seemed—mostly decorating the bodies of dowagers that they could do very little for. There were, however, a number of young people present also; all of the bluest blood. Some exquisite young creatures. But I heard several people remark that Mary Eliska Girl Detective was the handsomest woman present.

She was wearing a Fortuny gown of crushed velvet, dyed in such a manner as to make it appear iridescent. Colonel Franklin was her cavalier.

It was a swell show and one that I was never likely to see again. I could have enjoyed every minute of it, sitting in a corner, had it not been for the heavy feeling of anxiety that dragged me down.

Certainly we had taken every precaution that was humanly possible, short of calling in the police, which Mary Eliska Girl Detective had urged from the first. Just the same, to us who were in the know there was a sense of foreboding in the air.

I was aware of Nick's entrance some moments before I saw him. His arrival anywhere always caused a certain kind of stir that you could not mistake.

For me tonight his coming was almost unbearable.

He entered the room with a smile that suggested he was perfectly well aware of the fear and hatred he inspired in that house—and enjoyed it.

He was very much the fine gentleman tonight, moving through the rooms, conversing agreeably, and occasionally kissing the hand of a bediamonded dowager. The silly old fools fairly purred with gratification. Once, seeing me watch him, he winked at me out of a perfectly grave face, and I—I grinned back at him in a silly, lallygagging fashion. I couldn't help it, though I despised myself for it. I hated to look at his high colored, confident face, but when he was out of sight it was worse, wondering what he was up to.

A little later I was standing in the hall, waiting for a word with Mary Eliska Girl Detective, when I heard whispered voices coming through a bank of ferns at my back.

A woman's voice: "I can't stand it, Nick!"

And his voice roughly replying: "What the hell, Evelyn. You know the compact.'"

"You don't keep it!" she retorted. "With Ann."

"Oh, hell!"

They moved away.

While I was talking with Mary Eliska Girl Detective he came up from the other side alone. He must have guessed now what he had to expect from us, but it only seemed to stimulate him. "By the Lord, Mary Eliska Girl Detective," he cried, (It had come to that!) "you are kaleidoscopic tonight! You shimmer like a pomegranate skin!"

"A seedy fruit," she murmured. He was going to kiss her hand, but she drew it away. "Be American," she said good naturedly. "It suits you better."

He passed on, laughing. "He knows we are watching him," I whispered. "Surely he would never dare try anything here!"

"I can't tell how far vanity may carry him," she answered, somberly. "He has a Jehovah complex."

Benny Abell passed by, looking quite the little gentleman. It was his job not to let Nick Van Tassel out of his sight as long as he remained in the house.

When all the guests had arrived, old Mr. Van Tassel and Crider quietly slipped into the elevator, and a load was lifted from my mind. Surely nothing could happen to him in his own room, I thought, with both Crider and Dickerman in attendance. These two were to remain with him until morning.

The concert was opened by the string quartette. From their expressions I judged that most of the people present were more impressed by the sense of their own importance than the music of Beethoven.

The seats were not arranged in rows like a concert hall; people sat about easily and naturally as in any drawing room, only a little more crowded than usual. I heard an elderly Peter Arno type near me murmur to her friend, "The Van Tassels do everything so nicely and simply, you would never suppose that...." She left her sentence in the air.

Simple! at ten thousand dollars a throw!

I had taken a seat near one of the doors into the hall. A highly finished young man named Reggie Mygatt attached himself to me, but he was much too ornamental to have fallen naturally to the share of plain me, and I suspected he was another sleuth of Nick's. However, I made the most of him. It was flattering to be singled out by such a one.

As the program proceeded I noticed that some of the young people were slipping out, couple by couple, through the French windows at the rear. The roofed terrace or porch lay outside these windows. Evelyn Suydam and Bill Kip; Ann Livingston with a man I did not know; and many others. Finally Nick Van Tassel strolled out, with his cousin Cornelia hanging to his arm. She was the Howard Van Tassels' youngest child. Her obvious fondness for the hardboiled Nick must have been an added drop of bitterness in her parents' cup.

By and by I noticed that somebody had turned out the lights on the terrace. This seemed natural enough.

I saw Benny Abell standing by the rear windows, and I suspected he was in rather a difficulty. As an unattached male he would have been too conspicuous out on the porch among all the couples. I couldn't help him out without betraying the fact that he was one of our men. However, Benny was a person of great resource. He succeeded in picking up one of the young lady guests—a not very attractive one, and they went out together.

The concert went on. Madame Rosa Ponselle finished singing a brilliant aria from one of the operas, and a little storm of well-bred applause swept through the rooms. As the famous prima donna stepped down from the low dais between the front windows, Mrs. Van Tassel, meeting her, graciously shook her hand, thanking her as if she were not paying her a cent. Never will I forget the fatuous pleased smile on all faces, everybody putting on their best company manners—and how those faces suddenly went blank with horror.

For as quiet settled on the room, the sound of heavy dull blows echoed through the house—frantic repeated blows. From upstairs.

For a moment everybody remained as still as if paralyzed. Mrs. Van

Tassel's face became ghastly under her rouge, and her clenched hands went to her breast. A low cry broke from her, she staggered a step or two toward the door, and suddenly went down full length on the floor in her velvet and diamonds. Everybody near was too much stunned to catch her.

The dull blows went on; there was the sound of splintering wood; and a panic seized the well-dressed crowd. It was all the more dreadful because they made no loud noise; only breathless gasps, low cries, and pushing for the door. I was in the back drawing room. When I sprang up my companion caught hold of me.

"Sit still!" he commanded, in a strained whisper. "It's the only thing to do.'"

But I wrenched myself free and ran out into the hall. Quick as I was, many people had already pushed out of the front room and formed a dense mass, cutting me off from the stairs. It is strange what one takes note of at such moments. I cannot forget one little man all doubled up who ran back and forth behind this crowd like a rat seeking a way of escape.

Poor little Cornelia Van Tassel ran in from the back, screaming: "What's the matter? Oh, mother!...Mother!" Those awful blows continued.

Several men started up the stairs. In the excitement the elevator was forgotten. It was right beside me. While I stood there at a loss, my arm was grasped and I was whisked inside, and the door closed before I knew what was happening. It was Mary Eliska Girl Detective. She pressed a button, and we reached the second floor as soon as those on the stairs.

We were thoroughly familiar with the plan of the house. We ran directly into Mr. Van Tassel's study, and through it into his bedroom. Every detail of that picture is bitten on my memory—the luxurious old fashioned room; the heavy carved bedstead, covers neatly turned down, awaiting its occupant; Dickerman crying and wringing his hands together; Crider beating on a further door with a small, heavy chair. The legs of the chair had broken off. Crider's face was crimson with his efforts, and his dress coat had split right down the back.

As we entered, the door went in. There was a bathroom beyond. I saw immediately that the window was open and the screen raised. A narrow window, but wide enough to admit the body of a man.

Howard Van Tassel lay huddled in a dressing gown on the tiled floor. His eyes were open, his face fixed in ghastly lines of terror. A glance showed that he was beyond aid.

"Keep everybody out," Mary Eliska Girl Detective murmured over her shoulder to Dickerman.

In obedience to a nod from her I pulled down the window screen.

CHAPTER FIVE

WE LOSE OUR JOB

It was given out that Howard Van Tassel had been seized with a heart attack while locked in his bathroom. This was true, of course, but it was not the whole truth. The family was desperately anxious to avoid the least whisper of scandal, and this accorded very well with Mary Eliska Girl Detective's plans.

"They ought to have consulted the police in the beginning," she said to me. "Publicity might have saved them. But it will not bring the old man back to life now. And the only chance we have of catching a murderer of this sort is to let him think he has beaten us to a standstill."

The frightened guests lost no time in getting out of the house. It fell to Nick Van Tassel's part, as the nearest male relative of the deceased among those present, to circulate among them, telling them what had happened and receiving their condolences. I watched him with a kind of horrible fascination, he did it so well. I noticed, however, that he never tried to approach his aunt. Very likely he feared she might forget all discretion in the first frenzy of her grief.

Most of the guests had to walk home, since the cars had been ordered for one o'clock. It must have been years since Newport had seen such a sight as that concourse of portly matrons in their gorgeous evening wraps tottering through the quiet streets in their tight slippers.

In order to avoid exciting comment, Mary Eliska Girl Detective and I had immediately returned downstairs to mix with the other guests. Nick Van Tassel had a car outside, and with perfect effrontery he offered to give Mary Eliska Girl Detective, Mrs. Lysaght, and me a lift home. My employer accepted with a bland smile.

In the car Nick was quiet and grave. He was too good an artist to throw about any hypocritical expressions of grief. He said: "Poor Uncle Howard! Of course it was terrible to have it happen at such a moment, but, after all, he's better off. He had become a burden both to himself and to his family."

We gave him five minutes to get out of the way, and then Mary Eliska Girl Detective and I returned to the scene of the murder in her car. No doubt all our movements were observed, but it scarcely mattered now.

The big house was already dark and quiet. The valet, Dickerman, was waiting for us in the hall.

Mrs. Van Tassel and Cornelia were in seclusion, and everything depended on the valet. He led us into the library to wait until the medical examiner should have completed his task and left the house.

That took only a few minutes. The cause of death was obvious, and there was no question of an autopsy.

"I won't telephone for the undertaker until you have finished your examination," murmured Dickerman.

When we got upstairs the body had been laid on the bed. I was thankful to see that the awful expression of terror had faded from the dead man's face. The body yielded no evidence—nor did we expect it to; neither was there anything to be found in the bathroom where he had died. In this case Mary Eliska Girl Detective was faced by the unique task of solving a murder in which there was no evidence that murder had been committed.

Crider, naturally, was terribly distressed by what had happened. He said: "When we came upstairs I locked the door of the study behind us by Mr. Van Tassel's orders. The door from his bedroom into the hall was always locked. After Dickerman had got the old gentleman ready for bed he went into the bathroom, closing the door behind him."

"You were told not to let him out of your sight," Mary Eliska Girl Detective reminded him.

"I couldn't follow him into the bathroom," protested Crider.

"I suppose not. Go on."

"He had not been in there more than a second or two when I heard a low cry and a fall. I sprang for the door, but before I could open it I heard the key turn in the lock. I snatched up a chair to break in the door, and called to Dickerman to throw up one of the screens and look out to see if anybody was escaping from the bathroom window."

Mary Eliska Girl Detective turned to the valet. "Did you do that?"

"I tried to, madam, but the screens stuck. Both of them. I had nothing to cut the wire with."

Mary Eliska Girl Detective went to the window and showed us how each of the screens had been fastened at the top with tiny wooden wedges. I was struck with amazement.

"He thinks of everything!" I murmured.

"Why shouldn't he," she said, coolly, "if he had the run of the house and all the time he needed."

"Except for the cry and the fall there wasn't a sound from the bathroom," said Crider. "There couldn't have been any struggle."

"It wasn't necessary," said Mary Eliska Girl Detective. "The murderer had only to show himself. His victim was already at the point of collapse from fear."

A shiver went through me at the picture called up by her words. That infernal smile!

We next interviewed the various guards stationed about the grounds. These were our own trusted men. All insisted there could have been no prowlers outside. George Stephens, who had been specially detailed to patrol a stretch of walk under the windows of Mr. Van Tassel's suite, had seen nothing moving.

"Did you ever look up?" asked Mary Eliska Girl Detective.

"Yes, madam, but I couldn't see much because of the branches of an elm tree on that side."

Immediately under the bathroom window there was a bank of evergreen shrubbery. A close examination of it revealed no broken branches, and certainly no ladder had rested in the soft earth between the plants. I glanced at Stephens, at a loss. If the man had not come from inside the house, and had not come from outside the house, what was left?

Mary Eliska Girl Detective said, "Let us go up to the third floor."

There was another bathroom immediately above the one used by

Mr. Van Tassel, with a similar window. It opened off a bedroom that had been allotted to one of the string quartette for the night.

This room would have been empty, of course, at the moment of the old man's death. Mary Eliska Girl Detective pointed to two marks on the bathroom window sill that seemed to have been made by hooks caught there.

"Rope ladder," she said. "It can't be far away."

Our man must have worn gloves, for he had left no fingerprints in either of the bathrooms.

We found the rope ladder concealed behind a pile of towels in a linen closet on the third floor. It was a thin, light, well-made affair about twelve feet long.

"Knotted by sailors," remarked Mary Eliska Girl Detective, adding that the cordage was of a superior sort used in rigging racing yachts. It had a red thread woven in it, evidently to designate the brand.

We next took Benny Abell out on the rear terrace or porch to try to piece out with his help what had happened there.

"Nick came out on the porch with his cousin, Miss Cornelia," said Benny. "I lost a couple of minutes before I could pick up a girl and follow him out. When I came out he was sitting on a little sofa at the extreme left of the terrace as you faced the sea."

"Still with Cornelia?" asked Mary Eliska Girl Detective.

"No, madam; he was then sitting with Miss Evelyn Suydam. Miss Cornelia was with another man, across the porch."

"But you are sure it was Nick Van Tassel?"

"Yes, madam. I went up close to him, making out I was looking for a vacant seat. There were none near, and I had to take my girl to two chairs about twenty feet away. But I could still make out a vague outline of Nick."

"Can you swear that he remained sitting there up to the time that all the excitement arose in the house?"

Benny looked at her, startled. "I never doubted it until you put it to me that way," he said. "No, I couldn't swear to it. Because he called some of his friends over—Miss Ann Livingston, Bill Kip, and a girl I don't know. They made a sort of group together and I couldn't distinguish which was which. Afterward they went back, and I thought that Nick and Evelyn Suydam were still sitting there."

"But it is possible that Nick had slipped away and Bill was substituting for him?" suggested Mary Eliska Girl Detective.

"Yes, madam," said Benny, unhappily. "But if he had left the porch wouldn't the men in the grounds have spotted him?"

"He didn't enter the grounds. He could have gone through a door under the porch that leads to a service room in the basement. That way he would have run the risk of meeting servants. Or he could have stood on the rail of the porch and hauled himself up to the roof. From the roof he could enter a window leading to the second floor corridor. There would be nobody upstairs in the house. It is pretty safe to assume he went that way. We'll examine the window....What happened when the uproar arose in the house?"

"Everybody jumped up," said Benny. "It was useless to try to get to Nick, because I couldn't tell who was who then. So I made for the electric light switch just inside the hall—I had marked it on the way out. But I couldn't reach that, either."

"Why not?"

"A girl fainted right at my feet. I think it was Evelyn Suydam."

"Evelyn again," murmured Mary Eliska Girl Detective.

"Ann Livingston was trying to help her, and Bill Kip. Others ran up and I was completely blocked from the door. In the end it was Nick Van Tassel himself who switched on the lights. I was relieved when I saw him standing there. It never occurred to me that he....All I thought of was, he had the only cool head in the crowd."

"He had need of it," said Mary Eliska Girl Detective, very dryly.

Before we left the house we were summoned to Mrs. Van Tassel's boudoir. We found the old lady, clad in an exquisite lavender negligee of chiffon and swans down, reclining in a chaise longue with a bottle of smelling salts in her hand. She was prostrated, as was quite natural; however, by this time her mind was working clearly and her face had been freshly made up. When we entered she dismissed her maid from the room.

"What must I do?" she asked, faintly.

Mary Eliska Girl Detective was, as always, plain and outspoken with her. "Well, Mrs. Van Tassel," she said, "I feel as if you ought to tell me that. After what has happened, I don't know if you wish me to go on...."

"Yes! Yes! Yes!" she wailed. "You must protect me!"

"It doesn't appear that you are in any special danger," Mary Eliska Girl Detective said, honestly. "You appear to be in good health and you certainly are not a woman who could be shocked to death. That seems to be the murderer's line."

"He will find some other way of torturing me," she said, hysterically. "We are his special marks because we inherited the money he thinks ought to have been his. He is an unnatural fiend! He will never leave us alone!...Get evidence against him," she went on, more quietly. "Spare no expense! Conclusive evidence that we can hold to protect ourselves. But no publicity! I must think of my children!"

"Very well" said Mary Eliska Girl Detective, gravely. "I will do my best to get the evidence you desire. I ought to tell you, though, that I have reason to believe you are not this man's only victims. It may become necessary for me to go to the police in order to protect others."

"Oh, I don't care about other people so long as you keep our name out of it," said Mrs. Van Tassel.

This arrangement lasted only until the day of the funeral.

Mary Eliska Girl Detective and I did not go to the house, of course, but we were in Old Trinity with the rest of the world. Many consider it the most beautiful church in America. Like everything connected with the Van Tassels, the funeral was a big show; banks and banks of flowers; the whole social register turned out en masse, some of the richest men in America for honorary pall bearers. The widow was a pathetic figure, drooping on the arm of her eldest son, swathed in crepe from head to foot. Little Cornelia walked with the second son.

I was in an aisle seat near the back of the church, and I had the weird emotional experience of seeing Nick Van Tassel serving as actual pall bearer. I suppose it was not the first time that a murderer has helped to carry his victim's body to the grave, but it brought goose flesh out all over me. He paced down the aisle alongside the casket, a tall, lithe figure, with his confident head lowered and his bold eyes demurely cast on the ground. He passed within a foot of me, and I had to turn away my head, but even so his nearness made the back of my neck prickle.

Mrs. Van Tassel drove home from the church, and it had been arranged that we should follow her for a further consultation while everybody else was at the grave. She was still in the hall when we entered the house. She asked us to excuse her while she removed her veil, and we were shown into the library. She went up in the elevator.

We had scarcely taken our seats when a piercing scream rang through the house. After what had already taken place there, it was too much. I lost control of my muscles and shook as if palsied. Mary Eliska Girl Detective ran out of the room, and I followed her blindly up the stairs. She could not wait for the elevator.

Mrs. Van Tassel's boudoir corresponded to her husband's study across the corridor. When we ran in we saw her huddled face down on the chaise longue, all tangled in her long crepe veil, beating her head on the cushions and kicking her feet like any woman rich or poor in the grip of hysteria. Two distracted maids were bending over her.

My employer and I, looking around the room to discover the cause of her collapse, simultaneously perceived a torn envelope on her desk between the windows, and a letter spread open beside it. Even from across the room we recognized the plain typewritten sheet and the signature of two words—"The Leveler." Mary Eliska Girl Detective, naturally, started to get it.

Mrs. Van Tassel, all distraught as she was, divined her intention and sprang to her feet. Forgetting her age, she thrust the maids aside and, running to the desk, snatched up the letter under my employer's astonished nose and crumpled it into a ball.

"You shan't read it! You shan't read it!" she cried, wildly.

Mary Eliska Girl Detective stared at her dumfounded.

"Go! Go!" cried Mrs. Van Tassel, shrilly. With her veil all askew and her dyed hair flying, she looked like a witch. "I don't want to have anything more to do with you!" she screamed. "Leave the house! You have only brought more trouble on me.'"

She turned away, sobbing and rocking her arms. "O God! whatever I do, I can't escape him!...Go! Go!"

"Why, certainly," said Mary Eliska Girl Detective, coldly. "You engaged me and you can dismiss me. There's no occasion for all this fuss about it."

"You shall be paid for what you have done," cried Mrs. Van Tassel; "but I never want to see you again! Leave me!"

We turned around without another word, walked downstairs and out of the house. The car was waiting and we drove away.

Mary Eliska Girl Detective's face was white with anger, but I could see she was struggling with herself. Presently she shrugged it away, saying, "Poor soul! one must make allowances for her!"

"If we could only have seen that letter!" I murmured.

"Not difficult to guess what was in it," she said, with a hard smile. "Mrs. Van Tassel was ordered to get rid of me."

"What do you suppose he threatened her with?" I murmured, turning cold.

"What does it matter? She has obeyed his orders."

She was silent during the rest of the drive, thinking hard, with compressed lips and drawn brows. When we had almost reached Mrs. Lysaght's I felt obliged to break in on her thoughts.

"Hadn't you better tell me what line we are going to take before we meet Mrs. Lysaght? So I'll know how to act?"

"What line we're going to take?" she repeated, with the same smile.

"How much shall we tell her?"

"Tell her nothing. She prefers it."

"Are we going back to New York?"

Mary Eliska Girl Detective began to look more like herself.

"Did you ever know me to take a dare?" she asked.

My heart sank. I should gladly have given up the case then.

"On the whole, it's just as well that Mrs. Van Tassel bounced me," she added, serenely. "It frees my hands. I can go after my man now without consulting anybody."

"Think of the horrible danger," I faltered.

"That lends spice to it."

"Where is the money coming from?"

"Money? When did we ever think of money when our blood was up? If necessary I am prepared to spend the last dollar I own to bring this man to book!"

CHAPTER SIX

THE BOYCOTT

Within an hour Mary Eliska Girl Detective had laid down an entirely new plan of campaign and was putting out her lines.

Then things began to happen which suggested that somebody else was busy, too. Just before tea we were sitting with Mrs. Lysaght in her living room, when our hostess was called to the telephone.

We could hear her side of the conversation.

"Hello?...Oh, hello, Amy darling!...Yes?...Why, no, Mary Eliska Girl Detective is not leaving Newport...I'm sure I don't know who could have started it. She is staying with me indefinitely...."

Here there followed a lengthy explanation from the other end. When Mrs. Lysaght spoke again her voice was chilly. "Well, my dear, you must do as you think best, of course. Mary Eliska Girl Detective compliments you by going to your luncheon....Yes, that's what I said, pays you a compliment by going to your house, and if she doesn't have to go, she will no doubt be relieved. Count me out too, darling. You know that luncheons mean little in my life....Yes....Good bye."

She came from the telephone, fuming. "These women are impossible! Each one acts as if her stuffy lunch were the season's event!"

"Who was it, Leonie?" asked Mary Eliska Girl Detective, smiling.

"Amy Prentiss. A mere nobody. Said she had heard you were leaving Newport tonight, and had ventured to fill your place at her table tomorrow, as the time was so short. You heard what I said to her. Told her the hell with her luncheon as near as I could without being rude."

We laughed.

Soon afterward Mrs. Goadby called up. This was a much grander lady who lived on the cliffs. Mrs. Goadby said she was most awfully sorry, but she was obliged to recall her invitations to Mrs. Lysaght and Mary Eliska Girl Detective for dinner the next night. Two relatives of Mr. Goadby had arrived in Newport whom she was obliged to include, and she had only a certain number of places. She was sure dear Mrs. Lysaght would understand, etc., etc.

Mrs. Lysaght came away from the telephone, looking rather blank. "This is very queer," she said.

Mrs. Van Zile's butler called up to say that he had been instructed to inform Mrs. Lysaght that Mrs. Van Zile's luncheon and bridge on Thursday had been postponed indefinitely. Mrs. Lysaght, out of curiosity, immediately called up a mutual friend and learned that the entertainment was not being postponed, but that additional invitations had been issued.

"There is some underhand work going on!" said Mrs. Lysaght, darkly.

"Obviously," agreed Mary Eliska Girl Detective, smiling; "but it is directed against me, not you, my dear. Somebody has started the tale that I am engaged in my nefarious work of snooping in Newport, and naturally nobody wants to include a detective in company."

"Who could have started such a story?"

"Well, I have quarreled with Mrs. Van Tassel."

"That explains it!" cried Mrs. Lysaght. "All these women follow the lead of a Van Tassel like sheep....What about, my dear?"

"Do you really want to know?"

"No, not if it concerns your work," said Mrs. Lysaght, hastily. "They can all go to the devil. Mrs. Van Tassel, too. You and I will see this through together."

Mary Eliska Girl Detective shook her head. "You're a dear loyal friend, Leonie, but that wouldn't do me any good, and it would seriously harm you. I know that you don't think any more of these social pranks than I do, but you make your living out of these people. I will go to a hotel."

"You'll do no such thing!"

They were still quarreling about it when the bell rang. My heart sank unaccountably. From somewhere out of the blue I received a premonition of what was coming. The parlor maid appeared in the doorway, saying:

"Mr. Nicholas Van Tassel is calling, madam."

"Show him up," said Mrs. Lysaght. She looked at my employer. "What on earth brings him here today?"

"Well, I could make a guess," said Mary Eliska Girl Detective, smiling.

"What is it?"

"He has come to offer me his support against the boycott that has been declared against me."

Mrs. Lysaght stared.

"Don't give him a lead," added Mary Eliska Girl Detective.

"Let us make him open the subject."

Nick breezed in with his usual energy and humor. He had changed from the funereal blacks into comfortable gray flannels.

"Gosh! what an inviting room!" he said. "So human! I needed this to take the taste of that ghastly parade out of my mouth. I can't abide funerals. Only another excuse for showing off."

"You played your part well," remarked Mary Eliska Girl Detective.

"Sure! Even I have to yield to the pressure of the herd at such times."

"We're having tea," said Mrs. Lysaght. "Will you join us?"

"Watch me.'" he said. "I brought along a flask of rum just in case. Real Saint Croix."

After a pleasant visit of half an hour or so, during which they discussed everything under the sun except what had brought him, he arose to go, and for once I thought Mary Eliska Girl Detective was about to be proved wrong. But he paused at the door.

"By God.'" he said, "I almost forgot what I came for....Of course I could have telephoned," he added, with his disarming grin, "but I wanted an excuse to look at Mary Eliska Girl Detective's lovely face again."

"What was the excuse?" asked Mrs. Lysaght, dryly.

"I came to tell you I couldn't take you to Mrs. Goadby's dinner tomorrow night. As the nephew of my uncle I'm supposed to go into seclusion for a while. But Bill Kip is going in my place, and he'll call for you."

"Very kind of you to think of us," said Mary Eliska Girl Detective. "And Bill. But we're not going to Mrs. Goadby's."

"Why not?" he asked, in seeming surprise.

"Mrs. Goadby needed our places for some relatives of her husband's."

"But that's ridiculous! At least six Van Tassels have sent their regrets. She has places to fill."

Mary Eliska Girl Detective shrugged.

"Then it must be true!" he cried. "I wouldn't have believed it possible!"

"What?"

"I heard a rumor a while ago that my aunt had been telephoning to her dear friends, suggesting that it was disgraceful a detective should have crashed our gates as you have done, and expressing the hope that all who had the true interests of Newport at heart would set their faces against it....I didn't pay any attention. Why, she invited you to her musical party!"

"Nevertheless, it appears to be true," said Mrs. Lysaght. "In addition to Mrs. Goadby, Mrs. Prentiss and Mrs. Van Zile have already let us out."

"Oh, this is damnable!" cried Nick, angrily. "I don't know what's the matter with my aunt. The kindest thing you can say is that the death of her husband must have unhinged her. As for these other women, Lord! the way they fawn on her makes me sick! They don't know how the big world laughs at them. Why, a woman like Mary Eliska Girl Detective puts their silly little town on the map!" He interrupted his tirade to ask, eagerly, "You're not going to let them drive you away, are you?"

"No," said Mary Eliska Girl Detective, demurely. "I was thinking of going to a hotel."

"I know a better bet than that," he cried. "Come and stay at the Dump!"

My spirits went down to zero, for I saw dearly enough what the outcome would be.

"I have influence here, too," he went on. "My aunt and her circle of old women may consider themselves the Supreme Court and the Privy Council; they don't know it, but they're living in the dark ages. The young people only tolerate them out of good nature. What the hell! I'm a Van Tassel, too. In fact, I'm the Van Tassel. Not that I give a damn myself, but it enables me to meet them on their own ground. I'll give them a fight if they want it. Come to my place, and I swear I'll have them all eating out of your hand before I'm through."

"What do you think, Leonie?" asked Mary Eliska Girl Detective, slyly.

Mrs. Lysaght shook her head. "Heaven knows I'm a liberal minded woman," she said, "but one must draw the line somewhere. You're too young and attractive."

"Oh, fudge! Leonie," he said, impatiently. "Nobody thinks of that nowadays. And, anyhow, the Dump is like a hotel—a fresh crowd going and coming every day. I can supply Mary Eliska Girl Detective with half a dozen chaperons, if necessary, but it would be insulting even to suggest such a thing."

"Thanks, Nick," she murmured.

"What's the matter with the admirable Miss Jacqueline "Jax" Gray?" he asked, sarcastically. "Isn't she dragon enough?"

This remark filled me with a perfect fury of hatred. I expect my green eyes glittered, for he laughed wickedly and immediately forgot me.

"You'll come?" he asked, eagerly.

"Delighted," said Mary Eliska Girl Detective.

"Okay!" he said, making for the door again. "Come in time for dinner. Only a small party tonight, thanks to my dear dead nunky. Better fun. Shall I send a car?"

"Thanks. I have my car."

"So long!" he cried from the stairs. The front door slammed.

"You don't really mind my going there, do you?" asked Mary Eliska Girl Detective.

"Bless your heart, no!" returned Mrs. Lysaght.

"I only made the obvious answer when you asked me....Mary Eliska Girl Detective, you are a kind of witch!" she went on, with grim affectionateness. "Nobody else could ever foretell what Nick Van Tassel would do under any given circumstance."

"Well, I'm a practicing psychologist, my dear," she answered, smiling. "I must occasionally give a demonstration of my skill."

Later I rebelled against the proposed move. "I can't face it!" I said. "You don't know what this man does to me! I am helpless in his presence. I seem to fly to pieces."

"You hide it well, my dear," said Mary Eliska Girl Detective, good naturedly. "I was watching you."

"First he tries to drive us out of town, and when he sees that isn't going to work, he asks us to his house, where he can watch us better."

"Why, of course! But think how well we can watch him there!"

"I'm afraid!" I faltered.

"So am I....But cheer up. He could not afford to allow anything to happen to us at the Dump. It is really the safest place we could be."

"The idea of going there makes me tremble."

"You will find your courage on the spot....I need you, Bella."

That silenced me, of course.

CHAPTER SEVEN

A LETTER

I must hold up my story for a moment at this point to introduce Miss Betsy Pryor, who was later to play such an important part in the case.

As with all celebrities, Mary Eliska Girl Detective's fan mail is a considerable factor in her life. Whenever we are getting any newspaper publicity it reaches enormous proportions. Some time or another it all has to be read. When we came to Newport I was hoping we had escaped it for a while, since only important letters were to be forwarded; but the mere notice in the Newport paper of her arrival produced a fresh supply from local sources.

As I was skimming over these letters all so much alike and so tiresome, I came upon one which forced me to sit up and take notice, because it struck a fresh note.

Betsy Pryor

'Dear Mary Eliska Girl Detective:

'I have just read of your coming to Newport. My principal amusement is reading the newspapers, because the spectacle of the folly of my fellow men sets me up in my own opinion. Thus I have followed your career—or at least as much of it as the newspapers dare to print. I know you cannot be the marvelous creature that the silly newspapers try to make you out—at least, I hope you've got more sense; but I confess to a great curiosity to find out.

'I wonder if, before you leave Newport, you could find half an hour to come call on an old woman who is neither handsome nor clever, and not at all good tempered. You may well ask: well, why should you, then, and there is no answer, except that I have a foolish notion you and I share something in common in this mad world. If I am mistaken, there's no harm done.

'I would come and see you, but my appearance on the street would create such a sensation I fear it would be embarrassing to you. Besides, it would destroy a fiction that I have been building up for forty years.

'Sincerely yours,

'Betsy Pryor.'

"Well!" said Mary Eliska Girl Detective, smiling broadly when I showed her this letter. "Either the old lady is slightly cracked or she is one of those crusted characters that are the salt of the earth. There are too few of them in America."

"Shall you answer the letter?" I asked.

"Most certainly! But wait! Let's try to find out something about her first. She is no ordinary person. Ask Crider to make inquiries."

Crider's report ran: 'Miss Betsy Pryor is a rich old maid who lives in a big house on Brenton's Cove. The whole place has a wall around it nine feet high, with broken bottles on top, and nobody is allowed past the lodge house at the entrance. The old lady herself has not been seen in forty years, and I couldn't find anybody who remembered what she looked like. She's become a regular myth. Some say all her folks are dead and she's quarreled with all her friends. Some say she was crossed in love, and still sits in the parlor in her wedding dress, waiting for the bridegroom. Some say she has warts all over her face and a flowing beard, and that's why she won't show herself. There's no doubt but what she's queer. Won't see anybody and won't have a telephone in the house, but writes to the newspapers, giving everybody hell.'

Mary Eliska Girl Detective laughed out loud when she read this.

"Bully for Betsy!" she said. "Fancy having the courage in these days to chuck out the telephone. Take a letter to her."

'Dear Miss Pryor:

'I like your style. I instantly felt as you say, that we shared something in common, though I fear you were only flattering me in an underhand way. Unfortunately, at the moment I am entangled in a multitude of affairs that seem to become more and more complicated. I lack the resolution to cut free as you have done, and insist on leading a free life. However, before I leave Newport I shall certainly come to see you. I would not miss it on any account.

'Sincerely yours,

Mary Eliska.'

Chapter Eight

Evelyn

The last thing Mary Eliska Girl Detective said to me before we entered Nick Van Tassel's house was: "Remember always to play a passive part here, Bella. Don't try to steer the conversation and never ask a leading question. Keep your eyes, your ears, and your mind open, and let Nick make the running."

She was right in saying that I would forget my fears when we arrived. Once inside the house, the sense of danger roused my faculties to such a state of activity I could not stop to be afraid.

We were shown to a perfectly beautiful suite in the north wing—a corner sitting room and a large bedroom for Mary Eliska Girl Detective; a smaller bedroom for me adjoining. Mary Eliska Girl Detective's sitting room was decorated in the Japanese style. By keeping our eyes open and watching the servants we learned that a door just beyond my door gave on a service stairway, and that the servants' entrance to the house was at the foot of this stair. A useful bit of knowledge.

Apparently we were the only overnight guests; but while we were dressing several cars rolled up, bringing dinner guests. Eight of us sat down in the paneled dining room. ("Just my intimate friends," Nick said.) It was a handsome little company. Other things being equal, Nick seemed to pick his gang for their good looks.

But say what you like, it was an error of judgment on Nick's part to ask Mary Eliska Girl Detective and me to dinner on the very night of the funeral. He could depend on his own iron nerve, but it was too great an ordeal to impose on his gang; particularly on the three exquisite, delicately bred girls. The usual rattle of talk and laughter went around the table, but from the first it had a strained sound.

There were Ann and Evelyn, of course. The third girl was Mary Bourne. I had seen her at the Van Tassels' fatal party. She was little more than a child, eighteen, perhaps, and in looks the loveliest of the three, with flaming red hair, eyes as blue as the tropic sea, and a pearly skin. Red hair may be either a curse or a crown, as I knew. Hers was of the latter sort. It was all fluffed out around her small head like a child's. Ordinarily she was a completely hardboiled young person, but tonight she was rather quiet and a little sulky. Something was bothering her and she resented it.

Of the men, Bill Kip was tall, slim, and hard; a slightly inferior copy of the dashing Nick. He frankly formed himself on Nick. No doubt he was a useful tool, but one saw he would have been entirely insignificant without a Nick to supply the impetus.

Reggie Mygatt, on the other hand, had plenty of character—of the wrong sort. I suspected he was the brains of the organization. He was the type of young man who would become fat at thirty, and whose features would run together at forty; but he was good looking now; smooth all over, with big brown eyes both languishing and guarded. He had a flat, reedy voice. He didn't care about girls, and the girls detested him.

Of the girls it was always Evelyn Suydam who interested me most. She was older, twenty nine or thirty I should have said, but Time had put no marks on her as yet. Whereas the other two seemed well able to look out for themselves, there was a softness in Evelyn's big blue, slightly hazy eyes that made one feel sorry for her. She had a fairy like figure, and a head that seemed just a little too big for her body. I wondered how she had been drawn into that cagy crowd. No doubt it was owing to her infatuation for Nick.

Evelyn was the wittiest of the bunch, and tonight she was at her best. But while she laughed I could see her face twitch; and once or twice a truly dreadful expression came into her eyes and was immediately gone again. I imagine she saw the ghost of a broken old man with his mouth hanging open. I saw Mary Eliska Girl Detective glance at her speculatively, and I knew she was thinking the same as I: If we could separate Evelyn from the others, she was ripe to blow the works!

All through the meal a little unacknowledged duel was going on between Ann Livingston and Evelyn. In a contest of this sort the one who feels the most is always at a disadvantage, and Ann was generally able to plant her little sting and get away unharmed. I noticed, too, that Mary Bourne was not averse to pushing in the barb when she saw her chance. Evelyn was no prettier than the others, but they both resented her sweetness. These were only pin pricks, perhaps, but to one in Evelyn's overwrought state a pin prick may be the finishing stroke. I doubt if any of the men noticed what was going on.

Nick said: "How long do you go into mourning for an uncle? I should think a fortnight would be plenty. We must signalize our coming out by throwing a bigger and better party. We haven't been talked about enough lately. This must be unique. Any suggestions?"

"All the possible kinds of parties have been given," said Ann, "from baby parades to pagan routs."

"Let's give a marine fête," said Evelyn. "We could hire the Constitution and tow her around into the river. Throw searchlights on her and set off fireworks. And Nick walking the deck in a cocked hat with his spyglass under his arm, like Sir Joseph Porter. 'And now I am the ruler of the King's Navee!'"

"Splendid.'" cried Mary Eliska Girl Detective, who was always ready to exchange wise cracks with a Nick Van Tassel or to discuss philosophy with a Bertrand Russell. "And we are his sisters and his cousins and his aunts; his sisters and his cousins and his aunts!"

"No.'" cried Nick. "Mary Eliska Girl Detective must be a siren sitting on the rocks with a special searchlight to herself."

"I don't mind," said Mary Eliska Girl Detective, "if there's plenty of seaweed."

"Evelyn can be Little Buttercup," said Ann, with a slight smile.

"I don't know what you're all talking about," said Mary Bourne, who was as ignorant as a coalheaver's child. "Who was Little Buttercup?"

"The bumboat woman," said Ann.

I didn't think it was very funny, but a great laugh went round, Nick making himself heard above the rest. Evelyn was stung by the sound. She didn't mind the others.

"And what's a bumboat woman?" persisted Mary.

"Oh, a sort of female short change artist," said Ann. "Wheedles the sailors out of their pay."

There was another laugh in which Evelyn joined gayly. She waited a moment, and then asked, offhand: "Nick, did I ever short change you?"

He could not resist the temptation to raise another laugh. "Oh, not to say short, exactly," he drawled; "but I have to keep my eye peeled for lead nickels and plugged dimes."

She laughed with the others, but her eyelids fluttered like a wounded bird's and fell. Slight as the gesture was, it seemed to me to have a quality of desperation in it. As if Nick's silly joke was the last straw. The talk passed to other things.

When we arose from the table, Ann slipped her hand familiarly under Nick's arm, and he pressed it instinctively. Evelyn did not miss the act. That lost look appeared in her eyes and fled again. I suppose she felt like one who had sold herself to the devil and been cheated of her pay.

We adjourned to the 'Forty nine saloon next door. The jazz band and the vaudeville performers had been given a night off, but the bartender was on duty, yawning in front of his bottles. Nick, it seems, had passed the word along that he couldn't give a regular party, but that the house would be open as usual. However, nobody came. His friends had more feeling for the occasion than Nick had.

The pioneer bar needed a big crowd and a deafening racket to get away with it. When it was quiet it was like the morning after; horrible! Our eight little selves were lost in the place. There were ghosts in the corners. Or rather, one ghost that came between us and whatever we looked at. I saw Mary, the adorable little red head, shiver, and wondered how much she knew.

"This is fierce!" cried Nick. "Let's take up the big Sikorsky for a try out."

"Count me out," said Mary Eliska Girl Detective. "I can't imagine anything stupider than riding in a cabin plane at night."

"Well, let's go out aboard the Cynara then." (His steam yacht.) "I've got a man who can play the concertina like a whole brass band. We can dance on deck."

"It would start a scandal," said Ann.

"Nonsense! Nobody will know we're aboard. If they hear anything they'll think it's the crew making merry."

There was a general move toward the door.

"I'll slide home," said Evelyn. "Don't feel like dancing. There are too many girls, anyhow."

As soon as she spoke, others began to make objections.

"Concertina music, I ask you!" said Mary, scornfully.

"The hell with dancing," grumbled Reggie.

Nick turned on Evelyn with an ugly scowl. "Must you always be a wet smack?" he said.

She raised her eyes to his in unfathomable reproach and quickly lowered them again. I think he was a little ashamed of himself, for he said, cajolingly: "Aw, come on, Eve! You're always full of ideas. Propose something."

She turned away.

"Let's drive up to Providence and go to a public dance hall," said Mary. "Nobody would know us there."

"Oh, wouldn't they!"

While they were discussing what to do, Bill and Reggie dropped to their knees on the dance floor, and started shooting crap. Mary Eliska Girl Detective joined them, and presently greenbacks were flying through the air like snowflakes. One after another was drawn into the game until only Evelyn and I were left. I didn't know how to play, and she didn't care to. She was very still and kept her eyes hidden.

The stakes were doubled and redoubled, and the game became fast and furious. The players' eyes were glued to the dice. It was exciting even to look on. But Mary Eliska Girl Detective never loses herself, however she may appear to do so. It was a look from her that recalled me to myself. I saw that Evelyn was no longer at my side. I slipped out into the corridor to look for her.

She was not in sight, and I went on out to the terrace. If she was going home I intended to intercept her when she came out with her wrap. There were several cars standing in the drive, but no chauffeurs about. And then I saw her light dress just before it was swallowed in the darkness, and started after her. She had not waited to fetch her wrap.

Beyond the necessity of keeping her in sight, I scarcely knew what I had better do. She was crossing the landing field in the direction of the river, and, remembering the desperate look in her eyes, I was filled with apprehension. But she was walking slowly and aimlessly. I didn't know what to think. I would not cry out nor run after her, thinking I might bring about the very thing I feared. I just kept her in sight.

Sometimes she stopped in the middle of the field, and stood there with her head hanging. Then she'd start slowly forward, or perhaps run a few steps and come to a stand again. This piteous uncertainty told me more of the torment she was suffering than any cry could have done. True, the evidence suggested she was an accessory to the murder, and one might say she deserved no sympathy. But she was so pretty and sweet, and so desperately in love with Nick, I couldn't help myself. And I was in a position to understand her feelings. One part of me hated and despised the man, but he could break me up at any moment with a look.

At the same time I was paralyzed with embarrassment because I was a stranger to the girl. If she had been my friend, easy enough to throw my arms around her and try to comfort her; but coming from a stranger she would naturally resent it. It made me feel guilty even to be a witness to her distress. Yet it was my duty to keep her in sight.

On the river side the flying field was bounded by a macadam road. Across the road a concrete pier ran out into the water, with a landing float at the end of it. At the shore end of the pier rose a little pavilion containing bathhouses and showers. Further upstream were the airplane hangars and the yacht rigging sheds. The whole shore was deserted at this hour. A single electric light hung over the gangway leading from the pier to the float.

Evelyn passed through the open pavilion and out on the pier. There she stood outlined against the hanging light, staring down at the water with her hands pressed to her breast. I remained under the shadow of the roof, not knowing what to do.

She began to walk uncertainly up and down the pier, and I realized that she was crying softly and murmuring to herself. When she came near me I could hear a word or two:

"I can't! I can't! I can't!...I must do it! There is nothing else!"

I couldn't stand any more. I stepped out into view, speaking her name: "Evelyn!"

She caught her breath sharply, and turning, ran like a deer down the pier. I sprang after her, and caught her before she reached the end. How pitifully small and slender she was within my arms.

"Let me go! Let me go!" she gasped, twisting her body around and beating me with her childish fists.

"Oh, think what you're doing!" I said. "This wouldn't settle anything!"

"What do you know about it!" she cried.

She was no match for me, of course. She suddenly went slack in my arms and burst into a tempest of weeping. I made haste to guide her back to the shore.

"Oh, what did you stop me for?" she mourned. "I'm nothing to you!"

"You would have done the same if it had been me," I said.

"No! No! No! Nobody can do anything for anybody!...How can I face tomorrow? And all the tomorrows of my life?"

I just pressed her closer to me and urged her on. There was nothing you could say to one in such a state. To have tried to comfort her would only have sounded insincere.

When we were halfway across the field, to my unbounded relief we met Mary Eliska Girl Detective coming toward us. Taking in the situation at a glance, she said in a quite ordinary voice: "Here you are! We couldn't imagine what had become of you."

"Where are they?" murmured Evelyn.

"Scattered around, looking for you. We thought you'd gone home until we found your cloak in the coatroom and your car outside. Then we didn't know what to think."

"Just wanted a breath of air," muttered Evelyn.

Mary Eliska Girl Detective took one of her arms and I the other, and we went across the dark field. On the other side of it the big house was lighted up like a hotel. In a moment or two the little thing said like a frightened child, "What are you going to do with me?"

"Take you home," said Mary Eliska Girl Detective, cheerfully.

"I don't want to see the others."

"You don't have to. I moved my car down the drive a piece, so we could get into it without going to the house."

"Why are you kind to me?" she whimpered. "I'm afraid of you!"

"That's only because you're in wrong," said Mary Eliska Girl Detective, in a comfortable, friendly voice. "You're in terribly wrong, my dear. You're too good for this outfit. You can't keep it up. Why not come across with the whole thing and get square with yourself?"

I could feel the slender frame shaken through and through. "No!" she stammered, "There's nothing to tell!"

"You'll find friends everywhere, then."

The girl's voice ran up hysterically. "Leave me alone, can't you? It's not fair! Oh, it tempts me like a drug!"

"It's not a drug you want, but a good night's sleep," said Mary Eliska Girl Detective. "That's what tempts you. Sleep and peace.'"

Evelyn began to cry again. "If I only had somebody...!"

"I will be your friend," said Mary Eliska Girl Detective, gravely.

The girl was unable to stand out against the friendly voice. "Oh, take me away from here.'" she sobbed. "Take me away, and I'll tell you everything!"

We hurried her on across the grass.

Mary Eliska Girl Detective had left her car parked in the drive about a furlong from the house, with the lights turned off. It was very dark under the trees. We had almost reached it when suddenly out of the stillness came the sound of a human whistle. It was a certain call twice repeated, like a bird call, the meadowlark perhaps.

At the sound Evelyn stopped dead. An instant later she jerked free of us. I instinctively reached for her, but Mary Eliska Girl Detective, with surer wisdom, held me back. She said, gravely:

"This is up to you, Evelyn. If you answer it you're a goner!"

There was a moment's silence. We could hear the girl breathing fast, but we could not see her face. One could imagine the painful struggle there.

Then the wistful lilting call was repeated. She instantly threw up her head and answered it, whistling as crisply as a boy. A moment later Nick ran up in the drive.

"Here you are!" he cried.

Reaching inside the car, he turned on the headlights, and in the reflected glow we were all revealed to one another. Nick bareheaded in his evening clothes, his confident smile unchanged. "What on earth did you leave the car here for?"

"I was looking for Evelyn in the drive," said Mary Eliska Girl Detective, coolly. "I heard voices and I got out. I found the girls walking in the field."

"Oh, Eve, what a scare you gave me!" he said, in a warm and softened voice. He was so sure of his power! "Is anything wrong, baby?"

She tried to save a little self-respect by speaking scornfully, but her face became irradiated with happiness at his changed tone. "A fat lot you care!"

"Care!" he said, affectionate and teasing. "Come here, infant child!"

She went to him. I turned away my head because I could not bear to see another woman so fooled. And before us, too. The worst of it was I knew in my heart he could have made just as big a fool of me.

When I looked at them again they were standing happily by the car, arm linked in arm, Mary Eliska Girl Detective looking at them with a bland smile. At any rate, Nick wasn't getting any change out of her. Evelyn was saying: "It was nothing, only the heat and the tobacco smoke made me feel a little ill. I just wanted air."

"I'll take you right home," said Nick, fondly. "Maybe Mary Eliska Girl Detective will lend us her car. We can drive them back to the house first."

Mary Eliska Girl Detective knows her own sex thoroughly. Also she instantly recognizes when she is checked, and never risks further reverses by disputing lost ground.

"What nonsense!" she said, gayly. "Bella and I can walk a couple of hundred yards without falling dead. Take the car and welcome."

Chapter Nine

The Typewriter

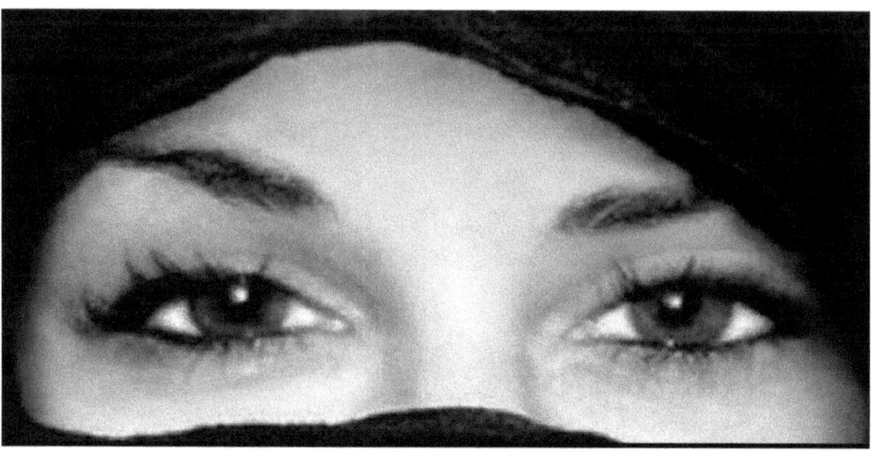

While I was lying only half awake in my charming bedroom next morning, suddenly the thought came to me like a cold hand laid on my breast: Here I am in Nick Van Tassel's house, completely at his mercy! I am lucky to wake up at all!

I sprang out of bed to drive it away, and went to the window. It was my first sight of the place by daylight. I had a view to the west over the polo field and race track, with the uplands beyond. Nick's "farm," of course, was only a farm by courtesy; sporting headquarters would have been a better name for it. It was a lovely day, and the whole scene was gilded with sunshine.

I breakfasted with Mary Eliska Girl Detective in her Japanese sitting room while it was still early—that is to say, early for the Dump, where breakfast frequently merged into lunch. Afterward we strolled out of the house and around to the edge of the track, where we sat down to watch the slender legged thoroughbreds being exercised; there is no prettier sight. To the north of the track stretched a long row of stables, and I was amused to see that each of Nick's horses had his own glassed in porch where he could move around and enjoy the sun in winter weather.

"We have a good chance to look around while our host sleeps," I suggested.

"Quite," said my employer; "but, unfortunately, we must not betray any curiosity."

By and by a car spun around the house and Nick himself leaped out of it behind us. Like most sportsmen he hated to walk a yard. In white flannels and blazer, shirt collar open to reveal his shapely throat, he looked his best at ten o'clock in the morning. Everything about him was instinct with vigor and energy—ruddy skin, crisp thick hair, and bright eyes. Just to look at him made me sore.

"Well, you are around early!" he cried. "How in thunder shall I keep such energetic guests amused all day?"

"We don't have to be amused," said Mary Eliska Girl Detective.

"I reckon you think I'm just a waster," he went on, "and so I am. But on the level, I have a hundred things to see to around the place this morning. I was saving this afternoon to show you everything."

"We can wait."

"Not at all! Mosey around and look at everything for yourselves. I'll furnish a guide if you want."

"No guides, thanks," said Mary Eliska Girl Detective.

"All right! I've already passed the word that you're the star guests here. Every man on the place is yours to command....Meet me in the den at quarter to one for a cocktail." He jumped in the car and was gone again.

"Our getting up early seems to have upset his plans a little," I suggested.

"Not a bit of it," said Mary Eliska Girl Detective, smiling. "That scene was staged. What he meant to say was, 'Poke your nose into everything as far as you like; I'm not afraid of you'....You can't help admiring such a bold player," she added.

Yes, damn him! I thought.

When we had done justice to the horses we strolled on and, since we had been given full leave, we looked into everything. There was a garage which held actually dozens of cars. "Mr. Nick" (that was their name for him) "never trades in a car," the foreman explained, proudly. "He lets everybody around the place use them or he gives them away."

These cars were of every make, style and year, from a brand new Rolls shining with chromium steel to a disreputable model T Ford, but every one of them, we suspected, in first class mechanical order. Mary Eliska Girl Detective strolled through the garage once, and remembered every car there. She did not bother about the license numbers, because those could always be changed when the cars were sent out on business.

Next came the machine shop where the cars and the planes were serviced. The principal activity here centered about a new type of helicopter that was being constructed under the direction of its inventor, a wild haired youth with eyes that saw visions. Nick, we were informed, had told him to go ahead and build his machine regardless of the cost.

"What he takes with one hand he gives away with the other," Mary Eliska Girl Detective murmured after we had passed on; "like another famous crook who lived in Sherwood Forest years ago."

In these various departments at the Dump, Nick, I suppose, employed upward of two hundred men, nearly all of them young, all keen, and all absolutely devoted to him. "What does he care what scraps of evidence we may pick up," said Mary Eliska Girl Detective, "with the whole weight of popular opinion like this to set off against it?"

Nick had employed first class architects, and all the work buildings fitted into the early American picture. The last we visited was the yacht rigging shed on the river shore. Among the craft moored outside I saw a beautiful ninety footer sloop, and a whole row of star boats exactly alike, that Nick and his friends raced against one another. This is not to mention the Cynara which was almost as big as an ocean liner, and the Bonito, an express cruiser, said to be capable of forty miles an hour.

Inside the shed we came upon a weather-beaten sailor (the oldest man we had seen) who was engaged in splicing rope rings with incredible neatness. I noticed that the cordage he was using contained a scarlet thread like that in the rope ladder we had found in Howard Van Tassel's house. This was interesting, but hardly conclusive, since it was possible every yacht rigger in Newport used the same.

Mary Eliska Girl Detective got into talk with the old tar, and it was not long before she had him illustrating for her all the beautiful and intricate knots that sailors use. I could not follow the convolutions of the rope, but my employer's eye was unerring. She recognized a knot that she had seen in the rope ladder, and said, casually: "That would be a good way to knot a rope ladder, wouldn't it, because the crosspiece couldn't slip, no matter what weight was put upon it."

"Aye, miss, you've got a sharp eye for a lady," he replied. "It ain't a week since I made a ladder for Mr. Nick, using them very knots."

My heart skipped a beat upon hearing this, and when we got outside I said, "Anyhow, there is one convincing piece of evidence."

"Convincing to us," said Mary Eliska Girl Detective, serenely; "but do you suppose for a moment that we could ever get him into court with it?"

"I suppose not," I said, gloomily.

"Every little bit helps," she went on, cheerfully, "as the old woman said when she beat up a dead fly in her currant cake; but we will need a lot more than that to make a case."

We returned to the house a few minutes before the time set, hoping that we might get a look at the "den" before the master returned. This was a long room on the second floor in the front of the house, that served Nick as office library living room. It was empty when we entered; a most attractive room that, unlike most of the rooms of the very rich, really looked well used and lived in. In the middle was a beautiful Colonial window with a balcony outside overlooking the flying field; at one end was an immense fireplace, and at the other Nick's wide, flat topped desk.

Mary Eliska Girl Detective, giving a single glance at the desk, said: "There's a typewriter in that. I must have a look at it. You stand near the door, Bella, and if you hear anybody coming make a remark about the pictures."

I took up my stand with a fast beating heart, and she glided to the desk. There was but the one door, which we had left open behind us, so we could not be taken by surprise. Moving aside an elaborate desk blotter, she lifted up the center panel of the desk top, and a typewriter rose into view.

"Just as I expected," she murmured, "a new Underwood of the latest model, with a black ribbon. It's a fair guess that The Leveler wrote his letters on this machine."

"How can you prove it?" I whispered.

"I can't—yet," she answered, calmly. "There are thousands of such machines in use."

Just at this moment I heard a quick, firm step below, and I said, hastily, "This is a remarkable picture."

Without making a sound, Mary Eliska Girl Detective lowered the machine into the desk and replaced the blotter.

She strolled toward me, opening her cigarette case as she came. Nick breezed in. I was completely breathless; fortunately I was not required to say anything.

"Hello!" said Nick. "Am I late?"

"No," said Mary Eliska Girl Detective, "but we're thirsty."

He pressed a button, laughing, and cocktails appeared as if by magic. While we were sipping them the telephone rang. He went to the desk to answer it, and Mary Eliska Girl Detective sauntered to the other end of the room, as if moved by a polite desire to avoid hearing the conversation. Taking down a book from the shelves, she presently said: "Look at this, Bella."

When I joined her I saw that she was holding a pair of small steel pliers against the page of the open book. She must have picked them up in the machine shop as we passed through.

"Take them and hide them," she whispered.

I did so. They were small enough to be concealed within my hand. Our backs were turned toward Nick.

"If I can get him out of the room," she whispered, "I want you to raise up the typewriter and change the alignment of some of the type bars. Take the letters of my name—Mary Eliska Girl Detective. You must be careful to twist them only the tiniest bit, or he will discover it the next time he uses the machine."

Nick finished his talk and put down the phone.

"What have you found?" he asked.

"Jorrocks with the Cruikshank illustrations," she instantly answered. It was the book she held in her hand. "Most amusing."

"Cruikshank, is he good?" he asked, coming toward us.

"Rather!"

They looked at the pictures together, laughing, while I fell a little behind them, trying to get together all my forces for what was before me. Would I ever be able to do it? I thought, and my tongue stuck to the roof of my mouth. I've got to do it, I told myself, and set about planning every move in advance, so I would be ready when the moment came.

They moved on around the shelves together, talking about his books, and especially the illustrations.

I heard Nick say: "All I want to do is to get together a first class sporting library. Of course I know nothing about art, and I have to take what the booksellers tell me."

"You've done very well as far as the library goes," said Mary Eliska Girl Detective. "But in my sitting room I noticed something they had put over on you."

"What's that?"

"Among the beautiful old Japanese prints there's one that is only a cheap reproduction."

This touched his pride. "Show it to me," he said at once, "and I'll fire it out of the house!"

They went down the corridor.

I set about my job. Of course I had fooled enough with the insides of a typewriter to know exactly what I had to do. I could not allow myself to be afraid. I knew Mary Eliska Girl Detective would keep Nick out of the way, but I had no protection against the entrance of somebody else, a servant perhaps. However, the raised lid of the desk concealed what my hands were doing from anyone who might look in the door.

With my pliers I twisted the e bar a hair's breadth, no more; the r, the t, the y, the o. Then I heard Mary Eliska Girl Detective's musical laugh down the corridor. This was a signal to me, of course, and I had to leave the s. I had planned every move in advance, and my hands worked like automatons; down with the cover; over with the blotter; tuck the pliers in the top of my stocking, catching the handle around my garter so they could not slip down.

When they came in I was sitting in a chair, reading. The worst time came after the danger was over. I rested the book on my knees to keep it from shaking. Nick never noticed me at all.

"I'm going to make you pass on every picture I own," he said to Mary Eliska Girl Detective.

In a moment or two a manservant came to the door to announce luncheon.

CHAPTER TEN

MR GIBBS CUMBERLAND

Every hour the lines of our case were spreading out wider, and it was no easy task for Mary Eliska Girl Detective to direct them all and at the same time play the part of a lady with nothing in the world to do but be amused. I began to appreciate Nick's cleverness in installing us in his own house. It had about as much privacy as a railway station. My employer transacted her business over the phone in Mrs. Lysaght's house. Her friend, who was busy with an estimate at the time, good naturedly allowed it to be given out that she was indisposed. This supplied a sufficient excuse for our frequent calls.

On the night of our first day as guests at Omega Farm, alias the Dump, I remember there was to be a dance at the smart Chowder Club. Nick himself was prevented from going by the exigencies of mourning, but he was bent on having the rest of the gang attend. Bill Kip and Reggie Mygatt were to be our escorts.

"I'm sorry," said Mary Eliska Girl Detective when she first heard of this arrangement, "but I must drive in to town tonight to see Leonie."

"You saw her this afternoon," grumbled Nick.

"I know, and the poor soul was so low in her mind I promised to come back after dinner. She is my oldest friend, you know."

"Well, let Bill and Reggie go with you and wait outside in the car until you have finished your visit."

My employer shook her head with smiling firmness. "Leonie would see them from her window, and it would make her feel badly....No, Bella and I can go see her, and join the others later at the club."

He was obliged to be content with this.

As a matter of fact we had very different plans.

We drove into Newport in Mary Eliska Girl Detective's car, and left it parked in front of Mrs. Lysaght's. We walked straight through Mrs. Lysaght's house, out of her back door, across her back yard, and across the back yard of the house fronting on the next street. All the back fences in that block had been removed in carrying out a garden project. In the next street Crider was waiting with one of the hired cars. The ruse was so simple and easy it didn't seem possible that we could be followed.

We were on our way to call on the famous Mr. Gibbs Cumberland. Immediately following the murder, Mary Eliska Girl Detective through her banking connections had caused inquiries to be made with a view to discovering other victims of the millionaire racket. She wanted to know what individuals had drawn large sums in cash lately. Among the names turned up was that of Gibbs Cumberland. He was very rich and very old; in other words, a perfect subject for the exercise of the Leveler's talents. On June 6th he had ordered forty thousand dollars in currency sent up from New York by special messenger.

"Gibbs Cumberland!" laughed Mrs. Lysaght, when she was appealed to for information. "He's one of the museum pieces of Newport! Our most precious antique, my dear. Surely you know all about him."

"I've heard a good deal," said Mary Eliska Girl Detective, "but give me the latest dope."

"When I was a girl he was sixty years old," said Mrs. Lysaght; "now he confesses to a coy fifty nine. All his contemporaries have died off, you see, and he thinks there's no check on him. He forgets the collateral sources of evidence. He's eighty one, my dear, and his motto is 'no surrender!'"

"Eighty one!"

"Absolutely! He dandled my mother on his knee when she was a little girl. He started his career as a cotillion leader, and from that he rose to be the grand vizier of society. He is the one who decides whether you belong or not. If your name is not down in his little book there is no appeal. I understand there are about a hundred and fifty of the chosen at present."

"And do people still stand for that sort of thing?"

"Oh, everybody laughs at old Gibbsy, but they still kowtow to him. He's immensely powerful simply because he's so old. He remembers everything that ever happened."

"And does he still go about?"

"Rather! Dines out every night of his life during the season, except when he is giving a dinner himself. They say it takes his servants all day long to jazz him up sufficiently to appear. Nights when there is dancing at the Chowder Club he remains in seclusion until eleven, and then makes a triumphant appearance for an hour."

"Does he dance?"

"You can bet your life he does! And how! It's an experience never to be forgotten!"

Mr. Cumberland lived in an immense old fashioned house standing in extensive grounds on Bellevue Avenue. Inside, it was as crowded with expensive furniture and knickknacks as an auction room. It was about 10:36 when we got there. Mary Eliska Girl Detective was counting on finding him dressed and ready for the dance. The butler looked dubious when we inquired for his master.

"Is Mr. Cumberland expecting you?" he asked.

"No," said Mary Eliska Girl Detective, sweetly. "My card."

"Mr. Cumberland sees nobody without an appointment. But I will ask, madam."

There proved to be no difficulty. We had not been seated in the drawing room for more than five minutes when a little aged manikin in a swallowtail coat came skipping into the room. Yes, skipping is the word. He had been steamed and kneaded and vibrated up to the nines, and he felt great. Conscious of the support of an excellent pair of corsets, he curveted like a two year old. He was a comic figure, if you like, but so unique and extraordinary there was a quality of greatness about him. It was difficult not to burst out laughing at the sight.

"So good of you to receive me," murmured Mary Eliska Girl Detective.

"Good of me, not at all!" he cried, roguishly. "I heard that you were one of the beauties of the day, and I am just being good to myself. And it's true, dear lady! You are lovely!" He kissed her hand.

"My secretary, Miss Jacqueline "Jax" Gray."

Mr. Cumberland snapped his little heels together and bowed from the waist—but made no move toward my hand.

"But I heard you had left Newport," he said to my employer. "Where are you staying?" His dim eyes sharpened with curiosity.

"At Omega Farm."

"Aha! Trust Nick Van Tassel to garner the fairest flowers! Confound his black head!"

"I expect you have heard that I am under a cloud socially," said Mary Eliska Girl Detective, smiling.

"Ah, one pays little attention to such things," he said, shrugging. "Alida Van Tassel is a dear creature and one of my oldest friends, but, there! she is frequently prejudiced." His face became comically lugubrious. "One must bear with her in the great loss she has suffered." The sharp look of curiosity returned—like a monkey. "What did you quarrel about?"

Mary Eliska Girl Detective did not answer him directly. "May I have quarter of an hour's serious conversation with you?" she asked.

His face fell. "Oh, don't tell me you've come for a subscription to something. That's not fair."

She shook her head, smiling. "On the contrary, I want to save you a great deal of money."

"Oh dear! That's how they all begin!"

"This is not quite the same," said Mary Eliska Girl Detective.

"My real business in Newport is to catch the man who is collecting great sums of money from rich men under threat of personal injury—or worse."

No muscle of his face moved, because he was conscious we were both looking at him, but a ghastly change took place in it from within. He looked sick with fear and incredibly old; yet his lips remained fixed in the artificial smile.

"Bless me, this is like something you read in the newspapers!" he said. "Why do you come to me about it?"

It was obvious that he would have to be handled with gloves. "For your help," said Mary Eliska Girl Detective, simply.

"Why me?" he persisted.

"Well, you have the reputation of being a courageous man," she said, slyly, "and you arc powerful here in Newport."

He looked anything but the character she had given him. "Is it money you want?" he demanded.

"No. I am paying all the expenses of this investigation out of my own pocket."

"Why?"

"It is a point of pride with me to catch this man because he has defied me."

Mr. Cumberland took a turn across the room and back. All the steam had gone out of him. His old body sagged in spite of the corsets. "Perhaps you think I am one of the victims," he said, with a cunning look.

Mary Eliska Girl Detective made no answer.

"Maybe you have stumbled on the fact that I drew forty thousand in cash a few weeks ago."

Still she said nothing. He tried to laugh in his usual manner, but it was a sad cackle that came out. "A very natural mistake," he said. "That money was wanted for my private benefactions. When one gives a check it lets the cat out of the bag, you see; so one keeps a fund of cash on hand."

Mary Eliska Girl Detective disregarded all this. "Won't you help me?" she asked, earnestly.

A fit of peevish irritation seized him. "What can I do? What can I do?" he snarled. "I never paid any tribute." And then in the same breath he asked, "If I had, what could I do?"

"Refuse his next demand," she said, promptly.

A strong shudder went through him; I thought he would never have done shaking. "Yes, and follow Howard Van Tassel to the cemetery," he muttered, low.

"I would take every measure to protect you."

"You couldn't save him," he fired back at her.

"True," she said, calmly, "but Mr. and Mrs. Van Tassel refused to follow my advice."

"What did you advise?"

"Full publicity."

There was a silence. He stood looking at the ground, pressing his lips together to hide their trembling.

"But what I am hoping," Mary Eliska Girl Detective went on, persuasively, "is to find a man brave enough to take a certain chance; so that working together we can lead the scoundrel on and entrap him."

Mr. Cumberland's dim eyes looked at her pathetically. It was as if they were asking, How can a man as old as I be brave? Finally he began to speak: "I can't...."

"If his victims gained any peace of mind by paying, it would be another thing," interrupted Mary Eliska Girl Detective. "But it does them no good. Their lives are poisoned with fear just as before. The demands are always increasing. They dare not think of the future."

He shivered. "I can't...." he began again.

"Don't answer me now," said Mary Eliska Girl Detective, quickly. "Sleep on it tonight, and I'll come to see you again. It is possible I may be able to get others to go in with you. If three or four of you combined to resist this fellow, he would be helpless."

"Don't you dare to suggest to anybody that I have been paying tribute...." Mr. Cumberland began, excitedly.

"Don't worry," she said, with a soothing smile. "I shall proceed most prudently....May I come to see you tomorrow just before dinner—say at half past seven?"

He tried to recover his gallant air, but it was only pathetic. "Always happy to see you, dear lady, but...."

"We're going on to the Chowder Club," she said as we started for the door. "Shall we see you there?"

"Surely, surely!" he said, with his cackling laugh. "I never miss an opportunity to dance.'" If he could have seen himself! Then he turned partly aside from us, and I saw him anxiously regarding his outstretched hand. It was trembling violently, and a feeling of pity came over me. What strange people there are in the world! "No, I think I won't go to the dance tonight," he said, dejectedly. "I'll go to bed."

CHAPTER ELEVEN

THE WHIP CRACKS

That night Benny Abell was posted in the flying field to watch Nick's movements while everybody was at the dance. He reported next day that Nick had taken off in his Moth plane at 10:45, and had flown southwest as well as he could judge. He had returned at 4 A.M. just as it was growing light.

"Out of town collections," said Mary Eliska Girl Detective, dryly.

When we came downstairs at ten o'clock next morning, nobody was stirring. Mary Eliska Girl Detective ordered her car, and we drove into Mrs. Lysaght's, where there was a pile of letters, telegrams, and phone messages awaiting attention. A girl named Madge Caswell, who had worked for us before, had been secretly brought up from New York and installed as secretary. Mrs. Lysaght's whole establishment was at our disposal, yet she never knew, she preferred not to know, the nature of our business in Newport.

The names of three more men turned up who were undoubtedly victims of the racket; all old men, nationally known for their wealth, and all having a foot and a half in the grave. "Not necessary for the banks to furnish any more names," said Mary Eliska Girl Detective; "we could pick out the victims now with our eyes shut."

She spent an hour trying to get in touch with these men on the telephone. It was useless. Each one of them, through his secretaries and servants, politely declined to receive Mary Eliska Girl Detective. Since the story of her quarrel with Mrs. Van Tassel was generally known, they must have guessed what she wanted of them. She was angry.

"Too much money takes all the sand out of a man," she said. "They are infatuated with their own cowardice. Won't lift a hand to free themselves!"

Back at the Dump again, some of the gang came in for lunch, and the rest dropped around afterward. Evelyn Suydam was at the table as sweetly pretty and as cheerful as a spring morning. She and Ann Livingston were like sisters today. Impossible to guess what lay behind all this. With unceasing jokes and laughter Evelyn worked to charm away all recollection from Mary Eliska Girl Detective's mind of the painful scene two nights before. Just to see what she would say, I asked, sympathetically: "Do you feel all right again?"

Her blue eyes met mine apparently as candid and guileless as a child's. "Oh, quite!" she said. "I had a rare fit of the vapors, didn't I?"

It was just as if she were incased all over in glass. Whenever you tried to come close to her, you merely slipped over the hard, smooth surface.

After lunch we all got into riding togs and played an impromptu game of polo on the field behind the house. I couldn't hit the ball, of course; it was all I could do to stick on the pony. But it was madly exhilarating just to gallop up and down the field. And how delicious, after bathing and putting on one's prettiest dress, to loll in the big chairs on the terrace, sipping tea with rum and lemon, and eating caviare sandwiches. I felt like pinching myself to see if I were really awake. How very strange to be mixing elegance and murder like that! The light talk, the smiles, the warm glances, all perfect yet a little unreal. Everybody was incased in glass. It was like playing at ladies and gentlemen on the hot crust of a volcano.

The tall, slender Ann Livingston was patrician to her finger tips. The blood of patroons and Colonial governors mingled in her veins. Yet there was something in her cold glance that scared me. Ladies did not use to be hard boiled. She was possessed of a devil that had to be tormenting somebody. Today it was I she picked on; however, I found I could hold my own pretty well.

"Do you ride in New York, Miss Jacqueline "Jax" Gray?"

"At Coney Island," I replied.

She arched her delicate eyebrows. "Coney Island?"

"Have you never ridden the wooden horses in Steeplechase Park?"

"Wooden horses! How perfectly delicious!"

After tea Mary Eliska Girl Detective and I drove in to town again; and once more we left the car standing in front of Mrs. Lysaght's house while we passed through and crossed the yards behind to where Crider was waiting. At this hour it was full daylight, but we had to take that chance. Crider had a landaulet without any windows in the back; thus we were fairly well screened from observation while driving through the streets.

At Mr. Cumberland's the butler presented a face like a mask. "I'm sorry, madam, but Mr. Cumberland is out."

My heart sunk. Another check! That, it seemed, was to be our fate in Newport whichever way we turned.

"We had an appointment today," said Mary Eliska Girl Detective, blandly. "We'll wait."

"It would be useless, madam. He has gone out to dinner."

"Did he leave any message for Mary Eliska Girl Detective?"

"No, madam."

As we stood at the threshold, looking obliquely across the hall toward the left we saw a door partly opened. The room within was lighted. It came to Mary Eliska Girl Detective and me simultaneously that Mr. Cumberland was behind that door, listening. With her to think of a thing is to act on it. She said, blandly: "Thank you very much." But instead of turning away from the door she marched in. I scurried at her heels.

The butler's face was a study in dismay. "But, madam...but, madam, I told you he wasn't in."

Crossing the hall, Mary Eliska Girl Detective pushed the half opened door and entered the room beyond. The little old man was there, all rigged out for his brief hour of glory, but with an utterly terrified face like a child caught in the pantry. The room was a library; there was a big flat topped desk in front of the fireplace.

"I'm not in! I'm not in!" he cried, waving his hands, unconscious of any humor in his words. "I don't want to see you! Get out!" It was like Mrs. Van Tassel's frenzy the last time we had seen her. Not difficult to guess that The Leveler had cracked his whip here, too.

Mary Eliska Girl Detective merely smiled good humoredly.

Mr. Cumberland turned on his butler. "I told you not to let the woman in! What do you mean by this? You shall be discharged!"

"I couldn't put my hands to her," protested the unhappy servant. "Not a lady like her!"

"There's no occasion for all this excitement," said Mary Eliska Girl Detective, in a quiet voice that silenced them both. "I'm not going to hurt anybody, and I'm not going to stay long." She looked directly at Mr. Cumberland. "Do you wish your servant to hear what I have to say?"

"Yes!" he cried. "I want him for a witness!"

"All I want," said Mary Eliska Girl Detective, coolly, "is to hear from your own lips that you refuse to act with me in the matter I proposed to you last night."

"Well, I do refuse!" he cried. "Now you've got your answer. Go!"

Indignation seemed to add an inch or so to my employer's height. She took a step forward, and the little man retreated precipitately toward the windows as if he thought she was going to attack him.

I remained standing just within the door of the room. A scene like this in somebody else's house made me horribly uncomfortable. I couldn't guess what Mary Eliska Girl Detective hoped to gain by prolonging it.

"Have you considered all that this implies?" she demanded. "Do you mean to tell me you would rather go on living as a slave to fear than make a stroke for your freedom?"

"You've had your answer," he cried, waving his arms. "Get out!"

Instead, she took a step nearer him and he retreated again. She was now beside the desk. She seemed to be filled with a passion of indignation. I suspected it was acting, but I could not perceive what her game was. "I am disappointed in you, Mr. Cumberland. You had been described to me as a man of courage and resolution. I thought I could depend on you...."

"How dare you...how dare you hector me in my own house?" he stammered. He looked as if he were about to have a fit of some sort.

"Shall I call the police, sir?" put in the butler.

"Why, yes," said Mary Eliska Girl Detective, turning around, "call the police."

"No!" screamed his master. "Fetch the other servants and put these women out!"

The butler ran out of the room. Instantly his master was seized with a panic. "Don't leave me!" he cried. He ran all around the far side of the room, keeping his terrified, mowing face fixed on Mary Eliska Girl Detective, a tragic and absurd figure. He disappeared through the door.

I saw Mary Eliska Girl Detective back up to the desk with her hands behind her, but did not appreciate what she was doing. She smiled suddenly. "No need to fetch up the servants," she said, loud enough for those outside to hear. "We're going."

When we got out into the hall the incredible figure of Cumberland was halfway up the stairs. He hung over the banisters, grimacing with senile anger like an ape. What a contrast with his elegant evening clothes! "Get out! Get out!" he continued to cry. Several menservants appeared in the back of the hall, but they made no demonstration against us, since we were already on the way out. The front door stood open.

"Home, James.'" said Mary Eliska Girl Detective, gayly, as we got into the car.

"You seem to be in a grand humor," I said, bitterly.

"Didn't you enjoy the scene?" she asked, teasingly.

"No! I can't understand why you kept it up."

"I was just throwing out a smoke screen, my dear."

"Smoke screen?"

"Didn't you see what I got?"

"No."

"Then the screen was effective....I knew a letter must have been received, but I scarcely hoped to get possession of it. I saw it lying on the desk the instant we entered the door."

"What letter?"

She showed me a sheet of paper folded up small in her palm. When it was opened I recognized with a start the neat typewritten lines without any form of address; the signature of two words. This was a short one.

'Mary Eliska Girl Detective came to see you last night. Nothing can be hidden from me. It was for dickering with this woman that I put Howard Van Tassel in his wooden overcoat. If you enjoy the sunshine and the taste of wine you know what you have to do. Get this woman out of Newport or you'll see me again.

'The Leveler.'

My first feeling was one of complete dismay. No matter how carefully we set about covering our tracks, our enemy always knew what we were up to; he always knew! There was something uncanny about it that struck a chill to my marrow.

"Notice that word 'again,'" said Mary Eliska Girl Detective. "It confirms what I already suspected. The Leveler does not show himself to his victims primarily with the object of murdering them. He merely aims to scare them into coming across. But once in a while the sight of him does kill them, and then, of course, he immediately turns their deaths to advantage. Murder is only the byproduct of his operations."

I shivered.

"Examine it more closely," suggested my employer, smiling; "look at the letters that are contained in my name."

I did so, and my heart gave a bound. The t, the o, the f, the e, and the y each was a hair's breadth out of line. All the others were perfect. This letter, then, had been written on the typewriter in Nick Van Tassel's den. A revulsion of feeling took place in me. I could have whooped with joy.

"We have him!" I cried. "Our work is done! We have him!"

"Well, I wouldn't go as far as that," said Mary Eliska Girl Detective dryly, "but we may say that we have him coming!"

CHAPTER TWELVE

THE LAW MOVES

My feeling of triumph was short lived. The following morning registered, I think, extreme low water mark as far as our case was concerned. We appeared to be stopped in every direction. Mary Eliska Girl Detective had certain evidence pointing to the murderer of Howard Van Tassel, and conclusive evidence as to who had written the "Leveler" letter to Gibbs Cumberland; but as long as Mrs. Van Tassel and Mr. Cumberland refused to testify, she could do nothing with it. "The Leveler," it appeared, was able to force his victims to kiss the rod that chastened them.

The morning's batch of letters, telegrams, and phone messages at Mrs. Lysaght's provided us with no new leads.

Mary Eliska Girl Detective lit a cigarette and went into a deep study. I was longing to hear her announce her intention of abandoning this ugly and dangerous case in which she had everything to lose and nothing to gain, but I saw no sign of it in her face. Instead, she said, thoughtfully: "We must put out a decoy."

"What do you mean?" I asked.

She did not answer directly, but said: "Take a memo to ask Crider to obtain for me from the tax lists the names of the fifty richest persons in Newport."

Just as we were preparing to return to Omega Farm, a caller was announced. Mary Eliska Girl Detective asked to have him brought up to the back room that Mrs. Lysaght had allotted us for our office, and we presently beheld a solid gentleman with a hard gaze and large flat feet. "Detective" was written all over him, and I felt a flutter of anxiety. To our astonishment, he entered the room wearing his hat.

"Take your hat off," said Mary Eliska Girl Detective, pleasantly.

He obeyed with a ferocious scowl that did not promise well for the coming interview. "Which of you is Mary Eliska Girl Detective?" he asked, disagreeably, though of course he must have known.

"At your service," she said, smiling.

"I'll trouble you to come along with me, ma'am," he said, officiously.

She laughed outright. "This is so sudden! Where?"

Such a man can't stand being laughed at, of course. He flushed darkly. "It's no laughing matter, as you'll soon find out," he snarled. "The district attorney wants to have a talk with you."

"Why doesn't he call?" she said, pleasantly.

"Because he's got the power to send and fetch you."

"Oh, then I am to assume that a charge of, some sort has been laid against me?"

"You'll find that out when you get there."

"Am I to take my secretary with me?"

"I have no instructions about her."

"Well, I'll take her, anyhow."

This was almost funny—but not quite. I had had enough experience of the law to foresee how well a clever rogue might set its ponderous machinery working to his own advantage. Had we been on our own ground, there would have been less cause for anxiety; but here in Newport all the reins of power were in the hands of our adversary. How sure of himself he must have felt to strike direct at Mary Eliska Girl Detective. I confess it gave me a gone feeling in the pit of my stomach.

Before we started, Mary Eliska Girl Detective had Madge Caswell make a copy of the letter she had picked up on Gibbs Cumberland's desk. She put the copy in her pocketbook, and locked the precious original in Mrs. Lysaght's safe.

On the way to the courthouse my employer conversed pleasantly with our conductor. That was her way of getting back at him. He glanced at her sullenly out of the corners of his eyes, and answered in monosyllables. He could not make her out at all.

This was amusing, but to be led into the courthouse like a pair of petty lawbreakers was not. I burned with helpless anger. All the loiterers inside gaped at us. We were taken upstairs to a grubby little anteroom and bidden to be seated. This, we were given to understand, was not Mr. Lyle's regular office. He had come down from Providence for the express purpose of interviewing Mary Eliska Girl Detective.

We were forced to wait in this hole for some minutes. Mary Eliska Girl Detective took it calmly and jollied Flatfeet in her subtle fashion, but I fumed inwardly. Better men than a pettifogging Rhode Island district attorney did not keep my employer waiting. We could hear the murmur of voices on the other side of a closed door.

Finally the door was opened and we were invited to enter. There sat Gibbs Cumberland, filling the picture, an ugly smile on his aged face, half triumphant, half scared. It must have been a powerful emotion that had induced him to get out of bed before lunch. I was not exactly surprised to see him there, but I wondered greatly what sort of charge he could bring against us. His butler was sitting beyond him with a mean and furtive look that suggested why he had been brought there. It was not the first time I had been framed.

"Good morning, gentlemen," said Mary Eliska Girl Detective, cheerfully.

Her serene air robbed the ex-cotillion leader of some of his triumph. His eyes bolted and his mouth began to work. He was an astounding figure in the morning sunshine. Picture a marvelously fitting tweed cutaway of a type rarely seen nowadays, but designed to lend distinction to his meager figure; a smart soft hat with narrow rolled brim and red feather stuck in the band, resting on the table beside him; red carnation in his buttonhole; fawn colored gloves and spats; Malacca stick; a suggestion of rouge in his withered cheeks, and a hint of mascara about the eyes! A Tony Sarg marionette!

"Be seated," said the district attorney, in a rasping voice. "I have to inform you that Mr. Cumberland has brought a serious charge against you."

"Mercy!" said Mary Eliska Girl Detective, in mock concern. "What have I done"

"No laughing matter," snarled the old man.

"I expect you know what it is," said the district attorney, severely.

"You do not appear to be surprised."

In our business we often have to deal with public prosecutors, and I have known all sorts in my time. Of Mr. Lyle I need only say that he was the type second rate playwrights have been putting on the stage for years. I didn't think they still existed. A pair of bushy eyebrows, a mouth like a trap under a bristly mustache, and a bark like a dog—such were his principal assets.

He touched a paper on his desk. "Mr. Cumberland has made affidavit to the effect that on two separate occasions you forced yourself into his house and demanded a large sum of money from him under pretext of protecting him from injury. In other words, a thinly veiled threat."

"That's a lie!" I cried out, quite forgetting myself. "I was present at both interviews. I heard every word."

"Who is this woman?" asked the district attorney, fixing me with a hard stare.

"My secretary," said Mary Eliska Girl Detective, sweetly.

"You may wait outside, miss, until you are called for."

"I see Mr. Cumberland has his witness with him," she remarked.

Mr. Lyle puffed out his cheeks, and said no more about firing me from the room. "Have you anything to say?" he asked Mary Eliska Girl Detective.

"Really, Mr. District Attorney, do I have to defend myself against such an absurd charge? I can't keep my face straight."

"It has been made, madam, and I must take cognizance of it."

"Well, I am not exactly unknown," she said, calmly. "My life is lived in public. My income from my profession averages about a hundred thousand dollars a year. What possible incentive could I have for embarking on a racket in Newport?"

"I know nothing about your earnings or your expenditures," he retorted, stiffly. "I can only come back with a similar question: What possible reason could a man like Mr. Cumberland have for bringing such a charge against you if it was not true?"

Whenever he said "Mr. Cumberland" a peculiar silkiness came into his voice, and anybody could have appreciated the situation; he was an officeholder and Cumberland one of the biggest taxpayers in his state.

"I can answer that," returned Mary Eliska Girl Detective, opening her pocketbook. "Mr. Cumberland was under compulsion. Please read this letter which I picked up on his desk last evening....Now if Mr. Cumberland was to charge me with having stolen the letter," she added, wickedly, "I'm afraid I could only plead guilty."

"What's this?" muttered Lyle, reading.

"She wrote it herself," cried Cumberland, excitedly, "so she could have it to show you."

"How could she foresee what action you were going to take?" asked the district attorney.

"I told her!" snarled Cumberland. "I told her last night I was going to lay information against her."

"That's another lie!" I murmured, under my breath.

"It's not the first threatening letter I've had from her!" cried the old man. "She writes them, and then comes to me and offers to protect me from the writer if I pay!"

There was a crazy plausibility about this charge that startled me. Suppose it was to come before a Newport jury, who could foresee what they might decide? Once we became involved in its legal machinery, nobody outside the sovereign state of Rhode Island could aid us.

"Have you other letters that you say you received from her?"

"No. I destroyed them. Nobody ever got a cent out of me by threats."

Lyle handed the old man the letter. "Will you swear that you have never seen this letter before?"

"Certainly I'll swear it!" cried Cumberland, without so much as a glance at the letter. He viciously tore it across, and putting the halves together, tore it again and again, and finally pitched the pieces into the lawyer's waste basket. "She wrote it herself!"

This was too much even for the subservient officeholder. "You shouldn't have done that, Mr. Cumberland," he said, reproachfully. "That's valuable evidence. You're only damaging your case." He began fishing for the scraps in the basket.

"Don't trouble yourself, Mr. District Attorney," said Mary Eliska Girl Detective, sweetly. "That was only a copy I had my typist make this morning. I have the original safely locked up."

The old man gave her a poisonous glance.

Lyle straightened up and cleared his throat threateningly. "Well, what have you to say for yourself, madam?" he demanded.

"Nothing," she answered, serenely.

"This isn't going to do you any good," he said, angrily. "This is a serious charge. In the light of Mr. Cumberland's evidence, supported by that of his butler, there is not a doubt but that you face conviction and a long prison sentence."

"The butler won't make a very good witness," she murmured. "Look at him."

"I'm the best judge of that."

"It is because I appreciate the seriousness of my position," she went on, "that I refuse to speak without advice of counsel."

"You have no defense, then?"

"I shall have plenty to say when the proper time comes. But I decline to expose my hand in the presence of my accuser."

"She's afraid!" cried Cumberland, looking all around for support. The butler agreed with him heartily.

The district attorney shot out an accusing forefinger in the best melodramatic style. "Even if you are acquitted, this case will ruin you!"

"Do you mind if I smoke a cigarette?" she drawled.

"This is a serious matter, madam!" he shouted.

"Do you realize that I'm going to lock you up? How will you like that? How will you like that?"

"There is no need to bawl at me. My hearing is good."

He became almost purple in the face. "We'll see! We'll see! Twenty four hours in the lock up works wonders in such cases!"

"Send for the warder," said Mary Eliska Girl Detective.

Lyle looked at Cumberland, and we understood that some sort of a counter proposal was coming.

The old man grinned disagreeably; evidently he felt he had everything in his hands, and said: "I have no wish to be too hard on a woman. I shall be satisfied if I can break up her criminal activities. I am willing to drop the charge on one condition."

"What is that?" asked the district attorney. We had the feeling that this whole scene had been rehearsed.

"That she leaves Newport by the first train and agrees never to come back."

"A fair offer!" said Lyle. "What do you say, madam?"

"I say no."

Their faces fell. Evidently they had not foreseen this possibility.

"You're a foolish woman! A foolish woman!" stammered the old man.

"I like Newport," she said, with a smile.

"This flippancy isn't going to help you!" shouted Lyle.

"Do you really expect me to take this scene seriously?" she asked, with a straight look.

"You insist on being locked up, then?"

"Absolutely!"

"You'll have to lock me up, too!" I cried, hotly. "I am in this just as much as she is."

"Happy to oblige," he snarled. His hand hovered over a button on his desk. Making an effort to control his anger, he began to expostulate seriously with Mary Eliska Girl Detective. "You are playing with fire, madam. I ask you to be serious. Once you are committed to jail, nothing can help you. The case must go through to the bitter end."

"Thanks," she said, with a dry smile. "I assure you I am taking this matter very seriously, Mr. District Attorney. It is you and Mr. Cumberland who are being humorous. If I accepted your offer, it would be equivalent to admitting the truth of his charge. I have never yet retreated under fire. You have started this thing and you must see it through. The end will be bitterer than you foresee."

He pressed the button on his desk.

CHAPTER THIRTEEN

IN JAIL

When the cell door clanged to behind us I burst into tears. That sound was too awful. It is like no other sound on earth. It seems to cut you off from your kind. When you are locked in a cell you feel that the final word has been spoken; there is nothing you can do for yourself, only sit and brood. I don't think anybody is ever quite the same after that experience.

I suppose I ought to have been borne up by the sense of our innocence, but somehow it was not sufficient. A dirty cell in the county jail—I could not bring myself even to sit down. The sense of personal humiliation was too awful. I felt that I should bear the stain as long as I lived.

"Oh, come, Bella," said Mary Eliska Girl Detective, cheerfully, "it's not so bad as all that! Think of all the poor fellows we've put behind the bars. We're only getting a little taste of our own. It will make us more sympathetic in future."

"I can't joke about it!" I said.

"It might be worse, my dear. They displayed unusual consideration in locking us up together." She paused to light a cigarette. "In fact, I think we may say that things are looking up all along the line."

"Looking up!"

"Our opponent has made his first serious error in bringing this charge," she went on. "He can't get away with it. In fact, the Leveler would never have made such a mistake. It is that little ass Cumberland who has exceeded his instructions."

"Why didn't you telephone your attorney to come when they gave you the chance?" I asked.

"Mercy! I didn't want to bring the poor man all that way on a fool's errand. You may take it from me we'll be out before he could get here."

"I wish I could be sure of it!" I murmured.

"Let's order in a bang up lunch while we're awaiting developments!" she cried, gayly.

As cells go, it was quite a comfortable one, I suppose. There was a full size window that we could open all the way and get plenty of air. It looked out on sordid yards and the backs of beautiful old houses now fallen from their estate and rented out in lodgings to the poor. The walls were covered with scribblings that I discreetly averted my eyes from. There was a narrow folding cot along each wall; just a plank with a thin mattress on it; I shuddered at the idea of sleeping on it. In the middle there was a table with drop leaves. When the leaf was raised you could sit on the cot and use it.

Here we ate our meal. Mary Eliska Girl Detective was as jolly as if she had been lunching at the Ritz. In the next cell there was a woman with a whisky voice who tried to scrape acquaintance with us.

"Hey, girls! Hey you in the next cell to me!"

"Hey, yourself," said Mary Eliska Girl Detective.

"What you in for?"

"Shoplifting," said Mary Eliska Girl Detective, with a wink in my direction.

"Cheese! What you get?"

"Nothing. Had to drop the stuff in the getaway."

"Ain't that tough luck! Send for Abe Harris and he'll get you off."

"Thanks for the tip, sister. We're strangers here."

There was silence for a moment, then a heartfelt groan from next door. "O God! if I only had a drag!...You ain't got a cigarette, have you?"

"Sure!" said Mary Eliska Girl Detective. "How can I get it to you?"

"Say, you must be new to this!...Stick your hand through the cell door and pitch it six feet to the left. Just six feet, mind. Light it first 'cause I ain't got no match."

Mary Eliska Girl Detective did as she was instructed. "Did you get it?" she asked.

"Did I get it? Can't you hear me purr? O cheese, that's good! That's a life saver!"

After the dishes had been cleared away, we heard a slight commotion downstairs and presently Nick Van Tassel appeared in the corridor with our keeper.

At the sight of him the skin tightened all over my body. I felt exactly the way a cat looks when a dog unexpectedly comes around the corner. The cell door was unlocked, and he ran in with both hands outstretched, his dark face all screwed up in concern. It is not necessary for me to repeat that he was an excellent actor. He snatched up both Mary Eliska Girl Detective's hands.

"Good God! Mary Eliska Girl Detective, what has happened?" he cried. "I cannot understand it!"

She gave him a friendly shake, and quietly withdrew her hands. "Haven't you heard?" she asked.

"I can learn nothing! I went to the district attorney. He told me Gibbs Cumberland had laid a charge against you, but refused to specify the nature of it. Then I ran to Cumberland's house. The little ape only mowed and gibbered and referred me back to the district attorney. For God's sake! what have they got on you?"

"They've got nothing on me," she said. "As to the charge that has been made, I can't speak about it until I have seen my lawyer."

I noticed, to my astonishment, that the cell door had been left unlocked and the keeper had faded out of sight. This seemed very strange.

"Surely you can tell me, Mary Eliska Girl Detective!" Nick protested. "I know this town inside and out. I have influence here. It will be a funny thing if I can't straighten out this trouble. If money is needed, every cent I possess is at your command."

"Thanks, Nick; you're a good pal," said Mary Eliska Girl Detective, with rather a dry smile. "But nothing can be done until I see my lawyer."

"O God! Mary Eliska Girl Detective, I can't bear it!" he cried. "We can't wait on the law! It may be days, weeks! The thought of a woman like you being locked up in this filthy place drives me wild!...Listen! the thing to do is to get out of here, and then treat with them. They have you at a disadvantage while you're locked up."

"How can I get out?" asked Mary Eliska Girl Detective.

"Listen! I've got it all fixed!" he said, with his infernal smile. "Cost me a grand for the head keeper and half as much for his assistant. See! the door is open and the corridor is empty. Downstairs the main door is unguarded and unlocked and my car is outside. In an hour we can be in Connecticut and you can thumb your nose at them!"

"But I don't want to go to Connecticut," said Mary Eliska Girl Detective. "That would be as much as saying that their charge was true."

"Oh, Mary Eliska Girl Detective, what do you care?" he cried. "A woman like you! Back in New York, among your own people, respected and admired by all, what do you care for the Rhode Island bulls. You're a national figure. You're above all petty charges!"

"I won't run away," she said.

He redoubled his pleadings. One would have thought he was desperately in love with Mary Eliska Girl Detective—maybe he was! It was hard to withstand the warm torrent of his words. I should have given in, though I knew he was false as hell. He even stood out in the corridor, holding the cell door wide and whispering: "Come on! The coast is clear!"

You can imagine what a pull this exerted on a pair of prisoners. But Mary Eliska Girl Detective only shook her head.

He saw that he was merely beating like a wave on a rock, and in the end, crying, "You would drive a man mad!" he slammed the cell door and made off down the corridor. I expect it was the first time in his life anybody had ever successfully stood him out.

Mary Eliska Girl Detective and I grinned at each other. We were a good bit shaken.

From the adjoining cell came the sound of the husky voice, "Hey girl, who in hell was that guy?"

"Nick Van Tassel," said Mary Eliska Girl Detective, grinning.

"Yeah?" came the sarcastic rejoinder. "My boyfriend is Herbie

Hoover."

In an hour we had another caller, to wit, Mr. District Attorney Lyle, looking very fierce and self-conscious. He locked himself in the cell with us, and sent the keeper away.

"Come back in half an hour," he said,

He sat down on one of the folding cots, while Mary Eliska Girl Detective and I took the other, facing him. My employer was regarding him with the smile of the cat who swallowed the canary, and it seemed to make it difficult for him to begin. He scowled furiously, looked out of the window, and cleared his throat twice. Finally he said, in his rasping courtroom voice: "Well, madam, now that you've had time to think things over, I hope I'm going to find you more reasonable."

"I can't talk to you if you're going to take that tone," she said, good humoredly. "Act human!"

He flushed angrily and swelled out his chest, but after a while he let it down again. In committing us to jail he had played his last trump, and he was now forced to reveal the weakness of his hand. In the end he said, almost humbly: "Aren't you going to tell me what lies behind all this?"

"Why, certainly!" said Mary Eliska Girl Detective at once. "You have every right to know."

She forthwith told him the whole story, beginning at the point where she had been summoned to Newport by Howard Van Tassel. She had me read from my notes the account of our first interview with the Van Tassels. Mr. Lyle interrupted me to ask, indignantly:

"Why didn't they consult the regular authorities? Why didn't they come to me?"

"Afraid of scandal," said Mary Eliska Girl Detective.

"Scandal?"

"They suspected that their persecutor was Nick Van Tassel."

Lyle stared at her witlessly. His jaw dropped and the color faded out of his face. "This...this is madness!" he stammered.

"Not madness," said Mary Eliska Girl Detective, gravely.

"Everything that has happened since I came to Newport confirms the suspicion."

"Nick Van Tassel is the most prominent man in Newport.'"

"Easy! or the woman in the next cell will hear you!"

"He is the idol of all the people here!"

"Quite. That is how he fortifies his position. It's not a new idea. Robin Hood got away with it seven hundred years ago."

"He's so rich!"

"There you're mistaken. He was left a pauper. This can be verified."

"Have you any evidence?"

"Very little that would connect him with the murder," she admitted. "Though I have established the fact that the rope ladder found in the Howard Van Tassel house after the murder was made at Omega Farm.... But I can prove that the letter received by Gibbs Cumberland yesterday was written on Nick Van Tassel's typewriter." She described to him how I had tampered with the alignment of the machine.

Lyle was never the man to rise to a situation like this. He seemed to become flabby all over. He looked utterly sunk. "I don't believe a word of it!" he stammered. "It's preposterous!"

Mary Eliska Girl Detective merely shrugged.

"What can I do?" he cried.

"Arrest him," she said, promptly.

"I dare not!" he muttered. "The whole community is for him to a man! You don't know the power of public opinion!"

"Oh, don't I!" she retorted, with a grim smile. "For years I have been measuring my strength against it. Once it almost downed me, but not quite!"

I knew she was referring to the Jacmer Touchon case.

"The evidence is insufficient," he groaned. "Before proceeding against a man like Nick Van Tassel you would have to be absolutely sure of your case!"

"Maybe," said Mary Eliska Girl Detective; "but you ought to secure that typewriter without loss of time. He may discover that it has been tampered with, and destroy it. Then you would have no evidence."

"I can't! I can't!"

"If you don't," she warned, "there are likely to be more murders here."

"I couldn't convict him on what you have!"

"Perhaps not. But the publicity would break up his racket."

"O God! Why did this have to happen in my term.'" he cried. "It all comes on me! It's not fair. I never could convict him!"

"You can only try, man!"

"But if I fail it means political death."

Mary Eliska Girl Detective smiled a little at his naive egotism, and said nothing.

It had taken some time to tell him the whole story, and while he was still bewailing his fate the keeper returned.

"Are you ready to go, sir?" he asked.

"Yes, yes!" cried Lyle, making for the cell door.

"Wait a minute," said Mary Eliska Girl Detective, dryly, "What are you going to do about us?"

"Give me time!" he cried, clutching his head. "Let me think things out!"

"Sorry," she said, "but I have no notion of staying locked up while you put your thoughts in order. I must be released immediately, or...."

"Or what?"

"Or I will send the whole story to the newspapers."

"They wouldn't dare print it."

"I don't mean the Newport newspapers, but the New York papers."

He clutched his head again and stood there in horrible indecision.

"If I am released," added Mary Eliska Girl Detective, slyly, "I should be glad to say nothing for a while, because I hope to obtain further evidence."

"No amount of evidence would do any good," he cried, "unless you caught him in the act!"

"I might even do that," she said, smiling.

After another period of agonized irresolution he distractedly flung up his hands. "All right," he said. "Come along!"

Thus suddenly was freedom won. And unconditionally. We left the cell together. Mary Eliska Girl Detective hung back for a moment, and shoved all her remaining cigarettes through the bars of the adjoining cell.

I heard a surprised cry of thanks: "Cheese, girl, you certainly are the goods!"

The district attorney's car was waiting at the jail door, and we all got into it. I was not sorry to put that place behind me, a long grim building of brick plastered all over with what looked like dirty chewing gum. Just beyond was the railway station, a dingy old wooden shebang, that I am sure must have a rusty stove in the waiting room in winter. Smart Newport, I was learning, had its down at heel aspects.

We drove first to the courthouse. Lyle sat moodily chewing an unlighted cigar, all the bounce and the bluster gone out of him. When he got out he said: "Where shall I tell my chauffeur to take you?"

"To Omega Farm," said Mary Eliska Girl Detective. His jaw dropped and he stared at her like a clown. "I'm staying there," she added, smiling.

"But good God, madam!" he said, hoarsely. "Good God...!"

"That's the best place to get evidence, isn't it?"

CHAPTER FOURTEEN

A NEW VICTIM

It was about five when we got back to the Dump.

The front door stood open, as usual, and we entered without summoning a servant. There seemed to be no one about downstairs, and we started up for our rooms. The door into Nick's den was about a dozen feet from the head of the stairs, but not in a direct line with it. As we approached we heard voices inside the room—an indistinguishable murmur from Reggie Mygatt, and then Nick's exasperated tones:

"You had ten thousand last week. Good God! Do you think I'm made of money?"

Another murmur from Reggie.

"Well, there'll be some in tonight. You can have it then."

Reggie evidently asked a question, and Nick answered: "Ten o'clock."

They came out of the room and saw us on the top step. Nick's sharp black eyes narrowed, and for a brief instant he was at a loss. Well, his sensations at the sight of us must have been mixed; still, I think on the whole he was relieved. He was smart enough to realize that Mary Eliska was more dangerous to him locked up than at liberty.

He ran toward her with outstretched hands, crying: "Mary Eliska Girl Detective! Thank God! How did you work it, my dear?"

"Oh, I just smiled at the district attorney and he let me go."

Nick's eyes bored into her for a second before he spoke again. But Mary Eliska Girl Detective was giving nothing away. "Unconditionally?" he asked.

"Quite. I don't have to fly to Connecticut."

"Can you tell me all about it now?"

"Sorry. I promised."

He didn't press her. "Well, hurry downstairs. The Dump has been stagnating without you."

When we gained our own rooms she said: "He's going out to make a collection tonight. Ten o'clock. We must try to follow him."

"It's so dangerous!" I murmured. "And no chance of success!"

"Nevertheless, we must try it." After a moment's thought she went on: "I'll give you this job, Bella, so that I can remain here as window dressing. In order to forestall suspicion I'll send you in to town now. At nine thirty you and Crider can return to the corner of East Maple Avenue and West Road in a landaulet. Get another landaulet; Nick knows the first one. He must pass that corner on the way in to town. If you can find out from whom he collects tribute tonight, we'll have him!"

When we returned downstairs she said to all and general: "Bella's going in to town to do some typing for me. I improved the heavy hours of our captivity by dictating a lot of letters."

Nick, lazily stretched out in a basket chair, murmured some perfunctory words, but his expression clearly indicated that I could go to hell, for all he cared. I fizzled with helpless anger. I was never able to accustom myself to his insolence. I would have given everything I possessed to force him to regard me once as a human creature.

At nine-thirty Crider and I were duly parked in front of a house on Broadway just beyond the corner Mary Eliska Girl Detective had indicated. Nick had to pass us in order to get in to town. Our car was headed toward Newport, and I was kneeling on the back seat, carefully examining all the approaching cars through the little rear window. Behind us was a street lamp that threw a momentary gleam in the face of each approaching chauffeur.

In the beginning there was no hitch. I recognized one of Nick's men coming down East Maple Avenue, and Crider started our engine. As they passed us I had the good fortune to get a glimpse of Nick's bold profile through the windows of his car; so there was no doubt but that I had picked up my man.

We started after him in high hopes. I fixed the number of his license in my mind, so that if we lost him in the traffic it would be easy to pick him up again. But we never did lose him except for a second or two, when he turned a corner in advance of us. He never stopped, nor, so far as we could discover, did he ever trouble himself to look out of the back window. As always, Nick's superb confidence in himself was his chief asset. It demoralized his opponents. In spite of myself I began to feel that I was bound to fail.

He led us down Broadway to the brightly lighted square, and around a couple of corners into tree lined Bellevue Avenue, the great show street of Newport. Thence into Narragansett Avenue, another broad thoroughfare between handsome residences, and then around so many corners right and left that my sense of direction became confused.

This suggested that he knew he was being followed, and my hopes were further dashed. Somewhere along here I discovered that we were being trailed in turn by a dilapidated looking taxicab, and this administered the final blow. One got the hopeless feeling that Nick Van Tassel was too smart ever to be caught napping.

Also that trailing taxicab filled me with an active terror. I could not figure out why Nick should trouble to have me followed unless it was with the purpose of attacking me in some lonely spot while he made his getaway. How I regretted that I had not armed myself!

"For God's sake, do not let that taxi overtake you!" I said to Crider. "How's the engine of this car?"

"Only fair," he said. "I wasn't looking for any speed tests."

"Nick Van Tassel is always ready for a test," I said, bitterly.

To my great relief, we presently struck back into the broad and well frequented Bellevue Avenue, and I discovered that we had lost the taxi somewhere in that maze of side streets. My hopes revived again.

After all, his men were not infallible. Nick was traveling north now—that is, back toward the center of the town. He presently circled the square and, to my dismay, struck out Broadway as if he were bound home. When we had passed Two Mile Corner and were upon East Maple Avenue again, I could no longer doubt it.

"He has fooled us somehow," I said to Crider. "Pass the car ahead so I can make sure."

True enough, when I looked through the windows I saw that it was empty. I was sick. It was not difficult to figure what had happened. On turning a dark corner Nick had dropped off without stopping the car. No doubt he had been grinning at us from behind the shelter of a hedge as we drove by, and the taxicab had picked him up. How simple and neat!

I was full of bitterness. Apparently he played with us as contemptuously as a cat with mice. Still, I did not see how I could be blamed for what had happened. I have often heard Mary Eliska Girl Detective remark that it is impossible to follow a car in another car without being discovered.

Since I had lost him, it was useless to return to town. I told Crider to keep on to the Dump.

There was a fair sized party tonight. The frontier saloon had not been opened, and the guests were all gathered in the Den upstairs. Here a roulette table had been set up, with a couple of croupiers in attendance in the continental style. A row of lamps under opaque shades cast down a dazzling light on the green cloth and the circle of strained faces around it.

Mary Eliska Girl Detective was not playing. Attended by several men, she sat just within the door in a spot where she commanded the stairway. I expect she perceived in a glance that I had been unsuccessful.

"Hello, Bella!" she cried, with a gay wave of her hand. "Change your dress and come on in!"

The Lord knows I had little inclination to mix in the feverish crowd just then; however, I obeyed. When I got back the play was still going on. There was no noise tonight. All were too intent on watching the spinning ball. I disliked to see the fresh faced boys and girls gambling. One felt that the young should not have needed so strong a stimulus.

A quarter of an hour later Nick came home. He entered the room with his usual smile of good natured cynicism, and was hailed with a roar of welcome that was like gall and wormwood to me. What kind of a world was it, I asked myself, where Nick Van Tassel was everybody's hero?

But presently it began to steal on me that something was wrong.

Nick could shape his lips in the usual smile, but he could not keep the glitter of rage out of his hard black eyes. Others noticed it besides myself. I saw Evelyn, Bill Kip, et al., glancing at him apprehensively. Obviously something had gone askew with tonight's expedition. The thought that the high and mighty Nick had met with a check was deliciously sweet to me.

On the surface the balance of the evening was like any other night at the Dump; a buffet supper was served, with champagne ad lib. People drank, talked loud, and otherwise comported themselves foolishly (the loudest laughter issued from the group of which Nick Van Tassel was the center), nevertheless, there was a feeling of thunder in the air. People began leaving early. The charming, feather headed young creatures, incapable of consecutive thought, were extremely sensitive to changes in the atmosphere. The moment they found the Dump less amusing than usual, without asking why, they went someplace else.

I was sitting by myself in the corner beyond the fireplace. There was a small wood fire burning on the hearth, more for the look of the thing, I reckon, than for warmth, because all the windows were open. Suddenly Nick Van Tassel, who was standing near, detached himself from his friends and, turning around, stared into the fire.

Whether it was he didn't see me in my obscure corner, or whether he didn't care what I saw, at any rate for a moment the mask dropped from his face.

I was appalled by what I read there. A hell of rage and hatred. He hated life; he hated people; and most of all he hated himself! I wondered how I ever could have seen him merely as a comely, vigorous, energetic young fellow. In the firelight his distorted face looked as old as the Wandering Jew's.

He took a letter from his pocket and, tearing it into small pieces, tossed the fragments on the fire. Then with the usual wisecrack he turned around to his friends.

It was a long time before my shaken nerves quieted down. In a curious way that glimpse into the night of Nick's soul comforted me, by revealing that there was something extraordinary in him and set apart from all others. Thus my instinctive terror of the man was justified. The worst of it was, it increased the helpless infatuation I felt for him. What woman could resist the appeal of a Lucifer?

When we got to our own suite later, Mary Eliska Girl Detective took a tiny piece of paper from the little bag she carried in the evenings, and smoothed it on the table.

"What's that?" I asked.

"Nick Van Tassel tore up a letter and threw it on the fire," she said. "I spotted one little piece that escaped the flames, and a long time after I secured it."

We bent over it together. All we could make out was the word "to" with some letters on either side of it, thus: "o to he."

"Looks as if somebody might have told Nick to go to hell," said Mary Eliska Girl Detective, dryly.

"Oh, I hope so!" I said, involuntarily.

She laughed. "At any rate, he received a setback tonight. That's certain."

"And then—what next?" I murmured, with a shiver.

"Ha! You felt it too!" she cried, with a keen look.

"Felt what?" I asked, turning away my head.

"Murder in the air!"

CHAPTER FIFTEEN

MISS BETSY AGAIN

During our stay in Newport that queer old Miss Betsy Pryor used to write to Mary Eliska Girl Detective every day or so. Her letters were so original, so different from the rest of the fan mail, that my employer always made a point of answering them immediately. I ought to mention that Crider's delvings among the tax lists had revealed Miss Betsy as one of the richest women in Newport, if not in all America. On her last return she had reported on an income of more than one million dollars. Yet there she lived behind her nine foot wall, apparently forgotten by the world. Crider's piece of information made Mary Eliska Girl Detective thoughtful.

One of Miss Betsy's notes that I have kept by me read:

'Dear Mary Eliska Girl Detective:

'I am wondering if you are still in Newport, since I no longer see your name included among those present at fashionable entertainments. Reading the society column is a woman's last weakness. My opinion of you immediately went up. I never could understand why one like you was ever attracted to Newport. Society is the final refuge of the empty minded. Lunches, teas, and dinners! Dinners, teas and lunches! Always the same old bell wethers sitting beside you, or meek ewes ever bleating in the same fashion.

'I had enough of it forty years ago, but they tell me they're still doing it. They tell me Gibbs Cumberland is still dining out every night. Good God! he's eighty two. If you ever meet him tell him that you have it on the authority of Betsy Pryor that he's eighty two. It will please him.

'Conversation is the only proper social exercise for intelligent beings. I never found anybody worth talking to in Newport, so I retired within my own grounds and talked to myself. Conversations of unimaginable wit and brilliancy, I assure you. Myself never let me down. However, sometimes I grow aweary of Betsy's wit and long to match her against another, a fresher set. Therefor I am reminding you of your promise to come see the tiresome old woman, though I must repeat, I don't know why you should.

'Yours anyhow,

'Betsy Pryor.'

Until we saw her Mary Eliska Girl Detective and I were never able to decide whether Betsy was quite cracked or merely waggish. A little of both, Mary Eliska Girl Detective suggested. She answered:

'Dear Miss Betsy Pryor:

'Your letters are always stimulating. You are right in inferring that it was not the fashionable entertainments which brought me to Newport. I am engaged in an engrossing and baffling investigation the end of which is not yet in sight. Several times lately it has occurred to me that you might help me in this matter, you have such an appreciation of life, and that you would enjoy doing so. But up to the moment of writing this I have not been able to think of any expedient by which I might visit you without advertising the fact to the spies who swarm around me. Of course if we are to do anything together, no hint of our association must be allowed to get out. Within the next few days I will find some means of visiting you secretly or, if I find that it is impracticable for us to work together, I will come openly.

'In either case you may expect to see me soon. Please tear this up as soon as you have read it.

'Ever sincerely yours,

'Mary Eliska.'

Chapter Sixteen

Murder in the Air

On the morning following my unsuccessful chase of Nick Van Tassel through the streets of Newport, Mary Eliska Girl Detective and I decided to go downstairs to breakfast at Omega Farm. We knew the capacity of our adversary for striking quickly, and there was much to be done if we were to get ahead of him.

Nick joined us at the breakfast table. Apparently he was a stranger to bad dreams, for he looked the embodiment of health and vigor. His freshly shaven sunburnt cheeks were as smooth and ruddy as an Elberta peach. Talk about your deceptive appearances! I wondered if the original Lucifer had the same faculty of assuming a boyish and disarming aspect. Probably he had. Scrambled eggs, broiled kidneys, bacon, and toast disappeared between Nick's fine white teeth in a business-like manner.

"What a treat to see you at breakfast, Mary Eliska Girl Detective!" he cried. "After all, it's the breakfast women who hold us."

"Must you be held?" she drawled.

"Ha! you're as heartless as you are beautiful!" he cried.

"I expect we're a pair," she said.

"I wish we were," he said, with a contemptuous side glance at me. "Why don't you stay here always?"

"It wouldn't work, my dear," she answered, calmly. "You and I are too much of a character. Solitary birds."

He laughed.

By this time we were beginning to know our host pretty well, and in spite of his wisecracking we perceived that his thoughts were elsewhere. Behind the superficial brightness of his eyes brooded a remote thought which never nickered—the thought of murder. A pale blue eye is supposed to be typical of the killer; but there is a kind of bright inhuman black eye that is even more characteristic.

"What's the program for today?" asked Mary Eliska Girl Detective, idly.

"I have to spend the morning conferring with my various overseers and foremen," he said. "Beastly bore."

"That's all right," she said. "Bella and I are going in to town to sit with Leonie."

"Very mysterious, this illness of Leonie's," he said, dryly. "I suspect it provides you with an excuse whenever you are bored here."

"Well, that's up to you," she said, calmly.

He laughed. "Never get any change out of you! Will you lunch here?"

"I will if you will."

"I will." He flashed a sharp look at her and said, a little too carelessly: "By the way, they're going to dance at the Chowder Club tonight. Will you come with me?"

"Good Lord.'" said Mary Eliska Girl Detective. "It's only five days since your uncle's funeral. You'll create a scandal!"

"Oh, I've been scandalizing Newport ever since I put on long pants," he said, offhand. "They expect it of me now."

"Well, it's not my lookout," she said, lightly; "and, anyhow, I'm in as bad as I can be already. Sure I'll come, if you can find a cavalier for Bella."

"We'll all go in a body," he said, without looking at me.

As soon as Nick drove off to make his rounds of the place, Mary Eliska Girl Detective and I started in to town.

After a brief call at Mrs. Lysaght's to see if there was anything important in the mail (there was not) we drove to each of the banks in turn. My employer's object was to show her scrap of paper to the tellers of each institution to see if they could identify the writing. Her introductions from New York banks smoothed the way for us.

Nothing came of it. The written characters were too few. Though we limited our inquiry to a few of each bank's richest customers, none of the tellers were able to identify our scrap of writing.

Back at the Dump, we found Nick's whole crowd, with the exception of Mary Bourne, gathered in the den. Their light talk and laughter broke out with suspicious suddenness as we mounted the stairs.

Suggestions that a more serious conference had been in progress lingered in their imperfectly smoothed out faces; the somber thought still dwelling behind Nick's eyes; little Evelyn hastily rouging her cheeks to hide their pallor. In her eyes the haunted look we had not seen in several days came and went again. Clearly she had no stomach for the business in hand. Ann, on the other hand, seemed uplifted. She was a fit partner for Nick.

Luncheon was an uneasy meal. Everybody talked and laughed a little too much. The tension slowly increased until I felt I could bear no more. It was too terrible to be in the presence of that grisly secret without being able to drag it into the light.

Nick said: "How about a sail this afternoon? There's an A1 breeze."

"Count me out," said Mary Eliska Girl Detective. "When I was at Mrs. Lysaght's this morning I got a telegram from an old friend who is passing through Providence this afternoon. I must run over there for a couple of hours."

There were expressions of regret around the table, but I could see they were relieved. Very likely they still had preparations to make for the evening, and it seemed like a stroke of luck to get Mary Eliska Girl Detective out of the way.

At 3:30 we were in the office of District Attorney Lyle in Providence. He received us with an injured air. The sight of us reminded him of his recent humiliation.

Mary Eliska Girl Detective wasted no time in beating around the bush. "I have come," she said, "to urge you to have Nick Van Tassel arrested immediately."

He looked a little sick. "Have you any fresh evidence?" he asked.

"No."

"Then why?" he demanded, spreading out his hands helplessly and wagging them from side to side. "Why?...Why?" He could get no further.

"I have reason to believe that another murder is planned for tonight."

"Well, it's a simple matter to warn the victim, isn't it?"

"That's just the trouble," she said, gravely. "I have not been able to discover who it is."

"Another mare's nest!" he cried, ill temperedly. "What do you know?"

She described to him the events of the past twenty four hours.

"Mere supposition!" he snarled, stamping up and down his office. "I can't act on supposition. You've got to bring me evidence!"

"There's no occasion to lose your temper," my employer suggested mildly. "My interest in this matter is identical with yours—to protect the public."

"I'm a busy man, a busy man, madam, and it puts me out of temper to be interrupted by frivolous pretexts like this!"

"Frivolous pretexts?" echoed Mary Eliska Girl Detective, running up her eyebrows. "To solve the murder of one millionaire and to prevent the murder of another? I'm offering you the greatest case of your career."

It does no good to tell the truth to an unreasonable man, of course. "There's nothing in it!" he yelled. Then immediately afterward he asked, "Why tonight?"

"Because of the dance at the Chowder Club," she patiently explained. "Nick Van Tassel always uses a gathering of some sort to cover his operations. He had no intention of going to this dance until he needed it for a pretext. He will use the dance to establish an alibi."

"This is all poppycock!" cried Lyle. "You're just looking for personal publicity!"

She smiled. "Well, let's not get into an argument about that. Just give me a plain answer—will you or will you not arrest Nick Van Tassel this afternoon?"

"There isn't a man on the force who would carry out such an order!"

"Try it and see."

"Arrest Nick Van Tassel on such flimsy evidence as you have presented! I would only cover myself with ridicule! I would be laughed out of office. I could never show my face in Rhode Island again!"

"You have not answered my question," she pointed out.

"No, I will not!" he shouted. "It's plumb ridiculous!"

Mary Eliska Girl Detective quickly rose. "All right," she said cheerfully. "Then I must take my own measures."

"What are you going to do?" he demanded, sharply curious.

"I don't know. I shall be guided by the circumstances."

He shot out the courtroom forefinger. "Mind you," he rasped, "if you take the law into your own hands you need expect no special consideration from me."

She laughed. "I shall expect nothing from you."

We hastened out.

She had carried the interview off bravely, as she always does, but for all that I could not see but that we were completely blocked. Going home in the car I felt very blue. It was then nearly five o'clock.

It was too awful to think that murder was striding toward us moment by moment, and we powerless to prevent it. It was like one of these nightmares where you seem to be tied hand and foot. At last I asked, diffidently: "What did you mean by taking your own measures?"

"I mean taking Nick into custody ourselves," she said, coolly, "and keeping him until the danger is past."

"What!" I cried.

"That would be an effective way to prevent the murder, wouldn't it?"

My spirits rebounded. "Oh yes!" I cried. "It's the only answer! After all, he's a man like any other!" And then another thought chilled me. "But afterward," I faltered, "what then?"

"Afterward must take care of itself," she said, coolly.

Before returning to the Dump, we went on to Newport to confer with Crider and lay out a plan for the evening.

CHAPTER SEVENTEEN

AT THE CHOWDER CLUB

We were all sitting around in the Den, sipping coffee and liqueurs before going on to the dance. Nick and his set always liked to make a late and effective entrance anywhere.

Ann Livingston, sitting at Nick's desk, suddenly said: "Why, Nick, there's a secret compartment in the middle of this desk. How do you get into it?"

"Nothing secret about it," said Nick, lazily.

She moved the blotter to one side and lifted the center flap, bringing the typewriter into view. "Oh, a typewriter!" she cried. "How cunning! I didn't know you could typewrite."

"Useful accomplishment," said Nick.

"I've always been dying to learn how to typewrite!" she exclaimed. "Do give me a lesson."

Nick arose with a good natured air and, inserting a sheet of paper in the machine, told her to go ahead and do her worst. "All you have to do is strike the letters," he said.

"If she knows her letters," put in Bill.

Ann made a face at him. "What shall I write?" she asked at large.

"Such a concatenation of events is inconceivable," chanted Reggie.

"Go on!" she said. "Tell me another!"

"Oh, where and oh, where has my little dog gone?" sang Bill.

Ann commenced to spell out the words laboriously.

The whole scene rang a little false in my ears. It did not seem possible that Ann could have been ignorant of the existence of the machine. Moreover, the kittenish air she was displaying was not natural to her. I wondered with a sinking heart if the scene was being staged for our benefit. If Nick had discovered the trap we had set for him, it would be just like him to let us know it in this manner. I waited anxiously for confirmation.

Presently Ann said, "Nick, some of the letters print crookedly."

"That can't be," he answered, carelessly. "I've had the thing only a few weeks."

"Come and look," she said. "The e, the r, the t, the y, the o."

He went and looked over her shoulder. It seemed to me that the room grew very still, and my breath failed me a little. But their voices had sounded so casual I could not be sure yet.

Then Reggie Mygatt drawled in his unpleasant voice: "Funny! If you transpose those letters they make Mary Eliska Girl Detective's name, lacking only the s."

By that I knew that they knew. My skin prickled all over. I wondered if a general show down was coming. There we were, Mary Eliska Girl Detective and I helpless in Nick Van Tassel's house, surrounded by his gang and his servants. I had a moment of perfect fear. I dared not look at my employer.

She laughed lightly. "What an odd coincidence!"

"Oh, what the hell!" said Nick. "It can easily be fixed....Come on, let's go to the dance."

So he was at his old game of playing with us like a cat with mice! I ventured to breathe again. At any rate, we would be safe at a crowded dance.

Just before we set out, two extra young men came to balance the sexes. We went in two of Nick's limousines, Ann, Evelyn, Mary Bourne, Bill, and Reggie in the first; Mary Eliska Girl Detective, Nick, the two new young men (whose names I have forgotten, but it doesn't matter) and I in the second. Nick, Mary Eliska Girl Detective, and I were occupying the back seat in that order. The two young men, I remember, were impressed with Nick's greatness, and Nick was showing off a little. One of them had asked him how many cars he had, and he answered: "Don't ask me. The Dump is all cluttered up with cars. I've been meaning for a long time to weed them out and have an auction."

As we turned into the club grounds Nick said, in his warm, persuasive voice, "Give me the two first dances, Mary Eliska Girl Detective."

"Charmed," she said, and at the same time pressed my hand twice. This was to convey to me that I should warn our men she would lead Nick out of the clubhouse during the second dance.

Notwithstanding its plebeian name the Chowder Club is one of the smartest institutions in Newport. It occupies a rocky promontory sticking out into the bay and is almost completely surrounded by water. The clubhouse is a wide spreading one story building with deep verandas. The whole summit of the promontory is surrounded by a stout rustic fence of cedar logs to keep the members from rolling down the smooth rock slopes into the water.

We were late arrivals and there must have been upward of a hundred cars parked all around the open space in front of the clubhouse, and along both sides of the wide approach, each car with its rear bumper against the cedar fence, ready to start without interference. Mary Eliska Girl Detective pressed my hand again, and following the direction of her glance, I understood that she was calling my attention to a convertible coupe, painted maroon and bearing a Maryland license. It was one of the first cars in line, that is to say farthest from the clubhouse. With her unerring eye she had recognized it.

In getting out, my employer and I were left alone for a moment, and I asked, "What about the coupe with the Maryland license?"

She said, "That's the car that Nick means to conduct his operations in tonight."

"How can you be sure?"

"I looked into the machine shop after lunch and saw them overhauling it."

As we mounted the steps I saw George Stephens lolling against a post. He was our liaison officer for the evening. He was a handsome young fellow, and looked perfectly at home in that crowd. He had been given the job because both Crider and Benny Abell had been working inside the Van Tassel house on the night of the murder, and it was conceivable that Nick Van Tassel might have spotted them. But he could not have known Stephens.

I hung back a little, and Stephens slipped up beside me. I whispered Mary Eliska Girl Detective's message to him, and he went off to pass it to Crider, Abell, and Scarfe, who were concealed among the cars below. Their job, of course, would be to seize Nick when Mary Eliska Girl Detective led him away from the clubhouse.

Crider had hired a big Cadillac sedan for the evening. It was an old model and the bloom was off it, but mechanically it was in perfect order.

Nick and Mary Eliska Girl Detective danced. Amid that smart and well-dressed crowd Nick stood out with a peculiar distinction. He was not the handsomest man present, but there was a certain air of arrogance about him none could match. There was that in his smile which forced men and women alike to yield him a kind of slavish admiration. His whole crowd shared in his reflected glory—Ann, Evelyn, Mary, and the men; among the young people, anyhow, this little circle was looked upon as the most desirable in Newport.

I presently noticed that Ann and Reggie had disappeared from view, though I did not see them go. They never returned. Sent on outpost duty, I assumed. On such occasions I had good reason to believe that the aristocratic Ann donned boy's clothes. She had the figure of a graceful stripling.

At the beginning of the second dance I pleaded heat to the nameless young man who was squiring me, as an excuse to get him out on the veranda. We took up our stand at the head of the steps, and pretty soon Nick and Mary Eliska Girl Detective came strolling along. I heard her say: "Oh, for a breath of fresh air and a glimpse of the stars!"

"Sure!" said Nick. "Let's stroll down the drive."

My heart began to beat fast. If all went well, Nick was presently due to see some stars that were not in the firmament.

Before he went down the steps he turned around to speak to one of the club servants. He pressed something into the man's hand. It looked as if he were tipping him, but I kept my eye on the fellow and presently I saw him unfold a note. Nick had his spies and accomplices everywhere, and they served him with the sort of devotion money couldn't buy.

But this one was careless. He threw away the note, and I marked where it fell. On the pretext that I wanted to watch the dancers through the window, I moved over and put my foot on it, and presently I picked it up. Spreading it out unseen by my partner, I read:

'When I have gone a hundred yards, come after me and tell me I am wanted on the telephone.'

My hopes collapsed. The uncanny feeling returned to me that Nick bore a charmed existence. Apparently he was able to foresee every move we made. We could not touch him.

The servant had gone after him. Soon they were to be seen returning. Mary Eliska Girl Detective paused at my side, while Nick went inside to answer his imaginary telephone call. I got rid of my partner by sending him for a glass of punch, and I told my employer what had happened.

She laughed. "Well, we must try something else," she said.

After a moment's thought she went on: "Tell Stephens to tell Crider to find the convertible coupe with the Maryland license. He is to cut the wires leading to the main switch. If the doors are locked, let him raise the hood and cut the wires leading from the distributor. Crider and the other two are then to conceal themselves in the vicinity of that car and wait for Nick. Let them move their own car as near as possible to the coupe, so they won't have so far to carry him."

Nick returned, saying: "The call wasn't of the slightest importance. What a sell! Let's finish this dance."

Later Nick danced with Mary Bourne and with Evelyn, but he did not ask me. Wherever his tall figure moved he was followed by those curious glances, half admiring, half resentful, that he alone had the power of evoking. Apparently he made all the other young men feel inferior. Evelyn, while she was dancing with him, in spite of her training, could not keep the rapt look out of her eyes.

Upon finishing their dance these two went out on the veranda, where they ensconced themselves in the darkest corner on the bay side. This looked as if they might be intending to repeat the trick that had been played at the Van Tassel house, and Mary Eliska Girl Detective and I watched them as closely as we were able without calling attention to ourselves.

At her suggestion we fetched Stephens, and the three of us strolled as near as we could. She whispered to Stephens to strike a match and light a cigarette. In its brief flare we perceived that the substitution had already been effected. It was Bill Kip who sat beside Evelyn. Nick apparently had gone over the rail.

Making our way around the veranda as quickly as possible, we descended the steps. Couples were strolling back and forth across the open space in front of the clubhouse, but the driveway beyond was deserted. It was a warm night, with a haze rising from the cold water; no moon. We quickened our steps. When we came within sight of the maroon coupe we saw that it was still empty. Nick had to creep around over the rocks below the fence, and that was how we had beat him to it. We slipped behind another car, where we could watch the coupe through the windows, ourselves unseen.

In a moment we saw Nick creep under the fence and unlock his car. He softly closed the door and stepped on the starter. We could hear it whir, but of course nothing happened. Then three more figures seemed to rise from the ground without a sound. At sight of them Nick pressed the catch that locked his door on the inside, and ran up the glass. For the moment both sides were helpless. Our men could not reach Nick, and Nick could not make his engine go.

It was the resourceful Benny Abell who broke the deadlock. I saw him scramble up over the rear compartment of the coupe. I could not guess what he was after until I saw his arm make wide, slashing movements; he must have had a knife as sharp as a razor. He cut out three sides of the back of the khaki top, and the piece dropped down.

Crider joined Benny; they reached inside the car and started hauling Nick out by main strength. Nick struggled furiously but made no outcry. There was surprisingly little noise. Neither party to this fight could afford to call attention to it. Scarfe got his hands on Nick also, and the tall figure was drawn clear of the car in spite of his struggles. All four of them rolled down over the back of the car and hit the ground with a thud. Nick broke free, and vaulted over the fence like a flash. The others ducked after him.

We ran to the fence between two cars and looked over. Stephens slipped under the rail to go to the aid of his comrades. There was a confused struggle on the flat rock below. Apparently Nick was giving a good account of himself against such heavy odds. I heard the impact of fists on bare flesh. They moved closer to us, and I could distinguish the one figure so much taller than the others, swinging his long arms, and hear him cursing softly.

An extraordinary emotion seized me. Whatever he was, Nick was game. To see him at bay like that, a stag attacked by terriers, almost tore the heart out of my breast. A hair's breadth more and I should have leaped down there, screaming, to help him. I clung desperately to the fence to steady myself.

There was one moment when he actually had them all down, and leaped for the fence directly where we were standing. But some one caught him by a foot and he crashed down on the rock. Even so, it was not yet over. He wrenched himself free and rolled away to one side. He got to his feet and stood with his back to the fence. I could hear his hoarse panting. A voice seemed to be crying inside me: I don't care what you've done! I love you! I love you! It was a kind of madness.

His assailants divided, and two of them came at him from each side. That was the end. Like dogs they pulled him down. There was something most horrible in the way all four of them silently dropped on his prostrate body. Even then Nick never uttered a sound. There was a sort of fumbling struggle on the rock, then the four men arose, leaving Nick lying motionless. I thought they had killed him, and a low cry was forced from me.

"Blindfolded, gagged, and tied up," Mary Eliska Girl Detective murmured, reassuringly.

We heard the sound of running feet, and she whispered, quickly, "Carry him down out of sight!"

Snatching up the helpless body, they disappeared as quietly as shadows into the mist.

Several chauffeurs ran up to us. "What's the matter lady?" one asked.

"There were some men fighting down there," said Mary Eliska Girl

Detective. "They went that way." She pointed to the right.

They ducked under the fence and followed her direction, while we quietly turned the other way.

Our Cadillac was now the last car parked on that side of the drive. We stood beside it, waiting, until the four men appeared with their burden. They passed him under the rail and swung him into the back of the car. Mary Eliska Girl Detective, Stephens, and I climbed over him, while the other three squeezed into the front seat, and we started.

As the car began to move, somebody from up the line hailed us. Crider merely stepped on the gas. A pair of headlights flashed on and a car turned out to follow us. But it was only a halfhearted pursuit. We soon lost it in the streets of the town.

Chapter Eighteen

A Crowded Hour

"Where shall I take him?" asked Crider, who was driving.

Mary Eliska Girl Detective leaned forward to keep her voice from carrying to the prisoner's ears. "It doesn't matter," she whispered. "Drive around for an hour."

We rolled at a quiet pace through the deserted streets of the town and out by what they call the West Road, one of the two highways that connect the island of Rhode Island with the mainland. This route carried us past the public airport, a golf course, and the ancient windmill with its long arms that is one of the sights of the neighborhood.

Benny Abell unbuttoned his coat and produced a pair of curious objects that he had thrust inside.

"Found these in his car," he said. "Thought they might be useful as evidence."

It was a pair of heavy wooden sandals that strapped on over the ordinary shoes. There was a row of short steel spikes projecting from the square toe, and a row of longer spikes from under the ball of the foot, inclining forward and forming a sort of fulcrum.

"With these," murmured Mary Eliska Girl Detective, "he could go straight up the side of a wooden house if he had a rain leader or any other projection to steady himself....Search him," she added to Stephens.

This was not altogether easy while Nick was lying huddled on the bottom of the car, but Stephens went about it systematically.

"Take his money, too," said Mary Eliska Girl Detective. "It can be returned to him."

Stephens produced in turn a wallet, a handful of change, a pocket flash, a gun, and a curious furry object that at first we could not identify

Mary Eliska Girl Detective.

Mary Eliska Girl Detective handed the gun to me to keep. It was an old fashioned six shooter of thirty eight caliber, a formidable weapon. I shoved it in my stocking.

She turned on the dome light, and we saw that the furry object was an ingeniously made wig, mask, and beard all in one. The wig part represented a completely bald pate, and when Nick drew it on and fastened it he must have been a truly horrible object and, of course, entirely unrecognizable.

Meanwhile Nick was groaning protestingly under his gag, and since we had left the town far behind, Mary Eliska Girl Detective whispered to Stephens to tell him we would take the gag off, but that if he made any outcry it would have to go back again. The gag was removed, and Nick rubbed his sore mouth gratefully against his shoulder.

"Why do I have to lie here under your feet?" he said, sullenly. "Can't you stick me in the corner of the seat?"

Mary Eliska Girl Detective could not deny a defeated enemy this small favor, and between them she and Stephens yanked him up and propped him in the corner.

Smiling, she stuck a cigarette in his mouth and lighted it, but after a puff or two he said: "Throw it away. It's no good when you can't see the smoke."

After a while he said, with restored good humor:

"What's to be gained by keeping me in blinders, anyhow? I know perfectly well that I am riding with the adorable Mary Eliska Girl Detective. I smelled her perfume when she lifted me up. What is its seductive name—Adieu Sagesse?"

Mary Eliska Girl Detective laughed and told Stephens to take off the blind. It was done, their eyes met, and both laughed. There was an extraordinary relation between those two. Each admired the other immensely, and neither would give an inch. Nick would have shot her down just as gladly as she would have sent him to the chair.

"All right, lady," said Nick, perfectly good humored. "My turn will come!"

After a while he said, ironically: "If it's a fair question, darling, why are you taking me for this delightful drive with all your gentlemen friends?"

"I don't mind telling you," she said, "if you will tell me where you were going tonight in the convertible coupe."

"That's easy," he said. "I've got a girl in the town. She's not in society, so I call on her secretly. You're a woman of the world; you understand these things."

"Is it necessary to take a pair of climbers, a gun, and a false face when you call on her?" she asked.

He ignored the question. "You have not answered me yet."

"I shall answer you more truthfully than you answered me," she returned. "I am taking you for this ride to keep you out of mischief."

"Good of you," he said.

We crossed the great Mount Hope suspension bridge, high above the water, and passed through the quiet streets of Bristol. Mary Eliska Girl Detective soon gave the word to return. In taking Nick's climbers, gun, and mask, she considered that she had rendered him harmless at least for the balance of the night. She told Stephens to untie his wrists and ankles.

"There are six of us, and all armed," she said, suggestively.

"You wouldn't dare shoot me, darling," he said, grinning. "At any rate, not in Newport county."

"Don't try me too far," she retorted, smiling back. "It has occurred to me more than once it would be the best way out."

After a while he asked, "Well, now you have me, what are you going to do with me?"

"It's quite a problem," said Mary Eliska Girl Detective, dryly.

"Yes. The district attorney won't entertain charges against me," (so he already knew that!), "and if you tried to turn me over to the police they'd set me free and arrest you for lèse majesté or something."

"Perhaps they would," she said, equably. "At any rate, I'm not going to risk it."

"Then what are you going to do with me?"

"When we come within five miles of the Dump I shall put you out and let you walk home."

Oddly enough, this angered him as no threat of danger could have done. To the arrogant Nick, who hated setting foot to the ground, the idea of being forced to foot it along the highway like a common tramp was intolerable. "Damn it! that's not sporting!" he cried. "That's a mean and petty advantage to take of me. It's humiliating! Look at the state I'm in!"

It was true his white shirt front was all slimed from having been rubbed against the wet rocks; his collar was torn, his coat ripped, his face bruised.

He had lost his hat, of course, and his black hair was wildly touseled. He looked like anything but the darling of Newport then.

"One of my boys will lend you a hat and coat," said Mary Eliska Girl Detective.

"For God's sake take me somewhere where I can hire a car!" he cried.

"It would not suit my plans," she answered, calmly.

Sure enough, soon after we had returned over the suspension bridge she forced him to get out in the road. In Benny Abell's hat, which was too big for him, and Benny Abell's topcoat, which was too short, he was an exquisitely comic figure. We had a good laugh at his expense. We left him grinding his teeth and savagely cursing. He had no money to hire a conveyance, and it was hardly likely anybody would stop and pick him up at that time of night.

"Where next?" asked Crider, when we drove on.

"To the Dump."

"It's dangerous," he said, scowling.

"I left jewels there and other things I want to secure," she said. "I also want the typewriter if it has not been made away with. It is my only evidence. Afterward you can drive us to a hotel."

In ten minutes we were there. The big house was dark except for lights in the corridors, and no cars were parked in the drive. When Mary Eliska Girl Detective and I got out, the Cadillac turned around and drove off as if to return to town, but it had been instructed to wait just out of sight of the front door. It was about one o'clock, and the watchman was on duty in the lower hall. This was an able looking ex pugilist known as Jack White.

"Has Mr. Van Tassel come home?" asked Mary Eliska Girl Detective, affably.

"No, ma'am."

"Any of his friends here?"

"No ma'am. I understand they're all at the Chowder Club. Nobody in the house but the servants, ma'am."

"We're going to bed," she said, smothering a yawn.

"How will we get past him, going out?" I whispered on the stairs.

"We'll go down by the back stairs and the service entry."

In our bedrooms we secured the most valuable of our belongings, and we also got long coats to replace the wraps left in the Chowder Club cloakroom. Also we put on hats which somehow render women less conspicuous at night. Then we stole noiselessly back along the corridor to the den. The corridor was lighted, but the big room was dark.

"Do you know how the typewriter is fastened to the desk?" whispered Mary Eliska Girl Detective.

"Sure," I said; "a couple of hooks over the frame that are fastened by thumbscrews below. I can release it in the dark."

"Good!" she said.

However, as soon as I raised the flap of the desk I realized that our errand was in vain. "It's gone!"

I said.

"Well, that was only to be expected," she said, serenely. "Come on!"

At that moment the electric light switch clicked and the lights flooded on. Between us and the way out stood Nick's five friends. Bill Kip had a gun in his hand. They must have been pressed back into the recesses on either side the fireplace when we entered. Reggie Mygatt was in rough clothes like a gardener and Ann Livingston was wearing a boy's suit. Even at that moment of terror I took note of what a handsome lad she made.

"What are you trying on?" asked Reggie, with a hateful sneer. "A little burglary?"

Mary Eliska Girl Detective made no answer. I saw her measuring the distance to the central window out of the corner of her eye. There was a small balcony outside. Unfortunately, the window was closed.

"Where's Nick?" demanded Evelyn, in a strained, high pitched voice.

"How should I know?" said Mary Eliska Girl Detective.

"You do know! You carried him away from the club! What have you done with him?"

"He is unhurt," said Mary Eliska Girl Detective, coolly.

"He had better be!"

Mary Eliska Girl Detective sprang for the window. Reggie, instantly after her, caught her by the shoulders, but not before she had succeeded in kicking out a pane of glass. "Crider! Benny!" she cried. "Come!"

At the same instant Bill shouted downstairs, "Bolt the door!"

I ran to my employer's assistance. Before I could reach her a heavy velvet portiere was thrown over my head, blinding and almost suffocating me. I was pulled down to the ground; a cord of some sort was thrown around and around my body and I found myself entirely helpless. As I heard no sounds of struggle, I judged that Mary Eliska Girl Detective had been treated in the same manner.

A voice said: "Quick! Down the back stairs with them!"

As we were carried out of the room, I heard a crash of glass downstairs, from which I gathered that our friends were coming in through the windows. Several shots followed, filling me with a sickening anxiety. Meanwhile we were being carried rapidly down the corridor, past our rooms and on down the service stairs.

There must have been a car standing outside the service entrance, for we were instantly thrown in the back, our captors piled in, and we started. This car was equipped with a cut out which was open, and we sped around the house and struck into the main drive beyond, making a tremendous roar. I could not understand why they were thus attracting attention to themselves, until I heard one of them say with satisfaction, "Here they come!" Then I knew they were trying to draw our friends away from the house.

Somebody said, "Put out the lights!" Immediately afterward, judging from the motion of the car, we made a complete circle and, I suppose, stole back through the gates and, turning out of the drive, bumped slowly over the field. Behind us I heard the sound of another car driven rapidly, and somebody said with a laugh, "There they go into Newport, looking for us." Our car stopped, and they held a consultation over us.

"What shall we do with them?"

"Throw them in the river," snarled Reggie.

"No!" cried Evelyn. "We can't do that without Nick's say so."

"Take them back to the house."

"No! They may have left a man on watch there. They may come back."

"Carry them up to the sail loft," said Reggie's voice. "If that is threatened, we can run them aboard the Bonito and carry them out to sea. Let Evelyn, Bill, and Mary watch over them while Ann and I go look for Nick."

Chapter Nineteen

In the Balance

I had been carried up an outside stairway, through a door, and laid down on a board floor. Mary Eliska Girl Detective I knew was near, because I had heard her body dropped beside me. There was a long wait.

Finding it useless to struggle against the cords that bound me, I submitted to my fate. I had fallen into a kind of lethargy in which one felt neither hope nor fear.

Finally I heard Ann and Reggie come back, bringing Nick. The sound of Nick's voice brought me cruelly back to life. I was plunged into a hell of feelings that I could not analyze—terror, regret, longing! I felt as if I were about to die without having really lived. Nick and his friends whispered together, and I could not hear a word.

Beside me, Mary Eliska Girl Detective began to moan feebly and to cry for water. Knowing her as well as I did, I suspected she was not as badly off as she sounded.

Evelyn's voice answered her: "There's no water up here."

"Take this thing off my head or I'll suffocate!" moaned Mary Eliska Girl Detective.

Evelyn approached us, and I heard the rip of goods alongside me. Presently she cut away the heavy velvet that swathed my head and I came out into the blessed air once more. I saw that Evelyn had one of the specially shaped knives that sail makers use. She returned to her friends without speaking to us.

Nick said: "Well, Mary Eliska Girl Detective, I told you my turn would come." He grinned evilly. He had not forgiven her his enforced walk along the highway.

"One good turn deserves another," she answered. "Cut me loose."

He turned his back on us.

Finding that I could see and hear again, could even whisper to my employer lying beside me, a measure of courage returned to me. I hastily took stock of our surroundings. We were lying on the floor of the sail loft over the yacht rigging shop. It was a polished hardwood floor so that the canvas would slip over it easily. Great piles of snowy half-finished sails were lying about.

As I have remarked before, this building was a barnlike structure in early American style. The roof ran up into a sharp peak over our heads. I remembered how it swept down almost to the ground in the rear, over a lean to addition to the shop below.

There was a row of dormer windows down each side of the loft. They were covered with pieces of canvas at present to keep the light from showing through. The loft was lighted by a line of naked electric bulbs suspended down the center.

Mary Eliska Girl Detective and I were lying near the door. Nick and his five friends moved to the other side of the loft to consult together. They lowered their voices as they thought, but as the talk went on they became excited, and in the stillness under the high roof I could hear almost every word. It gave me a sickening turn when I realized that our lives depended on it.

I heard Reggie say, "We've got to put them out or they'll certainly do for us!"

"No!" said Evelyn. "Our best hope of safety lies in turning them loose. They've got nothing on us. The typewriter's in the river. They've got nothing on us, and they can't get anything."

"Don't listen to Evelyn," put in Ann. "She's chicken hearted. She'd argue anything to keep from stepping on these women."

"How do you know they've got nothing on us?" Reggie demanded of Evelyn. "This woman works in the dark and strikes when she's damn good and ready. We know she's been tampering with Gibbs Cumberland. Maybe she's approached all our people. She'll never rest until she undermines the whole racket. We've got to step on her!"

"Reggie is right!" put in Ann again. Under her slim and elegant exterior that girl harbored the spirit of a fiend.

"Listen to what I say!" warned Evelyn, earnestly. "If Mary Eliska Girl Detective is put out of the way it will raise a storm throughout the country that will destroy us, evidence or no evidence!"

"Aah! talk sense!" snarled Reggie. "You can't convict without evidence! Listen! Her men can swear that she entered Nick's house and was never seen again. What of it? None of us five was seen. They can't testify that we had anything to do with it. And Nick can prove he wasn't on the scene."

"Jack White," suggested Evelyn.

"Jack can't rat on us," said Reggie. "We've got too much on him. If he should try it, we'll put him where he can't testify. He'd never be missed."

"Where is this going to end?" cried Evelyn, hysterically.

"I told you so!" cried Ann. "Her nerve is gone."

"Be quiet," growled Nick. "Let Reggie finish."

"You can't prove a murder without a body," Reggie went on, "and we'll take damn good care they are never found. Sure it will raise a storm. But it can't touch us. It will blow over in the end and we'll be in a stronger position than ever. Look! this woman has been to Gibbs Cumberland. Maybe she's been to Eversley and that's why he didn't come across last night. Maybe she's been to all of them. Well, if she disappears now, that will put the fear of God into them, won't it? They'll be glad enough then to pay on the nail. I say we've got to put these women out or go out of business ourselves."

A voice put in, "How could we dispose of the bodies?"

"That's easy. There's plenty of sheet lead downstairs. Roll them up in that and carry them out to sea."

"Cheese it!" said Nick. "They're listening."

They moved farther away and I could hear no more. God knows it was awful to lie there helpless, listening to the gang discussing whether or not we should be murdered, but it was worse not to hear what was said for and against. I felt as if I should go out of my mind. I heard somebody say, "Well, put it to the vote." There could be little doubt as to how the vote would go. Among the six there was only one voice raised in our favor.

Then Mary Eliska Girl Detective dropped a bombshell in my ear by whispering: "She left the knife with me. I have cut myself free. Turn partly on your side away from me and I will cut the ropes at your back. Be careful not to disarrange them until we're ready to make a break."

I obeyed in a dazed fashion, and presently she said: "You're free. Lie on your back to conceal the cut ends of the rope. They took my gun. Have you still got yours?"

"Yes," I whispered. "It's in my stocking."

"Can you pass it to me?"

"I'll try."

The velvet portiere still covered me to my feet, and under it I was able to pull up my dress a fraction of an inch at a time, and finally work my hand down into my stocking. I had to proceed with the greatest care to avoid pulling out the loose ends of the rope from under me. I got my hand on the gun and edged it out little by little. Still under cover of the portiere I passed it over to Mary Eliska Girl Detective's side, and she secured it. She whispered: "Lie perfectly still until the lights go out, then jump for the window immediately over your head. I know the windows are open, because I saw the canvas move. I'll take the next one. Remember the roof of the lean to is almost flat and comes down to within seven feet of the ground. Won't hurt you to drop off. If we become separated, meet me behind the first hangar."

A quarrel broke out among the gang—perhaps it was over the best method of giving us our quietus.

They disputed in angry whispers and forgot to watch us as closely as before. Glancing at Mary Eliska Girl Detective, I saw that she had turned partly on her side and had drawn up her right hand with the pistol to take aim. Her body still hid the pistol from any of the gang who might glance in our direction.

Apparently she was going to fire at the door, which seemed senseless to me; then I saw the electric light switch beside it.

The shot roared under the roof and was echoed by another report and a flash of blue flame from the switch. The loft was plunged in blackness. A yell broke simultaneously from the six throats of the gang, and they made for us as one.

"Quick! Roll back under the eaves until they pass," whispered Mary Eliska Girl Detective.

They fumbled for us in the darkness, continually falling over one another.

"Reggie and Bill!" roared Nick. "Hold the door! There's no other way out!"

"I'm here.'" answered Reggie, grimly.

"Try the switch.'"

"It's burned out!"

The search moved away from me a little, and I sprang for the window, and somehow precipitated myself out on the roof. I went down the steep part like a projectile, but slowed myself on the flatter part by spreading out arms and legs. Someone was above me at the window. Fearing a shot, I rolled off to one side. In my confusion I rolled the wrong way. There was no shot, but another body came hurtling down the roof and passed me. When I dropped to the ground it was between me and Mary Eliska Girl Detective.

Somebody clutched hold of me in the dark, and a shrill voice cried out: "Nick, I've got one of them! I've got one of them!"

This was little Mary Bourne. She had nerve to follow, us like that. I wasn't afraid of her. I picked her up in my arms and flung her with all my might on the ground. She squeaked like a mechanical doll when she struck. I jumped over her body and collided with Mary Eliska Girl Detective. Taking hands, we ran with all our might. We could hear the men pounding down the outside stairway, and Nick shouting orders: "Reggie; get a car and cut them off at the gate!...Bill! watch the dock and don't let them get a boat!...Ann! turn on the lights!"

When we came to the end of the building, instead of striking across the flying field direct for the gate, we turned to the right, and ran for the hangars bounding the field on the north side. They would never expect us to go that way. What we chiefly feared was the lights. The whole field was surrounded by tall poles bearing floodlights. We didn't know where the switch was. We strained every nerve to make the shelter of the hangars before the lights could be turned on.

It was a long run, and the lights came on when we had still a couple of hundred yards to go. We dropped in the grass and lay perfectly still, then crawled on our stomachs a foot at a time for the river bank. Rolling over the edge, we found partial shelter from the light on the stones below. Bent almost double, we ran over the stones, slipping and stumbling, until we had passed the hangars and were out of radius of the lights.

A short distance behind the hangars was a strip of woods that marked the boundary of Nick's property. We did not stop running until we had gained the shelter of the trees. There we flung ourselves down to give our pounding hearts a little ease. We could hear no sounds of pursuit.

CHAPTER TWENTY

A HITCH TO TOWN

As soon as we got our breath we resumed our way around the edge of Nick's outermost fields, passing behind the stables, and finally gaining the highway. We figured we were about five miles from town. Not exactly a pleasant prospect for a couple of lone women at two o'clock in the morning. The coats and hats we had secured in our rooms covered our conspicuous evening dresses, but our satin slippers were fouled with mud. We had lost the little valises we had taken, but Mary Eliska Girl Detective still had all her jewelry hanging about her under the coat. I figured she was worth between two and three hundred thousand as she stood. It made me nervous.

When we turned our faces toward town, Nick's polo field was on our left. "They'll be watching the main gate," I said, nervously.

"We'll make a détour," said Mary Eliska Girl Detective.

We had not gone far before we heard a car coming from the north. "Let's flag it," said Mary Eliska Girl Detective. "We can't come walking into town like this."

"Oh no!" I said, in terror. "Let's hide till it passes. You don't know who it might be at this time of night."

"It can't be Nick or his friends," she said, "and that's all I'm worrying about. I'm going to risk it."

When the headlights swung around a bend behind us, she raised an arm, and the car stopped with squeaking brakes beside us. It was a shabby little sedan. Two surprised young men looked out of the front window.

"Will you give us a lift to town?" asked Mary Eliska Girl Detective.

"What the hell are you doing out here?" asked the one at the wheel.

She instantly took his measure, and altered her style to suit. "Aah!

we didn't like the fellas we was with, and we got out and walked."

"Gee!" they said, sympathetically.

Their appearance was not reassuring. Well dressed, comely little fellows scarcely out of their teens, with smooth hard faces, they were of a type that we were familiar with in New York. Probably of Italian extraction. Their anxiety to butter their harsh voices and to ingratiate themselves made me more than ever uneasy. However, when they invited us to hop in, I had no choice but to follow my employer.

They were in no haste to proceed, but hung there at the side of the road, with the engine running, making friendly conversation. One produced a packet of cigarettes, and we lit up all around. I was uncomfortably aware that they were studying us sharply.

"Meet my friend Joe Mora," said the one at the wheel. "Me, I'm Pete Corioli."

"Pleased to meet ya," said Mary Eliska Girl Detective. "I'm Rosy Wilson, and my friend here is Bella Smith."

"Do you mean to say," asked Pete, incredulously, "that any fellas would put out a coupla swell looking girls like you in the road?"

"Take it any way you like," said Mary Eliska Girl Detective, carelessly. "We wouldn't stay with them."

"Wasn't you scared?"

"Scared as hell."

They laughed.

"Well, you're all right with us," said Joe. "We'll treat you good."

I didn't fancy the look in his eye when he said it.

"You don't live here," said Pete, "or I would 'a' seen you before. I wouldn't forget a face like yours."

"Just stoppin'," said Mary Eliska Girl Detective, vaguely.

"Where?"

"At the Allardyce Bowles Hotel."

"Yes, you are! That's where all the high muckamucks stop."

"Ain't we worth it?"

"You're all right, kid!" he said, laughing. "I'm for you! Change seats with Joe."

"Nothin' doin'!" she said, coolly. "You're one fast little worker, aint ya? Drive on, fella!"

"Drive on nottin'," he said. "What we gonna get out of it?"

"We can still walk," she said, making a move as if to open the door. "Our legs is good."

"Aah, don't be in such a sweat," he said. "I was just funnin'. Will you eat with us in town? We live over Mike's restaurant. We'll get him up and make him cook up a big sirloin. Oh boy! I could eat!"

"Come on!" added Joe, cajolingly. "We had a bit of luck tonight. Turned a trick up in Boston. We got the jack, girls. You better stick to us."

"Okay," said Mary Eliska Girl Detective.

Pete let in his clutch.

In a moment or two we came within sight of the main gates of Omega Farm. A big closed car was waiting in the road outside, with two or three men standing about it. Even at two hundred yards' distance we could recognize the tall figure of Nick.

"There they are," said Mary Eliska Girl Detective to Pete. "They're layin' for us. Are you game?"

"Sure!" said Pete.

"Then give her all she'll take!"

The little car jerked ahead, and Mary Eliska Girl Detective and I crouched down out of sight in the back. We could not see what was happening, but we gathered they were signaling Pete to stop, because he muttered, "You can go plumb to hell.'" When we passed them our engine was making so much noise we could hear only a confused shouting in the road.

Immediately afterward, it seemed, we were enveloped in the powerful lights of the pursuing car.

We had no chance against such a car. The lights grew stronger and stronger. It was like having a fiery beast at your heels. Yet the little car was bounding down the straight road. Pete and Joe were bent low in the front seat to keep our range of possible bullets through the rear window. I expect it was not the first time they had been chased in a car. We were swaying sickeningly. I expected a crash.

"O God! I wish I had my old Duesenberg under me!" groaned Pete. "This crate won't make but sixty three!"

"Go it, baby, go it!" Joe was crying to the car.

Presently I saw that the headlights were no longer streaming directly through the back window, and I realized the big car was drawing abreast of us. It held the road as solidly as a locomotive. We had no chance at all. One of Nick's chauffeurs was driving it, and Nick sat beside him. Reggie Mygatt was in the back. They looked in our car and saw us, but their faces gave no sign. Mary Eliska Girl Detective planted herself defiantly in the seat, and I sat beside her.

"You'd better stop," she said to Pete. "They'll force us off the road."

"To hell with them!" shouted Pete.

A moment later the two cars came together—not hard at first, just a grinding along the running boards.

"They've got me!" cried Pete. "There's a left curve ahead!"

"Oh, the devils!" muttered Mary Eliska Girl Detective.

"Hang on!" yelled Pete. "Here we go!"

We left the road. I cannot clearly describe what happened. We shot down an embankment at a crazy angle, and crashed through a board fence as easily as if it had been paper. We waited for the inevitable smash up. The little car seemed to bounce higher in the air every time it touched the ground. The successive shocks knocked all the breath out of me.

Finally it crashed over on its side.

I felt it coming and braced myself against the lower side. Mary Eliska Girl Detective fell heavily against me and we were showered with glass. Then an unnatural silence.

"Are you hurt?" she whispered.

"No."

"Then come on!"

She already had the uppermost door open, and we had scrambled out almost before the wheels stopped turning. We saw the limousine backing to the spot in the road opposite the break in the fence, about a hundred yards off. We seemed to be in a private park with ornamental trees and shrubbery. It was completely dark where we stood.

Men jumped out of the limousine, and we did not linger. As we turned to run we saw our two young friends climbing out of the front of the sedan, so we knew that they were at least not killed. We ran straight away from the men who were coming through the fence. The shrubbery soon swallowed us, and we slowed down to a walk. The sound of a noisy altercation arose behind us. So much the better if it hindered the search for us.

Turning at right angles, we shaped a course parallel with the road as far as we could judge. Presently we came to a private driveway, and followed it back to the public road. Here we sheltered behind an ornamental gatepost while we debated what to do next. We were, I suppose, about two hundred yards ahead of the limousine, but out of sight of it.

Mary Eliska Girl Detective thought that if the house in this park was occupied we had better frankly apply there for refuge.

Before we could put this into effect, we heard a car coming from the direction of Newport, and waited to see what it looked like. To our joy, we recognized the old Cadillac, with Crider at the wheel. We ran out into the road, signaling wildly. He ground to a stop, and backed his car into the private road. That was a glorious reunion.

However, we had no time to exchange notes on the evening's performance. Somebody at the wheel of the limousine had heard the other car stop and back, and a shout was raised. Mary Eliska Girl Detective and I flung ourselves into the Cadillac, and we started for Newport hell for leather.

When the road straightened out we saw the limousine flying after us, but in our big sedan it found its match. It could not overhaul us. When we struck the town we slowed down, and thereafter the limousine contented itself with keeping us in view. Five minutes later we drew up in front of the Allardyce Bowles on Bellevue Avenue.

"Go right on to the garage," Mary Eliska Girl Detective said to Crider. "We don't want a fracas in the street. Take care of the evidence. Bella and I will be safe here."

The Allardyce Bowles, as everybody knows, is one of the standbys of Newport. A congeries of mismated wooden buildings, hopelessly outmoded, it is nevertheless still the smart place at which to stop.

The fireproof hotel down the street angles in vain for the fashionable trade. Well, there's something very cozy about the old Allardyce with its white painted walls and crimson carpets.

When Mary Eliska Girl Detective asked for the register, the sleepy clerk roused himself, and peered somewhat dubiously over the counter at our mud encrusted slippers.

"Have you any baggage, madam?"

"I am Mary Eliska Girl Detective," she said, haughtily. "My baggage will arrive in the morning."

He smiled disagreeably. "I am sorry, madam...."

At this moment Nick Van Tassel entered the door.

He had procured a well-fitting overcoat from somewhere, and his hair was combed. His face still wore that infernal smile. At the sight of him I began to tremble violently, though I believed we were safe there. The clerk greeted Nick effusively.

"Ah, Nick," said Mary Eliska Girl Detective, coolly, "will you identify me to this man, please. I want a room here."

He hesitated for a second, still smiling evilly, debating, I suppose, which course would better serve his interests.

Mary Eliska Girl Detective said, quickly: "If they refuse to take me in I will telephone to the police. They are forbidden to turn travelers away."

Nick made up his mind. "What nonsense, Mary Eliska Girl Detective!" he said, with seeming good nature. "This lady is Mary Eliska Girl Detective," he went on to the clerk. "Give her the best in the house. I will be responsible for any bills she may run here."

"Certainly, Mr. Van Tassel; certainly, sir," burbled the clerk, hastily shoving the register toward us.

"I want one large room not connected with any other," said Mary Eliska Girl Detective.

"Yes, madam. We have the very thing. Number three hundred and seven. One of the choicest rooms in the house."

"Mary Eliska Girl Detective," said Nick, under his breath, "before you go upstairs come into the parlor a moment."

She shook her head.

"You will be quite safe," he whispered, smiling wickedly.

"Certainly I should be safe," she said, looking him full in the eye. "I am armed."

His good humor failed him momentarily. "You and I ought to talk things over," he said, scowling. "Best for both of us. All cards on the table."

"I have nothing to say to you now."

The lordly Nick was actually reduced to pleading for what we wanted. It did my heart good to hear it. "Aw, Mary Eliska Girl Detective, don't be a crab!" he murmured, with a hangdog air. "You and I are good sports. We play the game...."

"But not the same game," she said, smiling.

"Aw, Rosy...."

She turned to the clerk. "Will you please show us to our room?"

To our great satisfaction, the door of our bedroom was equipped with an old fashioned bolt. No way of forcing such a bolt has yet been discovered short of breaking in the door. We shot the bolt and turned it, and flung ourselves across the big bed with common groans of relief.

"Lord! what a night!"

Chapter Twenty-One

Red Flower in the Night

As our excitement died down in the quiet of our own room, Mary Eliska Girl Detective and I began to realize we had not escaped from the automobile crash so easily as we had supposed. True, neither of us had any broken bones, and by some miracle we had escaped being cut by the falling glass; but we felt as if we had been pounded all over with clubs. To move was torture.

Still there was to be no rest for us. The telephone rang, and Mary Eliska Girl Detective with a groan raised herself from the bed to answer it.

She said: "No, I won't see you," and I knew it was Nick Van Tassel. After a moment she said, "Well, tell me over the phone." When he refused to do so she said: "Well, that's your lookout. I have nothing to conceal." A long silence followed, broken only by Mary Eliska Girl Detective's muttered exclamations of impatience. Nick was evidently pleading. Finally she said, "This is merely absurd, Nick," and hung up abruptly.

"What did he say?" I asked.

"Vague threats," she said, scornfully. "The man is desperate. He has never been successfully opposed before, and it has shaken his belief in himself. He is apt to strike at us blindly now."

"Surely we are safe here in the hotel," I said, nervously.

"I don't know," she said, thoughtfully. "He has his spies and friends everywhere in this town. At any rate, we'll stand watch until morning. That's why I took only one room. Thank God, we still have the gun. It will be light in a couple of hours."

"Take a little rest," I urged.

She shook her head. "Got to do some telephoning first." She started looking for a number in the book.

"Who to?"

"I suppose you noticed that Reggie Mygatt let slip the name of the intended victim tonight."

A light broke on me. "Henry Eversley!" I exclaimed.

She commenced the patient business of trying to get a number in the small hours of morning. "Keep on ringing, please....Yes, I know, everybody in the house is probably asleep. Keep on ringing, please. It is important...."

Henry Eversley was one of the great railroad builders—or wreckers if you like—thirty years ago. He accumulated one of the greatest fortunes in the country. In those days his name was a household word, but since suffering a stroke some years ago, he has retired into seclusion and is rarely heard of. But he is just as rich as ever. His was one of the names that had already been turned up in the case. He had refused to receive Mary Eliska Girl Detective.

She finally succeeded in getting a servant on the phone, and as a result of persistent firmness managed to persuade him to connect her with his master's bedside phone. When she was satisfied that she had the multimillionaire on the wire, Mary Eliska Girl Detective said:

"This is Mary Eliska Girl Detective speaking. I think you know who I am. What you may not know is that my business in Newport is to run down the letter writer who signs himself The Leveler and who has been extorting large sums of money from various wealthy men here. I happen to know that he sent you a demand last night and that you refused to pay...." Here Mr. Eversley interrupted her with a dozen questions.

"Please let me finish first....You refused his demand, and in consequence he planned to attack you in your house tonight. I was able to prevent that, but I cannot tell what tomorrow may bring up, so I am taking this means of warning you. Unless he is prevented, he will certainly attack you tomorrow. You should, therefore, take whatever measures seem best to you. He is an extremely resourceful and ingenious man, and you should leave nothing to chance. I advise you to call in the police and publish the whole matter in the newspapers."

It appeared from the subsequent conversation that Mr. Eversley was angry. Mary Eliska Girl Detective expostulated with him helplessly. He accused her of being in the pay of The Leveler, and of using this early morning call as a means to frighten him into paying up. This was the result of the whispering campaign that had been instituted against us in Newport. It was passed from mouth to mouth that Mary Eliska Girl Detective herself was the racketeer, and we were powerless to combat it.

Mr. Eversley kept shouting that he wouldn't pay a cent, and refused to listen to what my employer had to say. She told him that the name of his persecutor was in the hands of the district attorney and advised him to consult Lyle. But it is doubtful if he heard her.

She finally hung up with a weary air. "Well, at any rate I've done my duty by him," she said.

Next she called up Lyle at his home in Providence, and once more had to go through with the weary business of getting a servant to the phone and persuading her to call her master. Lyle, she told me afterward, was in a villainous temper when she finally got him, nevertheless she forced him to listen to the whole story of what had happened that night.

One would have thought the attention of the operators must have been attracted by those long conversations in the small hours of morning. Mary Eliska Girl Detective did not name Nick over the phone, just the same, if anybody listened in, what strange matter he must have heard. But it never came out afterward. I suppose it was added to all the other strange stories, the inside dope about things that is passed along in whispers and never gets broadcasted.

Lyle as we already knew, was as pig headed as he was timid, and made out to pooh pooh the whole story. Mary Eliska Girl Detective had got no better than she deserved, he intimated, for trying to take the law into her own hands. But she beat him down with the deadly particulars. We still had Nick Van Tassel's gun, mask, and pair of climbers. In the end Lyle promised to come down to Newport first thing in the morning to consult with her.

"In the meantime," said Mary Eliska Girl Detective, "I think I am entitled to ask for protection. Will you telephone to the chief of police here and ask him to have this hotel sufficiently guarded until you get here?"

Lyle, still affecting to make light of the whole business, promised to do so. Whether or not he carried it out we never knew.

I persuaded Mary Eliska Girl Detective to lie down on the bed and take a sleep while I kept watch for daylight in the armchair. Neither of us took off any of our clothes. My employer was asleep as soon as her head touched the pillow.

I sat in the chair with the pistol in my lap and all my nerves taut, listening, watching—for I knew not what. We had a front corner room on the third floor. It had two windows looking out on Bellevue Avenue, and a third to the side. No other doors but the one on the corridor with the stout bolt. An old fashioned wardrobe for clothes.

At first I left the lights burning. A dozen times I got up and peeped around the window blinds. Nobody could have entered that way without a ladder.

Then I would go to the door and listen and reassure myself by trying the bolt. Not a sound outside. I decided it was the lights that were making me nervous and turned them out. Then I no longer felt as if I were making a target for somebody's bullet. When I ran up the window blinds I was assured nobody could appear outside without giving me warning.

The windows were open and had screens in. Nothing stirred in the street below.

I never would have believed it possible, in the state I was in, but I fell asleep, myself. I fell asleep while I imagined I was still sitting up watching and listening. Well, we had been through a terrific strain. I must have slept soundly, too, for I did not awaken until the full alarm was raised. I came back to consciousness with a hideous start, hearing doors slam, women screaming, running feet through the corridors, and that most dreadful of all cries in the night: "Fire!"

Mary Eliska Girl Detective sprang up at the same moment. My fears of Nick Van Tassel paled beside those dreadful sounds. I ran to the door. I switched on the lights and threw back the bolt. But the door resisted me. Shake it as I might, it was stoutly held.

"O God!" I screamed. "We're locked in! We're trapped!"

For a moment or two my nerve went utterly. I ran for the windows, screaming. Mary Eliska Girl Detective caught me round the waist and forced me down on the bed.

"Keep your wits about you!" she cried. "This may work to our advantage."

Work to our advantage! Her coolness nearly drove me mad. There was a dull explosion downstairs, and I could hear the mutter and crackle of flames.

She tried the door attentively. "Something has been wedged between the handle and the door frame. If we can take off the handle we'll be free." She examined it more attentively. "All depends on this one little screw. Think quickly, Bella. What have we that we can use for a screwdriver?"

"We have nothing!" I cried. "Let me call for help from the windows!"

"Nail file, scissors, pocket knife," she murmured.

"We have none of those! We'll burn up!" I screamed.

"Be quiet!" she said, harshly. "Let me think!"

I sat on the bed, gripping my head, almost suffocated by hysteria. A building all wood, at least seventy five years old! Such a building springs into flame all of a piece like a torch! Those dreadful sounds; the busy, busy murmur of flames gradually rising to an unchecked roar, with spiteful crackling overtones. The screaming had ceased. Everybody, apparently, had found a way out but us. Where were the firemen, the firemen? I could hear the flames roaring up the main stairway just around the corner from our room. Smoke began to seep under the door and to mount in lazy spirals.

"Garter buckle!" muttered Mary Eliska Girl Detective. In an instant she had torn it off her stocking. "It fits!"

Still, we were not out of the place. The thin piece of metal bent under the strain, and she had to hammer it flat on the floor with the heel of her slipper.

The roaring of the flames increased. The fire engines came, bringing fresh crowds of shouting people.

After all, it was only two or three minutes since the alarm had been raised. All over the hotel the window panes were going one by one with a pleasant, musical tinkle. There was a muffled sound beneath us and the floor began to get hot. The room was slowly filling with smoke, and the electric lights gleamed redly through it. I thought my heart would burst with terror.

The handle came off in Mary Eliska Girl Detective's hand.

"We're safe!" she cried. When she pulled the door by the knob of the bolt, it opened and a cloud of smoke rolled in. The shank of the handle was drawn through, and we heard a clatter of steel outside. "An iron bar jammed inside the handle and caught on both sides the door frame," she murmured.

I was already charging out of the room, but she caught hold of my arm. "Ten seconds!" she cried.

"There's time!" She dragged me to a front window, pulling the pins out of her hair as she went and shaking it around her shoulders. "Do as I do!" she cried. She thrust the screen out of the window and leaned out, waving her arms in pantomime of despair.

That glimpse out of the window will remain with me until I die. Every window below us was vomiting flames. It was too late to raise a ladder. Thousands of people standing in the street, all with their turned up white faces illuminated. A strange inhuman roar went up from them at the sight of us.

One might almost have thought they exulted in our fiery end. Individuals screamed, shouted directions to us, waved us back from the window. I wondered if Nick Van Tassel was down there somewhere, watching with a grin.

Just for a second we showed ourselves, then ran for it. Mary Eliska Girl Detective dropped her watch and an antique gold bracelet on the bureau as we passed. We gained the corridor not a moment too soon, for long tongues of flame were shooting around the corner from the main stairway. We ran in the other direction. All the lights in the hotel went out. There was a crash from below and a great soft burst of flame filled the corridor behind us, fanning us with its hot breath.

At the end there was a window with a fire escape outside. The platform was jammed with people waiting a chance to descend. Others were still coming down the ladder from the top floor. I was making to join them, but Mary Eliska Girl Detective pulled me into a side corridor.

"Everybody who escapes that way will be checked up," she murmured.

We felt our way along the corridor, turned to the left, always making toward the rear. We were stopped by a window opening on the flat roof of an extension. We climbed out and ran over the crackling tin. Looking over the edge, we saw another flat roof perhaps ten feet below. We made the drop without hurting ourselves. At the edge of the second extension there was a porch roof. From under it people were dragging all sorts of things they had saved from the building.

"We mustn't be seen," whispered Mary Eliska Girl Detective, holding me back.

The whole surrounding scene was lit up like a stage by the red glare of the flames, but we were in the shadow of the building itself. Peeping over the side of the roof we saw a shutter hooked back below that offered a foothold. With that and with the aid of the sill we climbed down. Nobody saw us.

An immense thankfulness filled me when my foot touched the good earth.

"What fiends!" I murmured. "To risk all those lives just to get at us!"

"I suppose we ought to feel flattered by our importance," said Mary Eliska Girl Detective dryly.

Chapter Twenty-Two

The Hide out

We were cut off from the side street by the people carrying things out of the back doors of the hotel, and by firemen dragging their lines of hose around from the front. So we turned in the other direction, forced our way through a hedge, crossed a couple of yards, and finally found ourselves looking out on another quiet little street running down to Bellevue Avenue.

People were making their way through it, bound for the scene of the fire, and we hid behind bushes until a chance came to scurry across unseen and lose ourselves in the yards of the next block. Thus we made a détour around the fire. When it seemed as if everybody in that part of town had gone to the fire, we ventured to cross Bellevue Avenue and struck into the maze of little streets to the east.

Looking down Bellevue Avenue, the burning hotel was like a gaudy torch in the night. There was no wind, and the flames mounted straight in the air. Never have I seen so complete, so obliterating a fire.

"Might as well have saved my watch and bracelet," murmured Mary Eliska Girl Detective. "Nothing will be found in the ruins." When we had gone on a little way we heard the interior fall in with a soft crash, and above the trees and the housetops we saw the pillar of sparks mounting to the sky.

From time to time we met people, of course, but their attention was riveted on the fire. The burden of Mary Eliska Girl Detective's thought was, "If we can only escape identification!" I understood what was passing through her mind, but I did not see how she could possibly get away with it.

We came into a street with a car line. It was lined with shops, lodgings overhead. Many of the upper windows on the east side were filled with heads watching the fire off to the west. Already the glare was dying down, and we realized with sinking hearts that day was at hand.

"Too late!" murmured Mary Eliska Girl Detective.

Over one of the darkened stores across the street we saw a sign that struck a chord of recollection—"Mike's Restaurant." Mary Eliska Girl Detective stopped. "The boys' hang out!" she murmured. "If we could only find them!" There were some heads at an upper window of this building, but only women. She crossed the street and tried the door alongside the restaurant. It opened, and she entered, with me following perforce at her heels.

"This is madness!" I whispered.

"It's a chance," she coolly retorted. "The only one we have."

We found ourselves in a narrow, fusty smelling passage, as dark as the inside of your hat. Mary Eliska Girl Detective.

Mary Eliska Girl Detective stumbled against a stairway and went up. At the top she felt along the wall until she came to a door, and knocked. There was no answer. While we were waiting we could hear the voices of the women upstairs.

"Why not apply to them?" I whispered.

"Women can't trust women," she said.

Feeling her way along the landing, she knocked at a middle door. No answer. When she knocked at the door of the front room a surly voice answered, "What do you want?"

"Pete Corioli," said Mary Eliska Girl Detective.

"Back room," said the voice, cursing us heartily for disturbing him.

Mary Eliska Girl Detective chuckled. "This is something new, Bella."

It was on the tip of my tongue to answer peevishly that she was welcome to it.

After knocking again at the door of the back room, we tried the handle. It was open. We walked in, and Mary Eliska Girl Detective switched on the lights. All my maidenly instincts (or what was left of them!) were revolted by the sight that met my eyes. A man's room in an appalling state of disorder; clothes strewn everywhere; a tumbled bed; a carpet black with soot and grime.

"Well, let's sit down and wait for them," said Mary Eliska Girl Detective, cheerfully. "Maybe they've just run to the fire."

"This is too dangerous!" I muttered.

"What, Bella," she said, drawing down the corners of her mouth mockingly, "don't you think I can handle these kids?"

In a moment or two the door banged open and they ran in. Their astonishment at the sight of us was comical to see. The two hard boiled faces that prided themselves on giving nothing away, each making a round of astonishment. Their first reaction was to delight.

"Cheese! Here's the girls! Damned if it ain't Rosy and Bella! Where the hell did you spring from? Cheese! Didn't we fool them high up guys nice! Did they look foolish when they found you was gone? I'll say! Where did you get to, anyhow? We thought the earth had swallered ya!"

And so on. And so on. Joe flung his arms around me and gave me a smack on the cheek.

"How did you find us here?" Pete kept asking.

"We saw the sign Mike's Restaurant, and we come right up," said Mary Eliska Girl Detective. "You promised us a meal."

"Yeah?" said Pete. An ugly mask of suspicion drew over his face and his jaw jutted out. "Say, who the hell are you, anyhow? You're no common pavement tapper like you tried to make out. That guy that was after you was Nick Van Tassel. I reco'nized him. He tried to make out it was accidental, and I laughed in his face. He paid us five hundred for the old Chevvie. Twice what 'twas worth. Say, what for do you want to run away from a fella like Nick Van Tassel?"

"I don't like him."

"Yeah?" he said with inimitable scorn. "Tell that to the dickey birds. I know women."

"Well, the truth is, he was trying to kill me."

Pete took this quite as a matter of course. "I wouldn't put it past him," he said, sagely. "He has the eye of a killer....But what I want to know is," he went on, stubbornly, "for why does a woman like you come after a coupla poor boys like Joe and me?"

"That's easy answered," said Mary Eliska Girl Detective, with an enchanting smile. "Bella and me are in a hole. We ain't got a friend in this burg. Well, you stood by us once tonight, though you never seen us before that minute. You were dead game! You were ready to drive that car plumb to hell for us. Is that answer enough? Such men ain't so easy to come by when a woman needs a friend."

No man could have resisted this from Mary Eliska Girl Detective. The ring of real feeling was in it. She meant every word. Pete scowled ferociously to try to save his face. "Aah!" he growled. "Aaah! That's all banana oil!" But in spite of himself the suspicious mask began to crack. "What is it you want of me and Joe?" he demanded.

"A hide out until tomorrow night."

"Ain't got no place we can put you but this room," he said.

"Could we stay here without being seen by anybody?"

"Sure! Nobody would come in here if we told them to keep the hell out!"

"How about the landlady?"

"She ain't particular, if she gets her rent. She keeps her nose in her face." He looked around the room, and a softened look came in his eyes. "But this ain't no fit place for a lady like you."

"I've lived in worse," said Mary Eliska Girl Detective. "Cut out the lady stuff, Pete. I'm just human like yourself."

He grinned at her sidelong. "Suits me," he said.

"Can you and Joe find a place outside to sleep?" she said, coolly.

His face hardened again. Their eyes engaged in an unspoken duel. Then he shrugged. "So me and Joe goes out," he said, pulling a droll face. "All right! But what is there in it for us? We may be dead game, but we're not suckers."

"Sure," she said, matching his tone. "Let's put it on a business basis. I'm in a hole but I'm not broke yet. I got no money on me but there's this."

Slipping her hand under her coat, she unfastened a short string of pearls that she was wearing. Her fine pearls, I learned later, she had dropped in her pocket.

Pete's eyes glistened at the sight of the necklace.

"Pearls!" he exclaimed, taking them eagerly. "Genuine!"

"How much are they worth to you?" she asked.

"Fella I know would give five hundred for them," said Pete, with an experienced air. "They're worth more."

"You're right they're worth more," she said. "If I come through this all right I'll buy them back from you for a grand at any time. If I don't, you can sell them for what they'll bring."

"Gee!" said Joe, softly. He was a weaker character than Pete.

The latter was looking at Mary Eliska Girl Detective in an extraordinary way. He sneered, yet there was a sound of hurt in his voice. "Aah! what's to stop me from keepin' them and puttin' you and Bella to the door, anyhow?"

"There's nothing to stop you," she said, meeting his eye, "but I don't think you're going to do it."

"Why ain't I?" he demanded, with jutting jaw.

"I don't know. I have a kind of feeling that you and I are friends."

"Aah!" He turned away to the window to avoid her candid gaze. There was some kind of an obscure struggle going on in him. He faced her from the other side of the room, scowling. "I'd do it for nottin'," he said, angrily, "I wouldn't take your beads offen you, if we was friends, if you was the same as us. But you ain't. You're the same as Nick Van Tassel. Way up. We're ag'in' the whole push of you!"

Mary Eliska Girl Detective made no answer.

"We don't mean nottin' to you," he went on, sorely. "It's on'y because you're up against it. We're useful to you. What are we? Coupla mutts! When you get out of it you won't know us no more. You'll be sending us round to the back door for a handout."

"That's not so!" she returned, indignantly. "If you had any sense you could see for yourself I'm not like that! What's the use of gassing? You've got to take it or leave it."

Her hurt voice won him. He returned to her with a smile pulling at the corners of his mouth, and a warm glint in his black eyes. Attractive little wretch! "Aah, I'm a fool!" he drawled, sneering still, but good humored now. "And that's the troot! I never believe what no woman says, but I t'ink you're on the level. You're not like a woman, any how, 'cept in looks. You talk out like a fella. I'm for you....If you're playin' me, you kin laugh!"

There was an irresistible quality of manliness in him, however depraved or ignorant he might be. Mary Eliska Girl Detective recognized it with a warm smile. I could see that he was becoming infected with the same complaint that many a better man had had before him, and I was a little sorry for him. "Are we on?" he asked his partner.

"Sure!" cried Joe.

"Well, shake!" said Pete to Mary Eliska Girl Detective. We had to shake hands all around. Pete's defenses against the sex were melting fast. He could not keep his eyes off Mary Eliska Girl Detective.

She said: "You can make another stake out of this if you want. The necklace is for giving us a hide out and for keeping your mouths shut about us tomorrow, no matter what you might get by telling. If you will go on keeping your mouths shut until I give you leave, I'll make it worth your while."

"Aah!" said Pete. "Don't you worry about us keepin' our traps shut. Joe and me ain't anxious to attrac' the attention of Nick Van Tassel. That guy carries this burg around in his pants pocket."

After the strain of the past hours a delicious relaxation began to steal over me, and I had to sit down. Gunmen though they were, I trusted them. You never know where you are going to find your friends. And in that deplorable room I felt we had a safer refuge than amid all the luxury of Omega Farm.

It was the same with Mary Eliska Girl Detective. She suddenly yawned greatly and exclaimed, "O God! I'm tired!"

"Shall we bring you something to eat?" asked Joe, solicitously.

By a common impulse we shook our heads. "Only sleep," said Mary Eliska Girl Detective. "We're all in."

"Well...we'll beat it," said Pete, with a wistful side glance. At that moment he looked like any nice lad who was falling in love in spite of himself.

"There's a good bolt on the door," he added, with a hangdog air. "Don't let anybody in till we come back. We'll knock four times. You'll be safe enough."

"Thanks, Pete and Joe," she said, simply.

"When can we come back?"

"Twelve o'clock. Bring food then. Bring newspapers. And see if you can buy me a good map of Newport in a stationery store. That's important."

"Okay, Rosie...Well...good night." He had his hand on the door.

"Come here, Pete!" she commanded.

He went up to her, swaggering and sheepish. She caught his face between her hands and kissed him on the mouth.

"There! I wanted to do that!" she said.

He paled. "Aah!" he sneered. "You're only making a fool of me!" But one could see that he was humming with delight.

They went out. When Mary Eliska Girl Detective turned around her eyes were misty. "Anyhow, I'm always on their side," she murmured. It sounded quite irrelevant, but I knew what she meant.

We pulled up the covers and lay down somewhat dubiously on the outside of that uninviting bed. But we soon forgot our doubts and everything else in the deepest sleep we had ever known.

Chapter Twenty-Three

Party of Four

When the four knocks sounded on the door Mary Eliska Girl Detective and I were still asleep. We roused ourselves with difficulty.

"Oh, Pete! Give us twenty minutes to wash and tidy up!" Mary Eliska Girl Detective sang out.

"Okay!" he answered from the other side of the door.

She smiled at the first sound of his voice. "He hasn't identified us yet," she whispered.

"We'll go get you some grub," Pete went on.

"Eat with us."

"Sure. Here's the newspaper and the map."

These articles were shoved under the door, and the boys ran down stairs. I need hardly say that we pounced on the newspaper. There are not many people who are privileged to read their own obituaries.

It gives one a very queer sensation indeed.

It was an extra that must have been brought out about breakfast time. There was a big two line full page spread:

THE ALLARDYCE BOWLES BURNS TO ASHES
MARY ELISKA GIRL DETECTIVE AND SECRETARY
MISSING

Also there was a striking photograph of the naming torch in the night. But the story itself, as is so often the case with small town papers, was flatly uninteresting. One wonders how they do it. They seem to go out of their way to leave out everything that matters.

This story had been written, in the first place, by an unskilled hand

and had then been heavily edited. There was an obvious desire to make as little as possible of it in order to save the fair name of the town. We wondered if Nick Van Tassel had had a hand in the editing. Probably it was not necessary for him to interfere. A small town paper soon learns to be prudent in naming the leading citizens.

There was no mention of the fact that we had registered at the hotel at two thirty, only an hour or so before the fire broke out; or that we had arrived without baggage; or that Nick Van Tassel had followed close at our heels. It was not even stated that we had been stopping at his place, and of course there was no suggestion that the fire might have been of incendiary origin; merely a brief statement that the fire chief was investigating the cause.

"Wait till the big metropolitan dailies begin digging into this!" said Mary Eliska Girl Detective, dryly.

It was both amusing and exasperating to read how the local sheet blamed us for losing our lives in the fire and so bringing discredit on the town.

While there was no claim that the hotel was fire proof—ye Gods! everybody in Newport had known for years that it was a fire trap!— there was ample provision of fire escapes and all were in good order. The fire did not immediately spread to the rear of the building where the fire escapes were situated, and all the other guests had plenty of time to get out.

Apparently Mary Eliska Girl Detective and Miss Jacqueline "Jax" Gray must have lost their heads completely. They appeared for a moment at a window of their room, and seemed to be about to fling themselves out, but were dissuaded by the horrified crowd below. The whole front of the hotel below them was then ablaze, and it was too late to raise a ladder. A myriad voices shouted to them to go to the back of the building, but they were incapable of acting upon the advice.

And so on. And so on. One would never have guessed from this story that Mary Eliska Girl Detective was a figure of national importance. I wondered what District Attorney Lyle's sensations were upon reading it. Impossible to figure out the mental processes of such a man. I suppose our deaths relieved him from an impossible situation, and he was not inclined to look into the matter too closely. At any rate, he never made a move.

"I'm just as glad the newspaper is so easily satisfied," said Mary Eliska Girl Detective. "It would be awkward for us if there was a nosy reporter on the ground."

"I don't see what you expect to make out of the situation," I said, helplessly.

"What!" she exclaimed. "If we can persuade Nick Van Tassel that we are dead!"

"Surely, I see that. But how can we hope to stay dead? As well known as you are? Where could we go? And if we succeed in getting out of Newport, how could we ever get back again to take up the case?"

"We're not going to leave Newport," she said, smiling.

I stared at her uncomprehendingly.

"That's what the map is for," she went on. "Pete and Joe are on the level with us, but I dare not trust them far enough to ask them what I want to know. Let's take a look at the map."

We spread it out on the bed, and with her forefinger she slowly traced the shore line of Newport.

Her finger came to a pause at a narrow inlet on the bay side of the town. "Brenton's Cove," she said; "that's our mark."

A light began to break on me. "Miss Betsy Pryor!" I exclaimed.

"Sure! Could anything be better?"

"How will we get beyond her gate?"

"We're going by water."

"How will we know the place?"

"It's got a nine foot wall around it covered with broken bottles."

We fell silent while we considered the possibilities of the plan. "The chief danger comes from our own men," I suggested. "What will Crider and Benny Abell do?"

"I'll send them a message."

The boys came in laden like a pair of Santa Clauses with what they considered adequate to furnish a breakfast for four. It included a dozen hot ham and egg sandwiches with wienies on the side; a couple of the largest size pumpkin pies and a cocoanut custard; a bag of oranges and ditto of apples; a bucket of coffee. We saw at once that our young friends had dressed for the occasion; each was wearing a new suit, with gay shirt, tie, handkerchief, and socks to match. Pete's eyes lighted up like lamps at the sight of Mary Eliska Girl Detective.

"Pete," she said, "while we're spreading the table will you send a phone message for me?"

His face fell. "Aah! Who to?"

"George Crider at the Viking Hotel....Be sure you give it to nobody but him."

"How will I know him?"

"Ask him his number. If he answers Number Two," (this was how Crider signed his confidential reports) "you will know that you have the right man. Tell him—Here, I'll write it out for you." She hastily scribbled on a piece of paper, "Wear mourning on your sleeve but not in your heart."

"What does that mean?" demanded Pete, scowling.

"It's a code message, Pete. I can't tell you."

"Aah! Is this guy your sweetheart?"

"No!"

He hesitated jealously.

"Listen, Pete," she went on, warmly, "I can't tell you anything now. But if I come through all right I swear I'll give you the whole story."

He went off with the message, half satisfied. He was back in five minutes. "Yeah, I got him," he said, scornfully, in reply to Mary Eliska Girl Detective's question. "The guy made out he was all broke up when I give him your message. 'God, man!' says he, 'that's the best piece of news I ever heard in my life!' 'Yeah?' says I. He says, 'Is the person what gave you this message in good health?' And I says, 'I wasn't supposed to tell you nottin' but what I told you.' And I hung up."

We laughed. "Poor Crider!" said Mary Eliska Girl Detective. "He's Bella's beau, Pete, not mine."

I blushed, and this seemed to reassure Pete. "Ah, to hell with him!" he said, turning to his food.

There was a table in the room which Joe had cleared by the simple expedient of shoving everything off on the floor with a sweep of his arm. As there were only two chairs, we pushed the table to the edge of the bed. Mary Eliska Girl Detective and I sat down, facing the two boys.

You can picture the incongruity of the scene: the elegant Mary Eliska Girl Detective in a white satin evening gown all creased and stained and torn, and me in my magenta and silver, likewise the worse for our adventures; the two flashily dressed youthful gunmen; the heap of coarse food on the table; the slatternly bedroom. But I have seldom eaten a better meal. I had no idea that ham and egg sandwiches an inch thick could go down so well.

Mary Eliska Girl Detective knew how to make herself one with our two young friends. "I reckon you know this town through and through," she said.

"Yeah," said Pete, carelessly, "but we never do no business here. It's too small a burg, and the rich guys are too well protected. This is our home town, our hide out. When we want to turn a trick we roll up to Providence or Boston."

"And New York?"

"Nah! New York's too well organized. No outside boy wouldn't stand a half hour's show with the police."

"The native sons seem to get by all right," suggested Mary Eliska Girl Detective.

"Nachelly. They've got the inside track."

Under the expanding influences of food and hot coffee Pete and Joe began to talk somewhat indiscreetly. With two sympathetic female listeners they could not resist bragging about their exploits.

"Me and Pete specializes in men's shops," said Joe.

"Aah, tie up your mouth!" said Pete, with a lingering impulse of prudence. "The string's broke!"

"Go to hell!" said Joe, amiably. "We're all pals together."

"Why men's shops?" asked Mary Eliska Girl Detective.

"Aah, the sales guys in them places is 'most always Nancies. I don't know why. Easier to han'le than women. Don't holler so much. They wilt right down when you show 'em a gun."

"And you can always pick up something tasty in shirts and ties, I reckon," she said, smiling at his purple ensemble.

Joe's pride was touched. "Nah! Whatever I wear I pay cash money for!"

"Go on!" put in Pete. "You couldn't leave the stuff alone unless I made you....No sensible fella ever lifts anything offen the counter," he explained to us. "Often we run out of the shop and mix in with the crowd that's gathering to see what's the matter, and they can't hang anything on us. The clerks is too scared to identify us. But if we had goods out of the store, they'd have us dead to rights."

Pete had the level gaze and the firm lips of one who would have been efficient in any line, and I felt that I was learning something.

Joe leaned back, laughing with his mouth full, and slapping his thigh. "Pete, 'member the time we made 'em take their pants off?" he spluttered.

Pete echoed his laughter. "Do I remember!"

"What was that?" asked Mary Eliska Girl Detective, laughing in anticipation.

"Well, we read in a New York paper how a gang down there that worked jewelry stores used to make the clerks take off their pants, so they couldn't run out in the street and holler. And Pete and me figured on trying it in Boston."

"Did it work?"

"Swell!" they cried, rolling in their chairs and hugging themselves with laughter.

"It worked too good," added Pete.

"Well, tell us about it."

"It was in the Bon Ton Men's Shop on Tremont street...."

"Let me tell it," interrupted Joe. "They had branches all over Boston, and we used to stick 'em up one after another. We had 'em scared right. Why, we went back to the same branch four times...."

"Let me tell.'" said Pete. "This was their biggest store, but at two thirty there was only three clerks in it. They do their biggest trade at lunchtime, so the clerks has to wait for theirs. So me and Joe fluffs into this swell store. There was a little elevator in the front to take you up to the second floor where they sold clothing. But no operator. The clerks run it when they take you up. And the chief clerk he comes up and he says in his Nancy voice, 'Can I serve you, boys?' And me and Pete each pulls a couple of rods—little automatics that lie snug in your hand...."

"Cheese! that guy turned green as Gorgonzola!" put in Joe.

"And I says, mockin' him," Pete resumed, "'Yes, dearie, back into the store. And you, Ferdie; and you, Percy'—to the udder two clerks...."

"I'll tell it!" interrupted Joe. "It was me made them take off their pants....Down in the rear of the store there's a little L, like, and I backs them in there while Pete is friskin' the cash registers. And I says, 'Take off your pants, boys!' Cheese! they begins to squeak like guinea pigs. 'Aw, mister; Aw, mister! Take my money but lea' me my pants! Don't expose me, mister! I would die with shame!'

"I up with my gun. 'Take 'em off!' I barks. And down comes them three pair of pants like the skins offen bananas. You would 'a' died laughin'! All dressed up on top and bare below like a pitcher on the screen. Real fancy B.V.D.s with colored stripes. And their bony knees shakin'! They steps out of their pants real quick and hands them over. I rolls 'em up and tucks 'em under my arm. Pete backs a customer into the rear, and he takes off his without waitin' to be ast...."

"Let me tell!" cried Pete. "I had cleaned out the cash registers already, so we backs out to the front real slow. Cheese! It was comical the way them skinny legged guys comes out to look, and scampers back when they seen we was still there. I sends the elevator upstairs, and Joe pitches the four pair of pants down the shaft. It was all greasy down there. Then we springs the catch on the door so it would lock behind us, and walks out of the store like gen'lemen. We knew we had a good five minutes before they could get new pants out of stock. There wasn't a peep raised behind us."

"O God!" cried Joe, almost helpless with laughter. "If you could have seen them guys dancin' in their garters!"

We laughed with them.

"What do you mean, it worked too good?" asked Mary Eliska Girl Detective.

"Aah!" said Pete, disgustedly. "Too much publicity. The papiss give it a front page spread. It was a regular sensation. Every Bon Ton Shop in Boston hired a dick with a gun to sit all day, and we hadda lay off and take a new line. We worked luncheonettes for a while."

"How did that pan out?"

"Not so good. We didn't know the ropes, see? And they have hard guys servin' them luncheonettes. You never know when they got a gun under the counter."

"Tough!" said Mary Eliska Girl Detective.

"But after a time the pants story was forgotten," resumed Joe. "The dicks were taken out of the Bon Ton stores and we went back. We've widened our field since. We take in Lowell and Lynn and Worcester and Springfield now."

"It's a nice, steady little business," said Pete, sagely. "We average a hundred or two every job. The newspapiss don't feature such small jobs, and so the police don't care. The risk is small."

"I see," said Mary Eliska Girl Detective.

"But me and Joe ain't satisfied," Pete went on. "We got ambition." He looked at her through his long curled lashes. "If you and Bella was to come in with us we could do something. With your looks and style and our nerve we could work up an unbeatable racket. I got ideas.... But you wouldn't do it," he added like a schoolboy, sullen and wistful.

"That would be great," said Mary Eliska Girl Detective. "But I got to stick to my own line. I'll tell you about it someday."

"Yeah," he said, sorely, "you're so good lookin' you don't have to work."

Chapter Twenty-Four

A Voyage

The boys, naturally, were curious to learn what our plans for the future were.

"We'll pull out of here about ten tonight," said Mary Eliska Girl Detective.

"Where you going?" demanded Pete.

She did not answer directly. "Is there a back way out of this building?" she asked.

"Sure. Through the yard, and through the yard of the next house into Thames Street."

"Pete and me wouldn't live in no house without a back way out," added Joe, grinning.

"Is that the waterfront street?" she asked.

"Yeah."

"Can you buy me a rowboat without attracting attention?" she asked.

"No," said Pete, bluntly. "If you don't want to attrac' attention I gotta swipe it."

"Well, swipe it," she said, "but let me know the owner's name so I can pay for it later."

Pete and Joe grinned at each other. This seemed like a quaint scruple to them. "What the hell do you want of a rowboat?" demanded Pete.

"To take a little voyage in."

"Can you row?"

"I can make a stab at it."

"Can Joe and me go?"

"No," she said, firmly. "We've got to say good bye in the yard."

"That ain't no stunt for a coupla girls," he said, scowling. "Out in a rowboat at night, and can't even row!"

"We can take care of ourselves," she said, coolly.

"I won't stand for it!" Pete said, truculently.

"Stand for it?" she said, running up her eyebrows. "Didn't you and me make a deal this morning and shake hands on it?"

He couldn't stand out against her powerful glance. "Oh, all right!" he mumbled, his eyes trailing away.

She forgave him because she realized there was a kind of chivalry at the back of his truculence.

"What the hell, Pete!" she said as man to man. "You ought to know by this time that I'm no candy girl! I won't melt."

Toward evening they went out to get some more food, to buy the latest papers, and to scout around before it got dark for a suitable boat that might be lifted later.

"Get me a New York and a Boston paper," said Mary Eliska Girl Detective, casually. "There's nothing in this Newport rag."

When they returned, our eyes flew to their faces to see if they had received any clue to our identities. Apparently not. The bundle of papers was still under Joe's arm, unfolded. He distributed them among us, and we sat down to read the news.

I drew the afternoon edition of a Boston sheet. The metropolitan newspaper instantly understood how big Mary Eliska Girl Detective loomed in the imaginations of its readers, and played up the story of her death accordingly. We occupied almost the entire front page. I gasped a little when I realized all that was set down here, and wondered what the outcome would be. There was a full biography of my employer, with a résumé of her more important cases. There was an excellent photograph of her, and one of those shapeless blobs labeled with my name, that even the best of newspapers will print when they have no real picture.

This paper had had a man on the ground in Newport since early morning, and he knew his business. He had wormed the circumstances of our arrival at the hotel out of the clerk, and had then set out to obtain an interview with Nick Van Tassel. Nick was too clever to refuse to be interviewed. He posed as the approachable millionaire. This is what the reporter had to say about him:

In addition to being the most prominent young man in the social colony, Nicholas Van Tassel is one of America's premier sportsmen. Besides owning a palace on the cliffs which he never uses and won't rent, he owns a farm a few miles out of town which is big enough to include a polo field, a racetrack, and a flying field. In spite of his wealth and prominence there is nothing exclusive about him. He is said to be the friend of every taxi driver and newsboy in Newport. His ready smile and friendly manner endear him to all alike.

Hm! I thought, as I pictured Nick's infernal smile, and the hard glance that had forced the reporter to take him at his own valuation. I quote part of the interview.

"Mr. Van Tassel, I am informed that Mary Eliska Girl Detective and Miss Jacqueline "Jax" Gray were guests at your place before they went to the Allardyce Bowles."

"That is right."

"I am told they registered at the hotel after two o'clock last night; that they were in evening dress without baggage; that you followed them there and pleaded with Mary Eliska Girl Detective for an interview which was refused. Is this true?"

"Yes."

"Well, this looks as if Mary Eliska Girl Detective had run away from your place in a hurry, doesn't it? Have you anything to say?"

He hesitated. "I don't see what this has got to do with the awful catastrophe that followed."

"It has nothing to do with it, but people will talk. I thought maybe you'd be glad of the opportunity to explain."

"You must understand this is very painful to me," he said, in a low voice. "It is the most terrible thing that has ever happened to me."

"The clerk said that the ladies' evening slippers were incrusted with mud when they came."

"That might occur to anybody."

"I know; but I have learned that there was a car smashed up alongside the road between your place and town early this morning."

"I know nothing about that. Can't you trace it through the license plates?"

"They had been removed. Was Mary Eliska Girl Detective in that car?"

"Not so far as I know."

"How did she get from your place in to town."

"I haven't inquired, but I presume it was in her own car that she kept at my place."

"Where is her car now?"

"I don't know."

"Had you and Mary Eliska Girl Detective quarreled?"

He lowered his head. "Unfortunately, yes. You can understand how that makes me feel now. It was not a serious quarrel. It was the sort of quarrel that often arises between two people who are strongly attached to each other."

"What was it about?"

"That I won't tell you. It concerns nobody but ourselves."

"Do you wish to say anything further? Were you and Mary Eliska Girl Detective engaged to be married?"

"If we weren't, it was not my fault. She was the finest woman I ever knew!"

The clever devil! I boiled inwardly. It drove me wild to see how ingeniously he could turn everything that happened to his own advantage.

I was recalled to the present by a movement from Pete. Looking up, I found him staring at Mary Eliska Girl Detective in an ugly fashion. Her head was still lowered over a newspaper. This was a more immediate danger, and I put the thought of Nick Van Tassel out of my mind.

"What the hell is this?" cried Pete, rapping the paper he was reading.

Mary Eliska Girl Detective looked up mildly. "Hey?"

"I know who you are!" snarled Pete. "You said you was goin' to the Allardyce Bowles. And didn't you come here while it was burnin?" He suddenly snatched the newspaper out of my hands. "Yeah! And here's a pitcher of you in this one. It's you, all right! You're Mary Eliska Girl Detective!"

"Well, I had to be somebody, didn't I?"

"Aah! Don't pull no cracks!" he cried. "That won't do you no good. You're nottin' but a bull! A dirty bull!" A whole string of curses followed.

Mary Eliska Girl Detective had risen. She was taller than he. She met his blazing eyes squarely. "Sure I'm what you call a bull," she said, still trying to be friendly. "What of it? I'm still me, myself. You're cracked on the subject. Bulls is just like anybody else."

"Not to me.'" he shouted. "I hate 'em!" Another string of foul oaths. "I fell for you!" he went on, almost weeping in his rage. "God! what a fool I was. You're the first and the last I'll ever fall for. I thought you was a swell girl, game like a fella, and on the level! And you're on'y a bull! You got all our business out of us, didn't ya?"

"I didn't ask you for it. You told me as a friend and I listened as a friend."

"Yeah? Well, I had enough of such a friend. You and she can get the hell out of here, see? I don't care if you do bring a cop back with you. You're lucky we don't beat you up first."

"Wait a minute!"

"Aah!" he snarled, sticking out his jaw. "Don't you think I'm man enough to put you out?"

"Sure," she answered, coolly. "And I wouldn't bring a cop back, neither. But just answer me one question first."

"What's that?" he demanded.

"Which do you hate the worst, a bull like me, or a high muckamuck like Nick Van Tassel?"

"I hate you all!" he said, with a violent gesture.

"Sure! But you got to decide, see? Because Nick Van Tassel is my mark. If you put us out of here I'll fail. If you help me like you agreed to do, I'll get him."

"Aah! What could you get on a man like Nick Van Tassel?" he sneered.

"I've got enough on him for him to want to kill me. You saw his first attempt last night. Later he burned the hotel down to try to get Bella and me."

"God!" said Pete, staring. "How do you know that?"

"Because we were fastened in our room by an iron bar across the door handle."

"Why don't you have him arrested?"

"I couldn't prove that he had the bar put across our door. He's a powerful man. I've got to have a perfect case against him before I open it."

No answer from Pete.

"That's why I want him to think that Bella and I are dead," she went on. "So I can work in the dark. So I can strike at him unexpectedly. You see I am putting myself completely in your hands. You can walk right out that door and wreck me if you have a mind."

"Aah! you're foolish!" he sneered.

"No, I'm not," she said, confidently. "I can see what you are. You couldn't go back on anybody that trusted you."

"Aaah!...What's Nick Van Tassel done, anyhow?"

"I can't tell you that. You'll hear all about it if I'm successful."

"Have you got any place to go tonight?"

"Yes, I've got a good place, but I can't tell you where it is. Bella and I will be dead to the world until I'm ready to strike."

Pete turned away from her. Mary Eliska Girl Detective, who possessed the art of never saying too much, went to the table and started unwrapping the food for our evening meal. After a while he gave her an extraordinary look out of the corners of his eyes—suspicion, wistfulness, sullenness, longing—I can't describe it.

"Aah!" he sneered. "You know what me and Joe's business is."

"'S nothin' to me," she said, cheerfully. "I'm not after you. I wouldn't take the case if it was offered to me."

"Wouldja eat wit a coupla stick up men?"

"Watch me."

"Don't you think me and Joe is pretty bad fellas?" he insisted.

"You can't draw me into any moral discussions," she said, smiling broadly. "I don't set up to be anybody's judge....But I will say I'm sorry for it."

"Why?" he snarled, all ready to lash out again.

"Because I like you so much," she answered, softly. "And the cops always get you in the end. You've been good friends to Bella and me. I would hate to think of boys like you and Joe sitting in a cell."

"Well, what are poor boys gonna do?" he snarled. "Feed a goddam machine all their lives? Might as well be in a cell."

"Don't ask me," she said, sadly. "I didn't make the world."

He flung away to the window. She let him alone. The rest of us sat down to the table, and presently he joined us with a swaggering, hangdog air, ready to blow up if anybody looked at him. But we ignored him, and gradually he smoothed down.

"Aah!" he said out of the corner of his mouth, "I picked up a boat for you. It's tied down at the foot of Extension Street."

"Thanks," said Mary Eliska Girl Detective.

He did not speak again, but there was a sort of a comfortable feeling in the room and we knew that the danger had passed. He kept looking at her in a rather piteous way through his lashes. The poor kid was hard hit.

At ten o'clock we started out. The boys led the way through a rear door into a dank and evil smelling yard. They opened a gate into an adjoining yard, whence there was a passage to the street beyond. Here we were to have said good bye to them, but Pete pleaded hard to accompany us to the boat.

"Aah! if any fellas tried to pick you up in the street, and you turned them down, they'd remember your faces, wouldn't they? Yeah, and if two girls was seen gettin' in a boat, people would talk about it. But if we was with you it wouldn't look funny."

So we let them come.

The boat was tied up at a rotting wharf. Pete had taken care to leave it in a spot remote from any electric light. I never shall forget the smell of the place—salt water, oil, sewage. I shivered with fear at the thought of setting forth in the dark in such a flimsy shell. Fortunately, there was no wind stirring.

There were brief, whispered good byes.

"You'll hear from us as soon as we come back to the world," said Mary Eliska Girl Detective.

"Oh, Rosy...!" mumbled Pete. All the hardness had gone out of him then.

"If you want to kiss me you can," she murmured.

He did.

We stepped in. "I'll take the first try at the oars," said Mary Eliska Girl Detective.

After a fashion she managed to pull the boat out beyond the end of the wharf. There she rested on her oars. There was a light fog on the water, just as on the night before, and the boys were already invisible to us. But sounds carry far on such a night, and we suspected they were listening for us.

"Which way is the tide carrying us?" whispered Mary Eliska Girl Detective.

After watching a moment, I said, "Out to sea."

"Good! We'll drift for a while."

I never took kindly to water in large quantities. I had rarely been so close to it as I was now. Its very stillness scared me. The little patch I could see overside was as smooth as oil, yet when Mary Eliska Girl Detective lay on her oars, the boat gently heaved up and down as if we were resting on the bosom of a breathing creature. There was some water in the bottom of the boat, and I was sure there was a leak and that it would gradually fill. I would not speak of it because I was afraid of Mary Eliska Girl Detective's laughter.

We drifted so slowly it was only by closely watching the lights on shore we could be sure we moved at all. While Mary Eliska Girl Detective rested she was trying to figure out her position. With that remarkable visual memory of hers, the map she had studied that day was spread before her eyes in the dark.

"That will be Goat Island ahead of us on your right, and that dark stretch along the shore on the left must be King Park. The bright light straight ahead is Lime Rock light. We have to pass it. It's a little less than halfway to Brenton's Cove." I began to be a little less certain that we were about to be swallowed up and lost in the foggy sea.

After a few minutes she started rowing again. As with everything she does, she applied her mind seriously to the business. "The theory of rowing is simple," she remarked; "the only difficulty is to make the oars coordinate."

I got a hideous fright hearing the loud put put of a motor boat and seeing a green light which suddenly appeared from I know not where, heading straight for us, as I thought. "Oh, they're going to run us down!" I cried.

"Now keep cool!" said Mary Eliska Girl Detective, a little sharply (she was frightened herself!) "and let me figure this out....Boats that run at night always carry a green light on the right side and a red light on the left side, each in a sort of box with two sides open....Therefore there can be no danger. That motor boat is going to pass us on your right. If she was heading straight for us we would see both the green and the red light."

And so it proved.

Mary Eliska Girl Detective's rowing improved as we went on.

We passed through a narrow channel inside Lime Rock, in order not to lose touch with the shore on my left. We had now left the clustered lights of the town far behind; all was dark alongshore except for the scattered lights of big houses standing in extensive grounds. A breeze came up and little waves began to lap against the sides of the boat in what seemed to me a very dangerous manner.

"How are you going to know which is Brenton's Cove?" I asked, nervously.

"If we keep close to this shore we'll find ourselves in it," she said. "When we can't go any further without turning around and rowing back, we'll know that's it."

What a gift it is to be able to translate the lines of a map into the actual physical features of a landscape! It turned out just as she said. We found ourselves in a little cove with a low shore on one side and a steep rocky shore on the other. From the lights here and there we judged that we were surrounded by four or five big estates. On the high side we could faintly make out the shape of a big house that showed no lights. Paddling around to investigate, we found that each estate had a little pier and landing stage, except the dark house.

"It's a fair guess that that is Miss Betsy's," said Mary Eliska Girl Detective. "What would she want with a pier? You stay with the boat and I'll make sure."

It was not any too easy landing from the boat to a steepish slope of rock. One of my legs went into the water above the knee, and I thought I was gone, but Mary Eliska Girl Detective grabbed me somehow. I sat on the rock, holding the rope attached to the boat, while she climbed away into the darkness.

When she came back she whispered: "This is it. I found the wall with the broken bottles."

"What shall we do with the boat?" I asked.

"Set it adrift."

"Ohh!" I protested. That miserable boat that I had detested in the beginning, now seemed like our only link with the land of the living. "What if she won't take us in?"

"Then we'll walk back to town."

With a strong thrust of her foot she started the boat on its way. We watched it until we made sure the tide was carrying it out of the cove, then turned and scrambled up the sloping face of rock. On the plateau above there was a lawn that smelled sweet in the night. It was clearer here, and we could make out the shapes of trees farther back and the mass of the big house outlined against the night sky. No light showed in any of the windows.

We went close to the house and circled part way round first one side, then the other, trying to get the hang of it. It was one of those fantastic wooden mansions they used to build during the 'eighties and 'nineties, with all the different kinds of gables, dormers, porches, pinnacles and what not that the architect could think of. There were scarcely two windows anywhere that matched. As a crowning touch he had stuck on one side a huge square tower of roughhewn stones.

"How do you propose to get in?" I whispered. My conventional soul didn't relish the prospect before us.

"Let's see if we can't dope out which is Miss Betsy's room," whispered Mary Eliska Girl Detective. "The view up the bay is on this side, therefore the best rooms must be facing us. On the second floor the windows to the right are closed. Guest rooms, probably. The windows on the other side are open. That ought to be the mistress's room. At any rate, let's try it. Wait here a second."

Disappearing, she presently returned with a handful of gravel from the drive, that she proceeded to throw pebble by pebble at the top sash of one of the open windows. She was a good shot. I heard the little stones ring against the glass and drop to the porch roof below.

After about a dozen tries we were rewarded by seeing a large whitish figure appear at the window.

It spoke in a deep woman's voice: "Who are you? And what do you want?" Her composure was astonishing.

"Are you Miss Betsy Pryor?" asked Mary Eliska Girl Detective.

"Yes."

My employer was not to be outdone in coolness. "I am Mary Eliska," she said, pleasantly. "This is my secretary. Miss Jacqueline "Jax" Gray. We have come to see you, as I promised. Please don't disturb your servants."

A sort of cavernous chuckle came down to us. "All right!" said Miss Betsy in a voice that quaked with laughter. "I'll come down and let you in myself. Have patience with me, because I move but slowly."

She disappeared from the window. Mary Eliska Girl Detective lit a cigarette. "I was not mistaken in my woman," she said, with quiet satisfaction.

CHAPTER TWENTY-FIVE

OUR HOSTESS

The lights in the hall went on, and the front door was opened wide. Apparently Miss Betsy was an utter stranger to fear. A magnificent old woman in more ways than one. She must have weighed three hundred pounds, and she used a stick as thick as my arm to help her along. At present she was enveloped in a most incongruous dressing gown of purple velvet. I lost myself in computing how many yards it had taken, with ruffles. Down her back hung two thick black braids that a girl might have envied.

There was scarcely a wrinkle in her massive face, and her little black eyes danced with youthful liveliness. I wondered what could have induced a woman of such force and vigor to shut herself up like this.

Perhaps the joking reason she had given was the true one. She was tired of fools.

"So this is what you're like!" she cried, drawing Mary Eliska Girl Detective inside. Her voice boomed like the deeper notes of an organ. "The photographs did not lie, then!...Glad to see you too, my dear," she added, turning to me with complete kindness. "I envy you your job!"

A few minutes before I had been ready to swap my job with anybody; now I began to feel proud of it again.

"You are not surprised to see us," said Mary Eliska Girl Detective in mock disappointment. "I was hoping to create a sensation."

"Ah, it was a shock to me to read that you had been lost in the fire!" said Miss Betsy, gravely. "But then I began to think: surely if all the fools were able to get out, Mary Eliska Girl Detective would not allow herself to be burned up. And if it happened to suit her plans to disappear, this would be her opportunity."

"You are a witch," said Mary Eliska Girl Detective.

"I ought to be," retorted Miss Betsy, chuckling—or it would be more correct to say that she rumbled in her diaphragm. "Come upstairs where we can be cozy, girls."

It was a slow and painful task for Miss Betsy to mount the stairs. "First time I have been down in years," she said. On the second floor we entered a big old fashioned room that was not grand at all, though Miss Betsy was one of the richest women in the world, but immensely comfortable. She called it her sittin' room. She had a masculine carelessness of speech.

"Sit ye down! Sit ye down!" she boomed. "How did you get here?"

"By rowboat," said Mary Eliska Girl Detective. "I set it adrift."

"Are you hungry?"

We were not.

She seemed to understand the situation without the necessity of any explanation. "You did right to come here. You can lie low here in absolute security. And direct your campaign from here—I assume that there is a campaign. You wrote me that I could help you, you know. I only make one condition."

"What's that?" asked Mary Eliska Girl Detective, smiling.

"You must tell me the whole story."

"I intended to do so."

"Start right in!" boomed Miss Betsy.

"But we got you out of bed!" protested my employer.

"Bed be damned!"

We laughed. "Do you mind if I smoke?" asked Mary Eliska Girl Detective.

"Not at all. I'm a smoker myself."

"Have one of mine?"

"Pah!" cried Miss Betsy. "Pimp sticks! Excuse my bluntness. I like something stronger." From a box beside her chair she took a little cigar, clipped the end, and nonchalantly lighted up. It seemed to complete the picture. She was a swell person. Hardboiled and kind. A unique combination!

Mary Eliska Girl Detective put my thought into words. "You're too good to be wasted in solitude."

Miss Betsy raised her massive shoulders. "I was born fifty years too soon. You can imagine what a misfit I was among the prim misses of my generation. Nowadays I might have stood a chance." The history of a lifetime was expressed in those simple words. "Start in!" she cried. "I can't wait!"

"We are safe from being overheard?" asked Mary Eliska Girl Detective.

"There is no one in this part of the house but my maid Catherine. The other servants sleep in the kitchen wing. We'll have to take Catherine into our confidence. She's been with me over thirty years. I'll vouch for her."

Mary Eliska Girl Detective had no more than started her tale when one of the doors opened and a scared white face looked in—a woman of fifty odd, plain and sensible looking.

"It's all right, Catherine," said Miss Betsy, offhand. "This is Mary Eliska Girl Detective and her secretary, Miss Jacqueline "Jax" Gray. They are going to stay with us awhile. The servants mustn't know anything about it. It will be quite a game!"

A sigh of blessed relief escaped the woman. "Oh, madam! I heard strange voices and I thought...I thought...."

"You thought I was being murdered in my bed," said Miss Betsy, composedly. "Well, I'm not, you see. Go down to the pantry like a good girl and make sandwiches. Make a lot. And fetch up some beer. We'll be hungry later."

My employer proceeded to tell Miss Betsy the same story that I have set down here, but more briefly. The old woman, greedy for details, continually interrupted her with questions. The tale had a special interest for her because she was familiar with the scene and many of the actors. She kept up a sort of rumbling comment throughout.

"Howard Van Tassel....never was anything but a cumberer of the earth.... Alida Van Tassel—she was a Bradley. A candy box beauty. It was her sort helped drive me into my hole....Ha! Omega Farm! Used to be the old Standish place. We practiced archery there....Gibbs

Cumberland! Good God! Is that little flea still hopping from tea to tea? He leaves an itch behind him wherever he goes. He's ten years older than me.... Chowder Club! I used to go there. They let me eat chowder, but nobody asked me to dance!..."

When Mary Eliska Girl Detective finally came to the end, Miss Betsy thumped her stick on the floor. "What a story!" she cried. "This is better than I expected. Good God! what a magnificent scoundrel! I'm half in love with him just from hearing your description!"

"Bella and I both are," said my employer, dryly.

"I used to know his father, the last Nicholas," Miss Betsy went on. "He was a stick like all the Van Tassels. This Nicholas must have got his vital qualities from the policeman."

"The policeman?"

"His mother was the daughter of a policeman. Her real name was Mary Ann Finnegan, they tell me, but it became Marian Finucane when she went on the stage. A comic opera star. 'La Mascotte,' 'The Grand Duchess,' 'The Bells of Normandy.' They say that Nick Van Tassel was trapped into the marriage, but I know nothing about that. I am sure she was far too good for him. However, it killed his father. An effusion of bile, I dare say. He lived only long enough to cut off his son with a beggarly six million.

"That Nicholas Van Tassel—I mean the grandfather of the present Nick—was the last man of ability in the family. Quadrupled his fortune. But he was a horrible little man; purse proud; arrogant to a degree. There was always something thin and sour in the Van Tassel blood. Ever since the first Nicholas Van Tassel, the fur trader, a superb old freebooter."

"What about our Nick's mother?" asked Mary Eliska Girl Detective.

"Nothing thin about her blood. I never saw her. A handsome wench, I understand. She and her husband got along well enough. At least there was no open scandal. He was like putty in her hands. She made the money fly. She brought color into the humdrum Newport season. Everybody accepted her and talked about her escapades. Perhaps you've heard about the monkey dinner or the living statuary ball about fifteen years ago. They wouldn't create a ripple nowadays."

"I have heard of them."

"Toward the end of her life Mrs. Van Tassel brought back a cheetah from India for a pet. Do you know what a cheetah is?"

"Not exactly."

"Well, neither do I. But that's the sort of woman she was. Irish exotic. Nine years ago she and her husband were killed together in an automobile accident in Switzerland."

"Double suicide?"

"Maybe," said Miss Betsy, coolly. "It never got around. If it was, it was certainly her idea. That Nick Van Tassel hadn't the spirit of a louse."

"And for nine years our Nick has been perfecting his racket," murmured Mary Eliska Girl Detective.

"Racket?"

"A new slang word."

"Nothing of the sort!" said Miss Betsy. "It's an old one revived. I get the meaning perfectly....Well, let's eat!" she cried, with gusto. "Story telling is hungry work!"

When she had sated her appetite and lighted another little cigar, she demanded to know what her part was going to be in the forthcoming drama.

"Well," said Mary Eliska Girl Detective, smiling at her with half closed eyes, "I was counting on using you as a sort of decoy."

"Ha!" cried Miss Betsy, delightedly. "I shall have a taste of life before I die....You mean a decoy to attract Nick Van Tassel?"

"Precisely."

"I only hope I set eyes on him!"

"But I must warn you it's dangerous," said Mary Eliska Girl Detective, earnestly. "It's so dangerous that every man I have put it up to has refused to face it."

Miss Betsy smiled in an amused fashion. "I can't understand how anybody over seventy fears for their life," she said. "....Why, Death and

I have been keeping company a long time back," laughing until the floor shook. "I'm expecting him to pop the question any night. That's one follower every woman can count on, however plain she may be."

"Well, thank God I've found you!" said Mary Eliska Girl Detective, simply.

"But look here; there's a serious obstacle in the way," said Miss Betsy, with an anxious frown. "How am I going to persuade anybody that I'm a fit subject to be scared to death?"

We all laughed.

"You can act, can't you?" suggested Mary Eliska Girl Detective.

"I'm not very good at it. Once I played a parlor maid in an amateur performance, and the audience thought I was a burglar in disguise."

"I'll teach you. We'll take plenty of time to make this thing go right."

"My voice is the healthiest thing about me," said Miss Betsy. "How can I strip its bark?"

"There are certain pastilles that actors put in their mouths to make their voices sound old and feeble."

"Bring 'em on!...And look you, here's an idea. Why not put me to bed and make out I have a dropsy?"

"Splendid! I never should have thought of that!"

Chapter Twenty-Six

Lying Low

Miss Betsy called her house the Priory in a spirit of fun. Mary Eliska Girl Detective and I were installed on the third floor, which had not been used in many years. It was never visited by the servants, with the exception of cleaning women who came in at stated intervals. We had a suite over the closed guest rooms, consequently nobody could hear our footfalls. Our doors were always locked, of course.

We were perfectly comfortable. The only drawback was the necessity of staying in all day. We gradually got in the habit of sleeping the greater part of the day, and staying up at night. This suited Miss Betsy to a T. Also at night we could get exercise out on the dark lawn.

Besides Catherine, the household consisted of a cook and three maids. Miss Betsy considered that butlers were nuisances. These four women slept in the kitchen wing, which was entirely distinct from our part of the house. All were elderly. Since Miss Betsy took her meals upstairs, they rarely saw her.

There was also a man and his wife (Mr. and Mrs. Baxter) who lived in a lodge by the gates. Baxter was a chauffeur, and his principal task was to take Catherine in to town every day to do her shopping.

Miss Betsy herself boasted that she had never been in a motor car. There were two gardeners who came by the day.

We became acquainted by degrees with the customs of that extraordinary household. The gates were kept locked at all times. When her husband was out with the car, Mrs. Baxter was forbidden to open the gates for any reason whatever. There was, however, an ancient telephone from the lodge to the house, so that she could transmit a message. There was no connection with the regular exchange. Miss Betsy's only visitor from the outside world was a certain Dr. Wickham, a very old man who had lost all his other patients, she said, because he told them the truth.

Catherine waited on us. A pale, subdued, enigmatic kind of woman, I was ill at ease with her at first. I discovered she was a treasure. She adored her queer mistress, and what was more, she understood Miss Betsy and could appreciate her funny side.

Once she learned that Mary Eliska Girl Detective and I also loved the grim old woman, she would have done anything for us. Catherine had no life apart from her mistress, and wanted no other.

Her greatest problem was to feed us without the knowledge of the other servants. She solved it cleverly. Among her other duties she was Miss Betsy's almoner; that is to say, she always had a dozen or more poor families on her list that she visited regularly. She carried a big wicker basket in the car, and had it filled at the grocer's. She carried it into each house she visited, and of course the chauffeur had no means of knowing if it was emptied when it came home. That was how our food entered the house.

She cooked it on an electric stove in our bathroom. Our bill of fare was somewhat restricted, but everything was delicious. Miss Betsy had a way of demanding food at all sorts of odd hours, so Catherine had had plenty of experience. She even smuggled a nursery ice box up to our bathroom, and kept it stored with ice. Our principal meal was usually eaten in the middle of the night with Miss Betsy. The old lady was more fun than a barrel of monkeys. In repose she had one of the saddest faces I ever saw. Mary Eliska Girl Detective said the two things went together.

"Ah, what will I do after you are gone?" Miss Betsy would say.

"Come with us," said Mary Eliska Girl Detective. "You've been shut up long enough."

But she always shook her head. "I don't like to be stared at."

In addition to the local sheet, Miss Betsy subscribed to a Boston and to a New York newspaper, so we were kept well advised of what was going on in the world. The sensation caused by the tragic death of Mary Eliska Girl Detective rolled up to an immense height, and subsided. I was a little shocked to see how quickly she was crowded off the front page.

Well, I suppose the President himself, once he was dead, would no longer be news.

The fire chief reported that the Allardyce Bowles fire had been caused by crossed wires. Same old gag.

There was no official investigation. District Attorney Lyle laid low. After the first day Nick Van Tassel managed to keep out of the papers. Henry Eversley left Newport in a hastily chartered yacht, "for a voyage around the world."

Mary Eliska Girl Detective immediately got in touch with her lawyer in New York by means of a letter which Miss Betsy addressed in her immense angular hand.

Through him a few people whom she could trust were informed of the real situation. But everything was allowed to take its course as if she were really dead. Her will was entered for probate and our offices on Gramercy Park closed up.

She was somewhat scandalized to learn that some friends who were not in the secret were getting up a memorial service for her at the Little Church Around the Corner. There was nothing she could do to stop it. I wondered if Nick would attend the service. It would be like him.

Crider and the bunch were ordered back to New York, and we were soon in daily communication with him. He addressed his letters to Miss Betsy Pryor. We were then ready to start our new campaign.

"We must first get some publicity for you," said Mary Eliska Girl Detective to Miss Betsy. "I hope you don't mind."

"I can stand it if I don't have to perform in public," she said.

"Only one appearance will be necessary, and that not in public."

My employer prepared some press notices, all much to the same effect, but differently worded. Like this:

It is not generally known that since the death of Hetty Green the richest woman in America is Miss Betsy Pryor of Newport. It is an established fact that Miss Pryor's income tax runs into the millions annually. In Newport Miss Betsy is more or less of a myth, because nobody has seen her for forty years except her servants. A few of the older residents remember her as a beautiful and brilliant girl who, in the full flush of her social triumphs, suddenly gave up everything and retired from the world.

Miss Betsy lives in a big house standing in extensive grounds on the shore of Brenton's Cove. Her place is surrounded by a nine foot wall topped by broken bottles imbedded in concrete. It is said that several fierce mastiffs are allowed to wander about at will inside. Night and day the gates are locked and guarded, and all communications must be made through the bars. There is no telephone.

Miss Betsy's only link with the world appears to be a faithful woman servant whom the storekeepers know as Miss Catherine. Miss Catherine has been holding down her present job as far back as the oldest inhabitant can remember. Every morning precisely at nine the gates swing open and a car appears bearing Miss Catherine to do her marketing. Miss Catherine, a severe, middle aged woman is about as communicative regarding her mistress' affairs as the proverbial clam. As for the chauffeur, he only turns his head away with a scowl when he is asked a question.

Yet Miss Betsy occasionally gives a sign of life from behind her well-guarded walls. It appears that she is a faithful reader of the newspapers. Every now and then she is displeased by some modern manifestation in the news, on which occasion she writes a peppery letter to the local paper. Her phobias include telephones, motor cars, phonographs, radios, airplanes—and in fact pretty much everything that has come in since 1890.

So far as is known, Miss Betsy has not a relative in the world and there is much speculation as to the disposal of her vast fortune when she passes on. She is over seventy years old.

Miss Betsy did not care much for this piece.

"Hum! Ha!" she snorted. "Beautiful! Brilliant! Pah!...Are you making game of me?"

"That's what they expect you to say," Mary Eliska Girl Detective pointed out. "It must sound like the usual tripe."

"Well, you know," she said, with an impatient shrug. "Send it out!"

Three notices were sent to an important press bureau, with instructions that they be sent to three papers only. To have covered the whole country simultaneously might have aroused suspicion. Mary

Eliska Girl Detective counted on other papers copying it, one from another.

And so it happened. Within a few days the story, now considerably garbled, trickled into the columns of a Newport newspaper. The editor added a little piece pointing out some of the obvious inaccuracies. This was exactly what we wanted.

"Richest woman in America" of course was news everywhere, and, once started, there was no stopping the story. It was like an endless chain. I think every newspaper from Panama to Alaska must have printed it eventually. As a result Miss Betsy's modest mail grew to such proportions that it had to be carried up from the lodge in a bushel basket. All these letters offered her suggestions for getting rid of her money.

Mary Eliska Girl Detective proposed that Miss Betsy write to the local newspaper about the matter. The old lady needed no help in composing this letter.

Sir:

Some idle minded fool has done me the doubtful honor of writing a piece about me and sending it to the newspapers. Apparently, since the original author remains anonymous, I have no recourse. It is outrageous that a law abiding citizen should be forced to submit to such an annoyance. I am not the richest woman in America, nor does my annual income tax run into the millions. Neither are there any fierce mastiffs at large in my grounds. If I choose to live in seclusion, that is my affair.

It seems that this story is being copied from paper to paper all over the country. It is a sad commentary on the quality of the mental pabulum that is required by our people. As a result I am being annoyed by hundreds of begging letters daily. I wish to advertise the fact that I don't propose to read these letters, much less answer them. I hope that my letter may be copied as widely as the original story, so that a lot of foolish people may be saved from wasting their time. I might also say, in case the label "richest woman in America" has attracted the attention of the light fingered gentry, that I possess no jewelry, and never keep money in the house.

Yours very truly,

Betsy Pryor.

I do not know how widely this sprightly communication may have been copied throughout the country, but it had not the slightest effect on the begging letters. They continued to arrive by the bushel.

We paid very little attention to the letters. What Mary Eliska Girl Detective was angling for was interviewers.

Night after night the old lady was coached for this ordeal. She entered into the game with spirit. We had a good deal of fun out of it. But it was true Miss Betsy was the world's worst actress, and in the end Mary Eliska Girl Detective had to abandon the idea of exhibiting her to the reporters.

The reporters came, of course, and like good reporters they refused to take no for an answer. Half a dozen times a day one of the Baxters telephoned from the lodge to the house to say that a man or a woman was hanging around the gates. They dogged Catherine's footsteps when she went in to town.

When they were balked they often went away and wrote spiteful stories about Miss Betsy. Finally one of the New York tabloids suggested there was a sinister mystery in the case. The inference was that "the tight lipped woman" (so they termed poor Catherine) had secretly made away with Miss Betsy, and was devoting her mistress' home and her income to her own purposes.

At this point Mary Eliska Girl Detective decided to take the doctor into her confidence. Miss Betsy assured us he was as honest and faithful as the day. When he next came to the house Catherine brought him up to our third floor sitting room. A gruff and hairy old man with a spotty waistcoat and eyes as gentle as a big dog's, if he was astonished to discover that Miss Betsy had two lodgers, he never showed it.

As a result of his conference with my employer, he sent the following letter to the tabloid newspaper:

Dear Sir:

Miss Betsy Pryor has been a patient of mine ever since I started to practice, forty three years ago. All the unsought publicity which has been raging in the press during the last few days is very distasteful to my patient, and the story which appeared in your columns yesterday seems to cap the climax. It does a serious wrong to an old and faithful servant.

Therefore I wish to assert as positively as I can for the benefit of you and your readers that Miss Pryor is very much alive. While she is not a well woman—she has been suffering for several years from a dropsical complaint due to a serious heart condition that confines her to her room—there is no reason, with the wonderful care she receives, why she should not live for many years to come. But the nervousness induced by these stories is very bad for her, and of course anything in the nature of a shock might terminate fatally.

I am therefore writing to ask you to give this letter as wide publicity as possible, so that these ridiculous stories may cease and be forgotten. All that my patient desires is to be let alone.

Yours very truly,

Jared Wickham, M.D.

Miss Betsy enjoyed a good laugh over this letter.

"That's our bait," said Mary Eliska Girl Detective. "We must sit back now and wait for a nibble."

"In what form do you expect to get a nibble?" asked Miss Betsy.

"The first thing our adversary must do is to inform himself of the real situation inside this house. He can only get that through Catherine. Either he or one of his agents will be making up to her shortly."

Catherine was in the room at the time. "Hm! Too bad she isn't a more promising subject for that sort of thing," said Miss Betsy, looking her over. "Maybe we ought to have put in somebody in her place."

"Not at all," said Mary Eliska Girl Detective. "Catherine is the best possible subject. She is known to all Newport. She's above suspicion."

"Let's warn her of what's in store," said Miss Betsy, with a wicked twinkle. "Catherine, my girl, has any young man been trying to flirt with you lately? I don't mean reporters."

"No indeed!" answered Catherine, with a toss of her head that suggested a young man had better not try it on.

"Well, you may expect it any time now."

"At my age!" said Catherine, scandalized.

"You are not too old," put in Mary Eliska Girl Detective, smiling. "Our antagonist is a good psychologist, and he knows you're not too old. He knows, too, that when a woman of your age falls for a man she falls very hard indeed. In fact, she can refuse him nothing. In the beginning you can repulse him if you choose, but after that you can appear to let yourself go without danger."

"I'll do my best," said Catherine, demurely casting down her eyes.

"Do your best!" said Miss Betsy, with affectionate scorn. "Listen at the woman! I only wish it was me. I'd give him a run for his money.'"

It is possible that Catherine in her quiet way had the same idea.

Chapter Twenty-Seven

The Trap Is Set

For a few days nothing happened. Meanwhile the storm of publicity blowing around Miss Betsy's head ceased as suddenly as it had arisen.

When they found it impossible to secure a photograph of her, the interest of the tabloids quickly waned. The life of a tabloid depends upon finding something new for its readers every day. Miss Betsy was forgotten by all the world, apparently—or all but one!

It was on Monday morning, I remember, that Catherine, upon her return from her daily shopping expedition, came up to the third floor and aroused us. She was in a state of considerable agitation—for her; a bright red spot burned in the middle of each pale cheek, and her eyes showed an unnatural glitter. This was the story she told us:

"This was my day for calling on Si Evans' family. He's the watchman who broke his hip six weeks ago and hasn't been able to work since. The eldest daughter has tuberculosis. They live in a poor house on Charles Street. Every week I take them jelly and soup from Miss Betsy, and make sure they have enough to go on with.

"Today when I went in, there was a young man in the dining room. Bob Dewar by name. They were all very friendly to him and grateful because he had bought a paper route for Johnny, the youngest boy, so Johnny could go back to school when it opens and still be earning something.

"The young man never said anything to me while I was in the house, but he kept looking at me funny."

Catherine averted her head. "I suppose it's the way a man does look at a woman, but I never realized it before. It was very...disturbing. He was a handsome young man.

"He left when I did, and as soon as we got outside the door he started speaking, 'When can I see you again?' You could have knocked me down with a feather! I didn't know what to say. I didn't say anything!"

"He was what they call a fast worker," said Mary Eliska Girl Detective.

"Yes'm. He said: 'Can't you see I'm just crazy about you? I been following you about. I only made friends with Johnny Evans so I could get acquainted with you. I must know you,' All this was standing in the walk in front of the Evans' house, with Baxter at the wheel of the car not twenty feet away.

"I finally managed to get out: 'What are you trying to do, make a fool of me? At my age?'

"'No! No!' he said. 'Look at me, and you'll see that I mean every word! You're not old to me. What do I care how old you are? There's something about you...I can't explain it. All I know is, you're the only one for me. When can I see you again?'

"I was so flustered I didn't know what to say.

"'Don't you ever get a night out?' he asked. 'I never go out at night,' I said, 'but I could go any time I wanted.' 'Then come into town tonight and go to the movies with me,' he begged. 'It's almost dark in there, and we can talk low. Meet me inside the Strand picture house at eight o'clock. I'll be waiting for you inside where it's dark and we can sit down together.'

"At first I said I wouldn't. 'Please come! Please come!' he begged. 'I swear I mean you no harm. Just want to make friends. I must know you! Please come!' So—" Catherine turned away her head again—"after a while I said I would...hoping I did right."

"Why, of course!" said Mary Eliska Girl Detective. "Everything is going splendidly!... What does this young man look like?"

"He's very good looking," said Catherine, self-consciously. "I couldn't quite make out if he was a real gentleman. He talked like one, but his clothes were too loud. He had big brown eyes—big as a woman's—and full red lips. His face was smooth all over. His voice was soft...."

Mary Eliska Girl Detective and I looked at each other. Reggie Mygatt!

"Are you sure it's the one you think?" Catherine asked, wistfully. The poor soul was hoping against hope she had made a genuine conquest.

"Absolutely," said Mary Eliska Girl Detective. "We know him."

"There might be some mistake."

"Listen! Doesn't he talk like this?" In an imitation of Reggie's flat, reedy voice, she said: "There's something about you!...I can't explain it!"

Catherine's head dropped lower. "That's him," she murmured. "Oh, what blackguards men are!" she went on, low voiced. "He looked at me in such a way, and spoke so soft and full of feeling you would have sworn he meant it!"

"Why, of course!" said Mary Eliska Girl Detective, crisply. "That's what men have been doing since the beginning....But as long as you know where you stand, it's all right, isn't it? You can go on with it just as if it was an amusing game, deceiving the deceiver!"

Catherine jerked her head up. "Sure I can go on with it," she said, with a hard smile. "I'll dress up for him tonight."

We did not learn in detail all that occurred at the movies, for Catherine was reticent. But it was evident that they had made a long stride toward intimacy. "I am learning more about men that I ever knew in all my life before," she said, with compressed lips.

He begged her to come into town the following night, but she said it would look too funny, after being such a home body, for her to start going out every night. He then asked her if it was true that there were dogs at large in the grounds, and when she said no, he offered to come in a boat at nine that night, and meet her outside the house.

She waited for him at the edge of the rocks. She told us he came in a small varnished boat that looked like a yacht dinghy. The name of the yacht was painted on the back of the stern seat, but something had been smeared over it and she could not read it.

They spent a couple of hours wandering around the grounds together.

After he had gone Catherine reported to Mary Eliska Girl Detective. Without appearing to betray any particular curiosity. Bob (or Reggie) had insinuated many questions about the layout of the house and the routine of the household, she said. She, of course, had taken pains to fill in the outline sketched in Dr. Wickham's letter. She represented her mistress as a sick and nervous old woman, just able to hobble from her bed to a chair and back. At all costs Miss Betsy must be saved from a shock, she had told him. And also that she and her mistress were alone in the main part of the house after nightfall.

"He's coming back tomorrow night," Catherine said, lowering her eyes.

"Bring him into the house," suggested Mary Eliska Girl Detective. "Tell him you're obliged to remain within hearing of your mistress's bell in case she wants anything."

On this occasion Catherine showed him all over the main house, excepting only Miss Betsy's bedroom and the third floor. No doubt he had used his eyes to good advantage. They entered and left the house by way of the conservatory, which opened off the rear of the main hall and had a door into the garden.

After the first meeting Catherine was chary of repeating the details of her young man's lovemaking, except in so far as it concerned Mary Eliska Girl Detective's plan. Well, we did not blame her. It was a strange experience for the elderly lady's maid. It made her cynical, yet I think she enjoyed it on the whole. We never could be sure how she felt, but there was no doubt she found it tremendously exciting.

After another visit, the young man began to talk guardedly of the possibility of marriage. The only thing in the way of it was a lack of money, it seemed.

From that it was only a step to suggesting ever so delicately that if they could only find some way of relieving Miss Betsy of a little of her surplus, she would never miss it and it would set them up for life.

"And what did you say to that?" Mary Eliska Girl Detective asked Catherine.

"I didn't say much," murmured Catherine, "but I let him see that I didn't mind if some way could be found without mixing me up in it.

He said I needn't have anything to do with it."

"And is he going ahead with it?"

Catherine nodded. "He thinks I'm completely gone on him."

"It's never hard to persuade a man of that," said Mary Eliska Girl Detective.

On the second morning following, the plot came to a head. Upon entering her sitting room, Miss Betsy found an envelope addressed to herself propped up on her writing desk.

Without opening it, she sent it up to Mary Eliska Girl Detective by Catherine. The plain white envelope, the sheet of typewriter paper within, covered with a few lines of type script—it was only too familiar to us. My heart pounded in my breast at the sight of it, and my old terrors flowed back. The only change was, in this letter the signature was typed in red. Evidently the writer had a new machine.

Miss Betsy Pryor:

My job is to collect from those who have too much money, and put it where it will do good. I have you down on my list. I want twenty five thousand dollars from you. I'll give you two days to get the cash in the house, then I'll send word how to pass it on.

If you attempt to stall me off, or to communicate with the police, you will see me in person. I will be the last thing your eyes will see on earth. No locks or guards can keep me from you. See how easy it is to put this letter on your table. I have my own way of working. Every member of your household is watched. Kip Havemeyer and Howard Van Tassel each received a visit from me. They both had magnificent funerals.

You are an old woman and a sick one. If you wish to spend your remaining days with a quiet mind, heed this letter. Remember, old women are easy to kill!

The Leveler.

When my employer read out the curt sentences I seemed to feel the wicked, grinning presence of Nick Van Tassel there in the room. The sudden reminder of that overwhelming personality turned me dizzy and made the palms of my hands sweat. I was unable to speak.

After making sure that the servants would be occupied elsewhere, Mary Eliska Girl Detective and I went down to Miss Betsy's sitting room to consult with her. The sturdy old woman chuckled when she heard the contents of the letter. How I envied her her unconcern!

"Ha!" she cried. "This time he's got a pig nut between his teeth when he thinks it's an almond!" She brandished the big stick. "I only hope I may get one good crack at him, that's all.'"

Mary Eliska Girl Detective shook her head gravely. "What good will that do you if he has a gun? However carefully we plan, there will be a serious danger. A gun can be fired so quickly.'"

"And I will make a pretty good mark, eh?" Miss Betsy's chair creaked warningly when she laughed. "Never mind. I'll chance it."

"I'll make it my job to disarm him," said Mary Eliska Girl Detective.

"What must I do about this?" asked Miss Betsy, shaking the letter. "I suppose I'll have to wait two days before I can hurl my defiance at him."

"No," said Mary Eliska Girl Detective. "Answer it at once—publicly."

"Publicly?"

"Write to the newspaper in your usual peppery style."

"Why?"

"To force the issue. Such a letter from you in the newspaper would put heart into all his other victims. He would have to strike at you instantly to keep them in line."

"But if he did for me, wouldn't that stop his game, anyhow? I mean if a letter from me had been published."

"Not if he shocked you to death. There would be no mark on you; no evidence of murder. Your death would be ascribed to heart disease."

"By God!" said Miss Betsy. "It's almost a shame to stop such a clever racket!"

With my employer's help she evolved the following letter to the editor of a Newport morning paper. Their principal care was not to say too much in it.

Sir:

As a result of the unsought and uncalled for attention lately devoted to my humble self in the columns of your newspaper along with many others, I am still being pestered by hundreds of letters daily from all the cranks and fools in Christendom. Today I have a letter signed by someone who calls himself "The Leveler," demanding twenty five thousand dollars in cash from me, under threat of death or injury.

I shall pay no attention to it, of course. It is obviously the work of either a practical joker or a madman. If his eyes fall on this, let him learn that his letter already reposes in my waste paper basket. I am writing this to call your attention, sir, to the endless annoyance (not to use a stronger word) which may result from the injudicious advertising you have given my name, and to express a hope that you will not subject me to any more of it in the future.

Yours very truly,
Betsy Pryor.

The letter was sealed and addressed, and Catherine sent for.

"If this brings him," I said, nervously, "there's only one man on the place, and all us women."

"I'll provide for that," said Mary Eliska Girl Detective. "I don't mean to take any chances." She weighed the envelope thoughtfully in her hand. "The question is, will the publication of this letter stir the district attorney into taking action. He knows that The Leveler is not making an idle threat. Surely, if there is a spark of decency in the man he will warn Miss Betsy of what she's up against."

"He took no action after the fire," I pointed out. "It may be dangerous for him to let anything come out now."

"You are right," she said. "I must prod him into action."

She addressed the maid. "Catherine, take this letter to the newspaper office, and make sure that it will be published in tomorrow's issue. Afterward you are to go to a telephone booth and call up District Attorney Lyle in Providence. Ask him in Miss Betsy's name to come call on her tomorrow morning at eleven on a matter of urgent importance.

"When he asks the nature of the business, tell him to read the Newport paper tomorrow and he will understand. Tell him to bring the Newport chief of police with him, if he thinks it desirable, and impress upon him the importance of saying nothing about his errand until after he has talked with your mistress."

"What! the district attorney, the chief of police! Won't all this publicity spoil our show?" asked Miss Betsy.

"Wait!" said Mary Eliska Girl Detective, with a smile.

She made Catherine repeat her instructions after her.

Chapter Twenty-Eight

The Trap Is Sprung

Miss Betsy's letter to the newspaper was published on the following morning.

Dr. Wickham made an early call, and through him we got in touch with the Westervelts, a family who had leased the adjoining place on Brenton's Cove. Mr. Westervelt had an express cruiser lying at his pier. Mary Eliska Girl Detective considered that it might come in useful later.

When Catherine returned from her shopping trip she reported that her young man had approached her outside one of the stores. This instantly suggested there was something important in the wind.

Well, we already knew our antagonist believed in striking swiftly. Bob (or Reggie) told Catherine he had been engaged as an entertainer at a smoking concert that night, and he wouldn't be able to meet her until eleven thirty. If she would wait for him down at the edge of the rocks, he said, they could go for a row.

This was obviously a ruse to get Catherine off the place while the chief paid his visit, and we therefore made all preparations to receive him that night. He knew, of course, that when Catherine went out of the house at night she left the conservatory door unlocked behind her.

At eleven Lyle and the chief of police duly presented themselves at Miss Betsy's gates. Mrs. Baxter had her orders, and they were refused admittance. One can picture their astonishment and indignation. There was quite a scene. Finally, as a great concession, Mrs. Baxter admitted them to the lodge and allowed Lyle to talk to the house over the private phone.

The instrument was in Miss Betsy's sitting room.

We were all there, waiting for the call. Mary Eliska Girl Detective answered it, speaking in the cracked and querulous voice of age. A wonderful piece of mimicry. How thunderstruck Mr. Lyle would have been had he suddenly been gifted with the power to see whom he was talking to! The real Miss Betsy listened to the conversation with a broad smile.

"Yes, this is Miss Pryor....No, I can't see you. I am too sick and nervous this morning. My doctor has forbidden it."

He reminded her that she had sent for him, and that he had driven all the way from Providence in answer to her summons.

"Yes, I know," she said, pettishly, "but I'm too sick to see you. And, anyway, I've changed my mind. I'm not going to do anything about the threatening letter I received. It is obviously a hoax."

Lyle said that she was very likely right, but just the same all proper precautions ought to be taken.

"No!" said the pretended Miss Betsy. "I'm not going to bother about it. I should feel like a fool."

When she continued to resist him, he was forced to change his tone. "There may be a real danger in this," he said. "I have heard rumors that there was something like this going on."

So there was a spark of decency in the man, though it was buried deep!

"What do you want to do?" she asked.

"If there is such a man it is my duty to catch him."

"Well, what do you want me to do?"

"Nothing, except to allow us to furnish you with adequate protection."

"If there is anybody, you'll never catch him that way," she retorted. "If he's got any sense at all he is certainly having me watched. And you, too. And if you fill up my place with police and detectives he'll simply stay away until you take them out again. You can't keep them here indefinitely. As soon as they're gone he'll strike at me."

Lyle could find no answer to this piece of obvious common sense except to say, helplessly, "But you must be protected, Miss Pryor."

"Fudge!" she said in Miss Betsy's impatient manner. "If you want to catch the man you've got to advertise that you're not trying to catch him."

"How can I do that, madam?" he demanded with asperity.

"Listen. Let you and the chief of police give out interviews to the press. Make sure they are going to be printed in the afternoon papers. Say that as soon as you read my letter in this morning's paper you hastened to my place to devote all the resources of the district attorney's office and the police force to my protection. That will sound well. Say that I refused your offers. You can ascribe it to my sickness, my nervous condition, or anything you like. But make it strong. Say that I refused to permit a single detective or policeman to enter my grounds, and that consequently your hands are tied. The chief of police might add that he intends to have the roads in the vicinity of my place well patrolled, anyhow."

"Why put that in?" he asked.

"Well, it sounds good," said the make believe Miss Betsy, winking at the real one. "And if anybody has the notion of attacking me, it may persuade him to come by water. It would be easier to catch him, wouldn't it, if he tried to escape by water? I am told that the result of an automobile chase is always doubtful."

Lyle admitted this was so.

"After you have talked to the reporters I suggest that you return to your office in Providence and work there all afternoon as usual. Tonight I will send up Mr. Westervelt's yacht to fetch you down here. The captain will telephone your residence when he arrives, say, about eight. Whenever he comes up from New York to visit his family Mr. Westervelt uses this boat to carry him from Providence to Brenton's Cove. Consequently, its appearance will cause no comment, whoever may be watching. Bring your special officers with you. I suggest that two will be enough. Land at Mr. Westervelt's pier, and I will have you brought secretly to my house."

"Tonight?" faltered Lyle.

"Well, I'm not going to guarantee that it isn't a wild goose chase. You insisted on it. If anybody is going to attack me, he will probably do it quickly for the sake of the moral effect."

"You are right, Miss Pryor."

It doubtless went very much against the grain with Lyle to accept a plan of action from an eccentric old woman who was supposed to be almost bedridden to boot, but as he could suggest nothing better he had no choice. The fact that Miss Betsy was called the richest woman in the world probably helped to sugar the pill.

"Very well, Miss Pryor, I will be expecting a call about eight,"

Thus Mary Eliska Girl Detective's simple plan was laid, and there was nothing further to do but wait for night to come.

We had to take Baxter into our confidence because we needed his assistance, but none of the women in the house were told what we expected. This Baxter was an innocent sort of fool who looked very smart in his chauffeur's uniform, and sported a big turned up mustache in the hope that people would think he was a foreigner. But he was faithful enough, poor fellow, and strong as an ox.

He was set to work that afternoon in the privacy of his own workshop, making a flexible ladder that could be thrown over the wall later for the district attorney. Afterward Baxter laid a wire from the door of the conservatory through the house and up to Miss Betsy's bedroom, where it was furnished with a tiny buzzer. This was to warn us of our man's coming.

I think that was the hardest day I have ever had to put in. Whenever I thought of the coming night I choked all up with an unbearable surge of excitement. I didn't see how I could ever go through with it. Most of the time my heart was right in my boots.

Nick Van Tassel had fooled us so many times; had always displayed such a devilish resourcefulness in a tight place, that I couldn't persuade myself we had a chance of catching him. It came back to me that there was something superhuman in the man. This was one of those feelings you can't reason with.

Mary Eliska Girl Detective slept calmly for many hours during the day, but I never closed my eyes.

That remarkable woman, Miss Betsy, looked forward with dancing eyes to what she termed "the fun." She refused point blank to leave her room during the time the visitor might be expected.

"But consider," said Mary Eliska Girl Detective, gravely, "when he visits his other victims it's all one with him whether they pass out with fear or not; he turns it to advantage either way. With you the case is different; he's got to kill you because you have publicly defied him. A man as clever as he is isn't leaving anything to chance. Believe me, in case he fails to shock you to death, he will have some other expedient in reserve. And we don't know what it is. It is too dangerous for you to remain in the room."

"You're going to be here, aren't you?" said Miss Betsy. "I'll take my chance." And nothing would budge her.

Dr. Wickham acted as go between with the people next door. It proved not to be necessary to take Mrs. Westervelt into our confidence. The doctor used the name of another patient, a Mr. Pembroke, who lived in the neighborhood. He told Mrs. Westervelt Mr. Pembroke's condition had taken a turn for the worse and that he wished to call other doctors in consultation. He hired the yacht in Mr. Pembroke's name to bring the doctors down from Providence, and furnished the captain with the phone number he was to call when he went for them. He further requested that captain and engineer sleep aboard that night in case the doctors had to return. Thus the yacht was available for purposes of pursuit, should we need it.

From an upstairs window in Miss Betsy's house I saw the cruiser nosing slowly out of the cove shortly before seven. Outside she shot away at full speed. They said she could do thirty five miles an hour or better. We expected her back soon after nine.

She did her job on time. Baxter brought Lyle and his two men through the patch of woods that separated the two estates, and over the formidable wall. The ladder was rolled up and hidden under a bush.

Mary Eliska Girl Detective and I were not present when Lyle was introduced to Miss Betsy. She told us about it later. When Lyle saw her planted in her chair with her big stick beside her, massive and composed, his jaw must have dropped almost to his chest. All the courtroom swagger went out of him.

"But I thought...I thought...." he stammered.

She finished his sentence for him. "You thought I was a frail wisp that was done with everything but the undertaker!" She shook with laughter, and the chair creaked under the strain.

The sound of the vigorous bass voice completed his demoralization. "There must be some mistake," he said, feebly. "Over the phone...."

"That was just part of my little game to catch this scoundrel," said Miss Betsy, airily. "I understand that his specialty lies in shocking old folks to death. I merely wanted to persuade him that I was a good subject."

"How did you learn so much about his methods?" he asked, staring.

"I will explain that presently."

"Then your pretense that you weren't going to take any action was just...."

"Just a hoax, Mr. District Attorney. Or, as they say nowadays, a stall."

When Mary Eliska Girl Detective and I entered the sitting room, Lyle turned as white as a sheet and clutched the back of a chair for support.

"I think you are acquainted with Mary Eliska Girl Detective and Miss Jacqueline "Jax" Gray," said the old lady, wickedly.

The eyes of the two detectives bolted wildly. Lyle was unable to get out a single word.

"I am not a phoenix risen from my ashes," said Mary Eliska Girl Detective, smiling. "I never was burned up."

Lyle was obliged to sit in the chair and to wipe the cold sweat off his face. The hardy old lady did not spare him.

"Aren't you glad they escaped?"

"Of course! Of course!" he stammered. "But this is such a shock...I don't understand it...."

"Perhaps you suspect there is a very ugly story behind the burning of the Allardyce Bowles."

"No!" he cried, wildly. "I made a private investigation. There was no evidence! Not a shred! Not a shred!"

"To hell with your evidence!" said Miss Betsy, pounding her stick. "You know perfectly well that Nick Van Tassel tried to burn them up!"

"What reason have you for saying such a thing?"

"It is very simple," put in Mary Eliska Girl Detective. "He chased us into the hotel. An hour later the fire broke out. When Miss Jacqueline "Jax" Gray and I tried to escape from our room, we found that the door had been fastened on the outside with an iron bar."

"O my God!" cried Lyle. "Why didn't you come to me? Why didn't you tell me? I would instantly have started proceedings."

"I thought we'd stand a better chance of getting him this way," said Mary Eliska Girl Detective, dryly. "You told me, you remember, that it would be useless to proceed against him unless we caught him in the act. Perhaps we will tonight."

During the rest of the night Mr. District Attorney sang pretty small.

Shortly after eleven Catherine went out to meet Reggie. All the lights in the house had been out for some time. Our final dispositions were quickly made.

Baxter was hidden behind the ferns in the conservatory, with an electric button in his hand. With this he was to signal us when our man entered the conservatory. The buzzer at the other end of the wire was in Mary Eliska Girl Detective's hand.

Since Miss Betsy insisted on remaining in the room, her chair was put in one of the front corners, and a screen placed around it. She said she was going to push the screen over with her stick when the fun began. She swore she could breathe as softly as a bird.

Mary Eliska Girl Detective was to stand just inside the door from the hall by which he would enter. A projection of the wall concealed her, should he cast a light inside before entering. She was armed with the same big revolver we had taken from Nick. Just beyond her was the foot of Miss Betsy's immense four poster. With pillows we had arranged the semblance of a human body under the covers, a small pillow covered with a boudoir cap sticking out at the top.

I was to crouch at the head of the bed in such a position that by straightening up I could press the light switch when the man was fairly inside the room. One of the detectives was to stand behind the door from the hall, ready to seize him, while Lyle and the other man were to wait just inside the sitting room door. This door was to be left open.

There was a long wait. Each separate nerve of my body seemed to be stretched like a violin string at the point of breaking. An agonizing feeling. Nobody was allowed to smoke, of course. Miss Betsy passed the time in ragging the district attorney in her rumbling whisper. She was a terrible old woman when she took a dislike to you.

No sound came through the open windows. We supposed that when our man entered the house he would have his outposts stationed in the grounds. It was a clear, cool night, with a gentle breeze stirring, a young moon preparing to set. I smelled honeysuckle somewhere. It filled me with a kind of wild regret.

Our man seemed to have a superstitious feeling for the hour of midnight. We heard it striking in a distant church tower, a lovely sound. Immediately afterward there was a click in Mary Eliska Girl Detective's hand.

She dropped the little buzzer on the rug and kicked it out of her way. I thought, clenching my hands, if I can live through the next two minutes I'll be all right. Lyle and the other man retreated silently into the sitting room.

The door from the hall opened. Peeping under the high bedstead, I saw it open; I saw his legs. He didn't make even the whisper of a sound. He used no light. There was still a dim suggestion of moonlight in the room.

When I understood he was carrying no flash, I ventured to peep over the top of the bed. O God! what a sight I saw! All the blood in my veins turned to ice. I understood at that moment what it feels like to die of fright.

Yet it was a mere theatrical trick; some luminous substance like phosphorus smeared on his mask and on his false beard; on his hands. A spectral masked face and a pair of pale hands, one holding a gun.

But this was not what frightened me most. Alongside the place where his body ought to have been floated a large globe or bubble faintly shining from within. It lazily rose and fell; swayed from side to side. It was too horrible! My voice froze in my throat.

He kicked the door shut behind him, and turning to the bed, said, in a voice more awful than anything I ever heard, "Wake up, old woman!"

I went completely daft then. They tell me I shrieked like a madwoman. However, I automatically pressed the switch.

After that things happened much more quickly than I can tell about them. When the lights came up Mary Eliska Girl Detective, holding her pistol by the barrel, cracked him over the wrist, and his gun clattered to the floor. She kicked it across the room. With her left hand she snatched the mask off; the beard came with it, and for a second we all saw Nick Van Tassel at bay, snarling lips rolled back, eyes darting. The thing tied to his waist was nothing but a child's balloon, only bigger. A child's balloon!

He exploded the balloon and billows of smoke spread out from it.

"Gas!" screamed Mary Eliska Girl Detective. "Don't breathe!"

I instinctively dropped to the floor. Under the smoke I could see legs; Nick's legs. He ran to the window and dived out head first, carrying the screen with him. I heard him roll down the porch roof and thud to the ground. He could not have been hurt, for instantly a shrill whistle pierced the night.

I saw Mary Eliska Girl Detective making her way toward the corner where Miss Betsy sat. Our first duty was toward the old woman, of course, and I followed.

The screen was down. Somehow we got the unwieldy body to its feet and ran her into the next room, holding our breaths. We slammed the door behind us. The others were in there. As we dropped Miss Betsy into a chair panting, she actually laughed.

"This is better than I expected!" she said.

Outside on the lawn we heard running feet followed by the sounds of a struggle. There was a shot and a fall; a long drawn groan. This was from Baxter. Then two pairs of feet running away on the turf.

"Come on!" cried Mary Eliska Girl Detective.

The gas was confined to the bedroom. We left Miss Betsy by the open window of the sitting room and, tearing down the main stairway of the house, banged open the front door. Filled with the madness of pursuit, I felt no fear then. Only a sickening rage because he had escaped us. We left Miss Betsy rocking her arms and groaning: "If I only had my legs! If I only had my legs!"

The two detectives set off pell mell across the lawn toward the rocks, but Mary Eliska Girl Detective caught hold of Lyle. "The speed boat is our best chance of catching him," she cried. "Show me where the ladder was left!"

Two or three minutes later we ran out on the Westervelt pier and, springing aboard the motor yacht, banged on the doors to awaken the skipper and the engineer. They must have been astonished at our violence. Mary Eliska Girl Detective briefly explained that Miss Betsy's house had been entered, and the engineer leaped to his engine. There were only the two men sleeping aboard.

During the brief moment of silence that elapsed before the engine started, we heard the sound of frantic oars nearby, and could just make out a dim shape lying outside the cove. When our engine started the generator started with it, and the searchlight came on. We picked up the craft outside, a smart motor cruiser not unlike our own. Four or five people were climbing over her side from a dinghy.

We had to back out from the pier and make a quarter turn. Before this was completed the other boat was gone. They left the dinghy drifting. There was a second dinghy floating in the cove. I wondered if Catherine were all right. When we got outside the cove we picked up the other cruiser with our searchlight. She was scooting north for the open bay. Running without lights, of course.

She rounded Fort Adams and disappeared. In a moment or two we followed, and picked her up again. It was now evident she was heading out to sea. The three of us were with the captain on a sort of little bridge amidships, behind a windshield.

Mary Eliska Girl Detective and I had been given slickers. We were boiling along through the dark sea at express train speed, yet we did not seem to gain a foot on the flying craft ahead. Below us, the engineer's body stuck out of his little door. He was likewise watching the boat ahead.

"It must be the Bonito, Nick Van Tassel's cruiser," muttered the captain. "Nothing else of her build has the speed. I reckon she was stolen."

Mary Eliska Girl Detective said nothing.

A chase at sea is an exasperating experience. There is nothing to do but sit still. You cannot help any. Your eyes are glued on the boat ahead, and its position never changes. The two boats are like fixed points with the sea roaring by. We left the land behind us and began to feel the long, slow Atlantic surges.

"Where the hell does he think he's going?" muttered the captain. "There's nothing in front of us short of the West Indies."

In the end it became evident that the Bonito was drawing away from us—very slowly, to be sure, nevertheless drawing away. We could just barely keep her in view with our searchlight now. Mary Eliska Girl Detective's face was stony. With the idea of cheering her, I said: "Just the same, we've got him hard and fast. When you unmasked him tonight there were six witnesses. A man like Nick Van Tassel can't escape for long."

"We shall never lay hands on him," she said, with grim certainty.

What happened, happened so swiftly that it stupefied me. The vessel ahead seemed to waver in her course, and for a second we saw her whole length dimly. I don't suppose it is given to many people to be actually looking at such a thing when it happens. She lifted up in the middle and broke in half as easily as one might break a breadstick between one's fingers. A vast burst of flame filled the heavens, followed by an appalling smash. Instantly the sea all round her seemed to be covered with fire. I was stunned. The cries of my companions seemed to come from far off. My first sensation was of blinding pain. I understood the purport of Mary Eliska Girl Detective's grave words then. Of course Nick was not one who would let himself be taken alive! He must have had the alternative in view from the beginning. Lucifer gone to death with his lips fixed in that infernal smile!

I wondered if his companions had been bold enough to face it out, too, or if he had dragged them with him willy nilly into eternity. One would never know. My heart bled at the thought of the three exquisite girls. What good had their beauty been to anyone? Especially the delicious Evelyn, betrayed by love.

We had to stop our engines until the spreading gasoline on the sea burned itself out. In the middle of the fiery circle the two halves of the yacht blazed separately. The long swell from the open sea indifferently raised and lowered them. The madly leaping, curling, entangling flames were like fiery hair blown in the wind. At no time did we see anything human in the fire or in the sea. They must have tied weights to their bodies so they would sink at once. Very likely they had jumped overboard before the explosion.

It was all over in a few minutes. Each part of the vessel slowly sank, disappearing suddenly at the last with an expiring hiss. The last flames on the sea nickered out and the night seemed darker than before.

We moved up close to the spot, playing our searchlight upon it. The surface of the sea was calm.

We lowered a small boat and Mary Eliska Girl Detective, Mr. Lyle, and the engineer got into it. The sea was covered with floating wreckage. Aided by the light from the yacht, they picked it over piece by piece, but found no suggestion of anything human. We knew we shouldn't find anything, yet we lingered for half an hour.

I kept my back turned to the searchers. I was only afraid they might find something. Leaning over the rail, staring down at the black water, I tried to argue myself back to sanity. What a fool I was to have allowed my imagination to become enslaved by a Nick Van Tassel! Shallow, cruel, and false, he had not a redeeming feature. But, oh! the splendor of that reckless life and fiery death! I gave it up with a shrug. My whole scheme of things was tottering.

When Mary Eliska Girl Detective came back up the ladder I stole a glance in her pale grave face. I was overjoyed to see she felt the same as I did. She was too big a woman to feel any jealousy because Death had cheated her of a personal triumph. Putting an arm around my shoulders, she murmured: "How much better to have it end this way than before a gaping courtroom!"

Mr. Lyle instantly agreed (for reasons of his own) that it would be better for the world if the truth were never allowed to come out now.

Consequently, when we got under way we made a long détour over toward Narragansett in order to avoid meeting the boats that we knew must have put out from Newport to investigate the disaster. Thus we avoided giving any explanation of our presence on the scene.

We returned to Brenton's Cove, where Mary Eliska Girl Detective and I were put ashore, and Lyle's two men taken aboard. The yacht then carried them back to Providence. The owner's family never knew that she had been out on any other errand. If the shot was heard, it was ascribed to an automobile back firing.

The two drifting dinghies were towed out into the bay and sunk.

We found Catherine safe, and in attendance upon her mistress, pale faced and tight lipped as she had been before it all happened. It seemed that when the warning whistle had sounded, Reggie Mygatt had unceremoniously dumped her ashore and rowed off to the Bonito. Catherine was never heard to speak of the matter afterward.

Mrs. Baxter had fetched Dr. Wickham to attend her husband. Baxter had been shot through the thigh, not a dangerous wound. From his description of the man who had run up, we guessed that it was Bill Kip who had shot him. By reason of Baxter's incapacitation Miss Betsy's car was useless to her for the time being, so Mary Eliska Girl Detective and I used it to make our get away. When morning broke we were far across the boundaries of Rhode Island. We slept all day, and continued our journey the following night.

Thus Newport provided a second sensation close on the heels of the first. Only about a dozen souls knew of the connection between the two, and they never told. According to the story in the papers, Nick Van Tassel had been entertaining a small party of his intimate friends at dinner at Omega Farm.

His guests were Ann Livingston, Evelyn Suydam, Mary Bourne, William Kip, and Reginald Mygatt, Jr.

About ten o'clock somebody had suggested they go for a sail out to sea in Nick's express cruiser the Bonito. As both the owner and young Kip were experienced pilots and well used to engines, they had left the crew of the vessel ashore. They had done this on former occasions. At a point about ten miles south of Newport the Bonito had blown up from causes that would never be known, and had no doubt instantly sunk. The fire had been seen from the Cliffs and word was telephoned to the police, but rescue boats had been unable to locate the spot until daylight, and then nothing was to be found but a little floating wreckage. No bodies ever were recovered.

It was the prominence of the families concerned that made it a unique sensation. Much space was devoted to the victims' genealogies and to accounts of their social triumphs. It was staggering to think of so many gilded scions being wiped out at one time. As for Nick Van Tassel, he bade fair to be enshrined forever as the premier patron of sport.

The other Van Tassels discreetly kept the amount of his estate out of the papers, and the public still thinks of him in terms of millions.

It was Miss Betsy Pryor, the seemingly cynical and hard boiled, who put up the good round sum that was considered necessary to insure the silence of the two detectives attached to Mr. Lyle's office and the two men on Mr. Westervelt's yacht. "What the devil!" (I can hear the deep voice bringing it out.) "All those youngsters have families. Why should the fathers and mothers have to suffer for the sins of their offspring'? There are enough scandals to tickle the ears of the mob without airing this one!"

Miss Betsy is still our very good friend. Mary Eliska Girl Detective has not been able to tempt her outside her walls, but we sometimes go to spend a week end with her.

All that remained was for Mary Eliska Girl Detective and I to resuscitate ourselves as plausibly as possible. We spent a week motoring through the White Mountains and Canada, to give the affair time to die down a little. Then, in order to divert attention as far as possible from Newport, we discovered ourselves to the world in a Minneapolis hotel.

There was a tremendous furor, of course, but, curiously enough, our coming back to life did not make so big a noise as our leaving it. The public seemed to feel a little cheated. Mary Eliska Girl Detective told the press the truth as far as she went. She said she had been engaged on a case that made it highly desirable for her to disappear for a while, and she had taken the accident of the fire as an opportunity to do so.

She refused all information about the case in question, and her story was not very well received. Her great popularity undoubtedly suffered a considerable diminution for a while. However, everything is forgotten in time. The brilliant piece of work she did in connection with the murder of Ram Lal, the so called crystal gazer, fully restored her in the public estimation.

THE END

ABOUT THE ORIGINAL AUTHOR

Hulbert Footner (1879–1944)

Hulbert Footner (1879–1944) was a Canadian writer of non-fiction and detective fiction. His most successful creation was the beautiful and brilliant Madame Rosika Storey and her plain assistant who explains the evolving solutions to her boss' cases. His Madame Storey mysteries fit the flapping 1920s like the long lizard gloves that graced her arms and did well supporting his traveling family's lifestyle. Mme. Storey, the lady dick, gets on the trail of a lad named Nick, a wellborn gent who is pretty slick at black-mailing people who're old and sick. If they don't come through, they pop off quick. Well, anyway, after being captured by the arch villain and his social registrite accomplices, Mme. S. and her secretary escape with the help of two gentlemanly gunmen, take refuge with the genial recluse, Betsy Pryor, and set a trap for Nick, into which——

ABOUT THE WRITER

About the Writer William A Stricklin:

Military Training and Service

- Life Member of "Military Order of World Wars" (MOWW);

- Bill received training initially at Ft. Lewis; basic infantry training, Ft. Benning, Georgia; followed by Fort Holabird, Counterintelligence Corps training for US Army service at Ft. McNair and in the Pentagon

- Honorable Discharge two years active service (wartime); and four years US Army Reserve

- Professional License History

- State Bar of California 036559 Active 1964-2025

- Hawai'i State Bar Association JD0962 Active 1970-2025

- Washington State Bar Attorney 10456 Active 1969-2025

- State of Washington General Contractor: Type I steel/concrete 1968-1970 Denny Building

- State of Hawai'i "B" General Contractor CT6406: 2/16/1973-4/30/1996 Amfac Center HI
- State of Hawai'i Real Estate Broker 1968-2015 ("inactive")
- State of California Real Estate Broker: Commercial, Residential real estate sales/leases 1958-99
- Financial Consultant, Montecito Bank & Trust. Santa Barbara 1997-1998
- Courts Admitted to Practice
- Supreme Court of the United States 1964-2025
- United States Court of Appeals for Ninth Circuit 1964-2025
- United States Tax Court 1964-2025
- United States District Court for the Northern District of California 1964-2025
- United States District Court, District of Hawai'i
- Supreme Court of State of California 1970-2025
- Supreme Court of Hawai'i 1970-2025
- Washington Supreme Court (Rule 18 reciprocity in 26 states) 1969-2025
- Green Building Certification
- LEED BD+C Project Manager 2010 to 2025
- Bar Affiliations, Activities and Memberships
- Hawai'i Bar's Model Rules Committee, rules of lawyers' conduct
- Hawai'i Bar's Government Lawyers Section
- Hawai'i Bar's Litigation Section
- Hawai'i Bar's Natural Resources Section
- Founding Charter Member Washington State Bar Association Civil Rights Section.
- Active Member of Bar Association of San Francisco (BASF) 162968
- Environmental Law Section of BASF
- Conference of Delegates Committee of the BASF

- Ethics Committee of BASF

- Member Race and Ethnicity Committee of BASF

- Member of Disability Rights Committee of BASF

  Union Member and Union Officer 2002-2025

- Sergeant at Arms AFGE Local 2275 District 12

- AFGE District 12 works with over 80 AFGE locals and over 82,000 workers in California, Arizona,

  Hawai'i, and Nevada. The District and its staff provide training and mentoring to local leaders and union members. We provide assistance with union contract negotiations, member representation, union organizing, union administration, local elections, legislative matters, and legal advice.

- Honors Philanthropic Affiliations and Awards

- Order of Golden Bear to promote statewide unity of University of California campuses

- Chair, University of California Alumni Association, Washington DC 1960-61

- Listed in National Trust for Historic Preservation Directory of Historic Preservation Lawyers

- Chair, Hawai'i Advisory Committee, American Arbitration Assn 1975 to 1985

- Master Mason 3° Berkeley 363 Blue Lodge 1959

- Scottish Rite 32° Mason Oakland Temple 1959

- Hawai'i Shriners Temple 1968 and Hawai'i Shriners Hospital Clown Corps

- Hawai'i Opera Theater Board of Trustees

- Hawai'i Ballet Board of Trustees

- National Board of Trustees, American Arbitration Assn, New York, 1990-1994

- Santa Barbara Board Trustees, Planned Giving Chair, American Red Cross 1998-2000

- Member Santa Barbara Board of Trustees, Catholic Charities, 1998-2000

- Member Santa Barbara Board of Trustees, Cottage Hospitals, 1998-2000

- Elected Member Montecito Santa Barbara All Saints by the Sea Episcopal Church Board, 2000-02

- Hawai'i's "Mediator of the Year" 1989 American Arbitration Association

- Robinson Cox Visiting Fellow, Law School, University of WA (Perth) 1989 to 1990.

- Facilitated the Australian Minister of Land's return of land to the traditional owners, Lama Lama Peoples

- Charter Member Founding Secretary, Hawai'i Lambda Alpha (Land Economics Honor Society)

- Confrere Order of Knights of the Hospital of St. John of Jerusalem, appointed by Her Majesty Queen Elizabeth II to help serve medical needs of children of all faiths caught up in the wars of the Middle East

Breast star of a Knight of Grace of Most Venerable Order of the Hospital of St John of Jerusalem

Queen Elizabeth II appointed me to become a confrère in the Venerable Order of St. John and appointed my son John Stricklin as a confrère. The Order of St John, formally The Most Venerable Order of the Hospital of St. John of Jerusalem (French: l'ordre très vénérable de l'Hôpital de Saint-Jean de Jérusalem) is a British royal order of chivalry first constituted in 1888 by royal charter from Queen Victoria. The Order traces its origins back to the Knights Hospitaller in the Middle Ages, the Order of Malta. A faction emerged in France in the 1820s and moved to Britain in the early 1830s, where, after operating under a succession of grand priors, it became associated with the founding in 1882 of the St John Ophthalmic Hospital near the old city of Jerusalem and the St John Ambulance Brigade in 1887. The order is found throughout the Commonwealth of Nations, Hong Kong, the Republic of Ireland, and the United States, with the worldwide mission "to prevent and relieve sickness and injury, and to act to enhance the health and well-being of people anywhere in the world." Recommendations are made by the Grand Council and those selected have generally acted in such a manner as to strengthen the spirit of mankind—as reflected in the order's first motto, Pro Fide—and to encourage and promote humanitarian and charitable work aiding those in sickness, suffering, and/or danger—as reflected in the order's other motto, Pro Utilitate Hominum. As Sovereign Head, Queen Elizabeth II confirms all appointments as she, in her absolute discretion, shall think fit. Individuals may not petition either the Grand Council nor the Queen for admission.

Published and © Copyrighted by William A. Stricklin

© 2017   Case 1-5600182531

- Nun of My Dreams © 2018 TXu 2-093-545 ISBN 978-1-48098-155-3

- Dollie's Secret – Survivor of the DeKalb, Texas, Indian Raid - Nonfiction – © 1-5564559089 © 2017 TXu 2-067-664

- A Pregnant Nun a historical novel - Nonfiction – Copyright © Case 1-8558966897 © 2019 Pau 3-833-744 - ISBN 978-1-09830-437-9

- A Hundred Secrets Volume 1 Books 1-20 nonfiction Copyright © Case 1-7072486931 © 2018 TXu 2-105-513 - ISBN 978-1-64530- 435-7 - &

- A Hundred Secrets Vol 2 Books 21-100 nonfiction 100 secrets © Case 1-6749127961 © 2018 TXu 2-105-513 - ISBN 978-1-64530-435-7

- Why Weren't the Kurds at Normandy? Parody Lyrics © 2019 Pau 3-998-562

- S'more Secrets - Sleepover Stories to be Told in Darkness Volume 1 Bedtime stories for kids ©2019 - TXu 2-129-150 - ISBN 978-1-64426-708-0

- S'more Secrets - Sleepover Stories to be Told in Darkness Volume 2 for tweens and teens - Fiction -© 2018 Case 1-7262889391 © 2018 TXu 2-129-150 - ISBN 798-1-64530-433-3

- S'more Secrets - Sleepover Stories to be Told in Darkness Volume 3 scary stories to be told in darkness to grownups – Fiction - © 2018 TXu 2-189-150 - ISBN 798-1-64530-454-0

- The Nurse's Secret - Kjellfrid's Secret - Nonfiction - ©2019 1-5985073311 © 2019 TXu 2-074-508

- Emily's Secret – Emily's Cargo Cult of 40 Mates in Irian Jaya - Nonfiction - © 1-5985016941 © 2019 TXu 2-074-514

- Katie's Secret – The Arsenic Murder Trials of Katie Browder Stricklin - Nonfiction - © 1-5714428421 © 2019 TXu 2-065-209

- Bad Breakup at 430 Lafayette Street - Nonfiction - Copyright © 2017 Case 1-5592907361 - © 2017 TXu 2-060-686

- Aesop Fables and The Candy Rabbit bedtime stories for kids - © 2019 - ISBN 978-1-54399-921-1

- The Prince and I - Miss Olive - historic novel - Unsolved murder of my nanny's former charge © 2019 TXu 2-139-737 - ISBN 978-1-64530-432-6

- One Corinthians nonfiction sermon delivered at Saint Clements' Church, Berkeley, 11AM December 11, 1949 © 2020 - ISBN 978-1-54389-951-8

- Senatorial Courtesy – nonfiction life-saving senatorial courtesy Senator John William Warner III - Nonfiction - Copyright © 2020 1-837259272592781 ©2020 - ISBN 978-1-54399-891-7

- Ladies Day – nonfiction account of misogyny at Harvard Law School professors during 1960s © 2020 ISBN 978-1-5499-920-4

- A Perfect Crime a historical novel © 2020 - ISBN 978-1-09830-140-8

- Four Score and More – nonfiction autobiography of a long life Case © 2019 TXu 2-167-560 ISBN 978-1-54399-922-8

- Easter Parade nonfiction COVID-19 © 2020 - ISBN 978-1-09830-945-9

- Ambrose Bierce anthology of Ambrose Bierce's 70 best of his 249 short stories © Case 1-8725184511 Copyright © 2020 - ISBN 978-1-09831-080-6

- George Sterling A Wine of Wizardry anthology of George Sterling's 20 best poems 1-8731197451 © 2020 - ISBN 978-1-09831-102-5

- The Boss – nonfiction 18-mos service to VP Richard M. Nixon © 2020 - ISBN 978-1-09830-750-9

- Epilogue – nonfiction account of crimes of President Richard M. Nixon and Presidential staff 1-8592617481 © 2020 - ISBN 978-1-54399-891-7

- White Fox and White Buffalo – Comanche abduction my maternal grandmother's maternal grandmother:

- White Fox – Book 1 Prequel to White Buffalo -Nonfiction Copyright © 2020 – Case 1-8842056821 and White Buffalo

- – Book 2 Sequel to White Fox -Nonfiction © 2020 – Case 1-8862149151 TXu2-093-545 ISBN 978-1-09831-836-9

- Roses Among the Thorns -- The Founders of the Bohemian Club – Nonfiction © 2020 TXu 2-195-967 Case No. 1-8791258541 ISBN 978-1-09831-738-6

- Crazy – Nonfiction plus five short stories that are fiction historical novels © 2020 Case No. 1-8946543741 – first edition ISBN 978-1-09832-149-9 and second edition ISBN 978-1-0983-2399-8

- Thistlewood Non©2020 TXu 2-206-871 ISBN 978-1-09832-390-5

- Twice Upon A Time – ©2020 Case 1-9245623151 ISBN 978-1-09833-861-9

- Alice Blue Gown –©2020 Nonfiction Case 1-9105640341 - ISBN 978-1-09833-191-7

- Day of Infamy – Pearl Harbor Day – The Ni'ihau Incident - Nonfiction - © Case No. 1-9381160911 © 2020 TXu 2-222-380 ISBN 978-1-09834-126-8

- The Plumbers Introduction – Non© 2020 TXu 2-217-462 Case No. 1-9185174771 ISBN 978-1-09833-500-7

- The Plumbers Volume 1 – United Airlines Flight No. 553 - Unsolved Mystery of Missing $2,000,000 – Watergate Burglars - Nonfiction Copyright © 2020 TXu 2-217-462 Case No. 1-9185174771 - ISBN 978-1-09833-400-0

- The Plumbers Volume 2 – Nonfiction Copyright © 2020 TXu 2-217-462 Case No. 1-9185174771 - ISBN 978-1-09833-401-7

- Ted: historical novel ©2020 Case 1-9620202411 TXu 2-225-762 - ISBN 978-1-09834-717-8

- Trump Plague – What did he know and when did he know it? Nonfiction - © 2020 TXu 2-219-947 Case No. 1-9264731081 ISBN 978-1-09833-825-1

- Reverse Santa Nonfiction Case 1-9990314981 © 2020 TXu 2-234-240 ISBN 978-1-09835-902-7

- Pardon Me Nonfiction Case 1-10029277321 © 2021 TXu 2-237-

084 ISBN 978-1-09836-275-9

- Tiny Hands Loser Non© 2021 TXu 2-237-155 Case No. 1-10029325830 ISBN 978-1-09836-204-1

- Widow of Friedrich Christian Anton "Fritz" Lang Non©2021 TXu 2-251-784 Hardcover ISBN 978-1-09837-577-5 ISBN 978-1-09837-157-9

- The Man in the Brown Suit by Agatha Christie - Fiction Republished 2021

- Poirot Investigates by Agatha Christie - Fiction 2021

- The Mysterious Affair at Styles by Agatha Christie - Fiction Republished 2021

- 125 Bedtime Stories Still Untold to My Most Beloved Daughter Sarai Stricklin (09.28.1959 – 06.19.2021) - Book 1

- – Stories 1-52 - Fiction by original authors Republished 2021- © 2021 ISBN 978-1-09837-566-9

- 125 Bedtime Stories Still Untold to My Most Beloved Daughter Sarai Stricklin (09.28.1959-06.19.2021) Book 1 Stories 1-52 - Fiction Anthology Republished in June 2021- © 2021 ISBN 978-1-09837-566-9

- Mary Eliska's Untold Stories - Bedtime Stories Still Untold to my Daughter Mary Eliska Books 1-26 © 2021-

- Mary Eliska's Untold Bedtime Stories of Japan, China, India, Israel, Europe and America - © 2021 TXu 2-254-154

- Mary Eliska's Untold Stories - Book 1 The Yellow Fairy Tales Book - © 2021 ISBN 978-1-09838-368-8

- Mary Eliska's Untold Stories - Book 2 The Red Fairy Tales Book - Tales of India by Rudyard Kipling - © 2021 ISBN 978-1-09838-424-1

- Mary Eliska's Untold Stories - Book 3 The Blue Fairy Tales Book - Jungle Books by Rudyard Kipling - © 2021 ISBN 978-1-09838-425-8

- Mary Eliska's Untold Stories - Book 4 The Orange Fairy Tales Book - Kim by Rudyard Kipling © 2021 ISBN 979-1-09838-438-4

- Mary Eliska's Untold Stories - Book 5 The Purple Fairy Tales Book – The Wind in the Willows by Kenneth Grahame; The Tale of Jimmy Rabbit by Albert Scott Bailey; The Velveteen Rabbit by Margery Williams; The Adventures of Danny the Meadow Mouse and The Adventures of Reddy Fox by Thornton W. Burgess; and, by Beatrix Potter: an anthology of Bedtime Stories; The Tale of Peter Rabbit; The Tale of Benjamin Bunny; The Tale of Johnny Town-Mouse; The Tale of Squirrel Nutkins; The Tale of Ginger and Pickles; and The Story of a Fierce Bad Rabbit. Mary Eliska's Untold Stories - Book 5 The Purple Fairy Tales Book – © 2021 Case 1-10518564131

- Mary Eliska Girl Detective – Volume 1 Books 1-13 borrowed from Mildred Augustine Wirt Benson's Penny Parker Stories -© 2021 ISBN 978-1-09837-244-6

- Mary Eliska Girl Detective - Book 1 - Clue of the Silken Ladder -© 2021 – Behind the Green Door - © 2021 – and The Deserted Yacht - © 2021 Case 1-10130208421 ISBN 978-1-09837-625-3

- Mary Eliska Girl Detective - Book 2 - Ghost Beyond the Gate - © 2021 – The Missing Formula – © 2021 - The Vanishing Comrade - © 2021 Case 1-10130208421 ISBN 978-1-09837-626-0

- Mary Eliska Girl Detective Professor Brankel's Secret Book 2 ©2023 TXu 2-358-212 ©2021 1-11299173361 98pp Mary Eliska Girl Detective - Book 3 - Guilt of the Brass Thieves – The Little French Girl - © 2021 Case 1-10130208421 ISBN 978-1-09837-627-7

- Mary Eliska Girl Detective - Book 4 - Hoofbeats on the Turnpike - © 2021 e 1-10130208421 ISBN 978-1-09837-249-1 ISBN 978-1-09837-628-4

- Mary Eliska Girl Detective - Book 5 - Saboteurs on the River - ©2021 Case 1-10130208421 ISBN 978-1-09837-245-3 ISBN 978-1-09837-629-1

- Mary Eliska Girl Detective - Book 6 - Signal in the Dark - © 2021 Case 1-10130208421 ISBN 978-1-09837-630-7 Hardcover 978-1-09837-251-4

- Mary Eliska Girl Detective - Book 7 - Swamp Island © 2021 –

The Clue of the Gold Coin - © 2021 TXu 2-265-659 – and The Silver Ring Mystery Book 570-© Case 1-10156100271 ©2021 TXu 2-265-652 Case 1-10574287601 and Case 1-10574287730 ISBN 978-1-09837-631-4

- Mary Eliska Girl Detective - Book 8 - The Wishing Well – The Lorelei Rupert Mystery – The Old Maid Fiction Case 1-10130208421 Case 1-10156100271 Case 1-10582290111 ISBN 978-1-09837-632-1

- Mary Eliska Girl Detective - Book 9 - The Cry at Midnight - © 2021 – The Stowmarket Mystery - © 2021 Case 1-10130208421 Case 1-10595752961 ISBN 978-1-09837-633-8

- Mary Eliska Girl Detective - Book 10 - The Secret Pact – © 2021 Case 1-10130208421 The Mystery at Dark Cedars Book 572 - © 2021 Case 1-10602161171 – The Mystery of the Fires Book 573 - © 2021 Case 1-10676148519 – The Mystery of the Secret Band Book 574 - © 2021 Case 1-10676090161 ISBN 978-1-09837-634-5

- Mary Eliska Girl Detective - Book 11 - Whispering Walls - © 2021 – The Phantom Friend Book 579 - © 2021 [Stave Two] – The Puzzle in the Pond Book 580 – [Stave Three] © 2021 Case 1-10130208421 ISBN 978-1-09837-635-2

- Mary Eliska Girl Detective - Book 12 - Voice from the Cave – The Orinda Mystery Book 50 - © 2021 Case 1-10130208421 © 2021 TXu 2-264-787 Case 1-10557865731 ISBN 978-1-09837-636-9

- Mary Eliska Girl Detective - Book 13 - The Clock Strikes Thirteen - © 2021 1-10130208421 ISBN 978-1-09837-637-6

- Mary Eliska Girl Detective - Book 14 - The Santa Claus Bank Robbery - © 2021 Case 1-10156100271 [Staves 5 & 6 Republished in Book 11]

- Mary Eliska Girl Detective - Book 15 - The Deserted Yacht - [Republished as Book 1 Stave 3]

- Mary Eliska Girl Detective - Book 16 - The Mystery of the Sundial - [Republished as Book 4 Stave Three]

- Mary Eliska Girl Detective - The Mystery of a Hansom Cab– Book

20 © 2022 TXu 2-307-367 Case No. © 2022 1-11231552371 318pp

- Mary Eliska Girl Detective – The Mystery of Madame Midas– Book 21 © 2022 TXu 2-314-023 Case No. 1-11299310531 327pp

- Mary Eliska Girl Detective - Book 28 – Behind the Green Door - [Republished as Book 1 Stave Two]

- Mary Eliska Girl Detective - Book 29 - The Missing Formula - [Republished as Book 2 Stave Two]

- Mary Eliska Girl Detective - Book 30 – Danger at the Drawbridge - [Republished as Book 1 Stave Two]

- Mary Eliska Girl Detective - Book 31 - The Mystery of 31 New Inn - © 2021 ISBN 978-1-09837-694-9

- Mary Eliska Girl Detective - Book 32 – Mary Eliska Finds A Clue - [Republished as Book 6 Stave Three]

- Mary Eliska Girl Detective - Book 36 - The Eye of Osiris - © 2021 ISBN 978-1-09837-705-2

- Mary Eliska Girl Detective - Book 37 - The Mystery of the Lost Key - [Republished as Book 6 Stave Two]

- Mary Eliska Girl Detective - Book 38 - The Mystery of the Red Thumb Mark -

- Mary Eliska Girl Detective - Book 39 - The Uttermost Farthing - © 2021 ISBN 978-1-09837-695-6

- Mary Eliska Girl Detective - Books 40-48 - Doctor Thorndyke's Cases - © 2021 ISBN 978-1-09837-706-9

- Mary Eliska Girl Detective - The Mystery of the Rainbow Feather – Book 41 © 2022 TXu 2-307370 Case No. 1-11231594691 234pp

- Mary Eliska Girl Detective - The Mystery of The Silent House– Book 45 © 2022

- Mary Eliska Girl Detective - Book 50 – The Orinda Mystery - ©2021 TXu 2-264-787 - [Book 12 Stave 2] The Orinda Mystery Book 50 - © 2021 Case 1-10130208421 © 2021 TXu 2-264-787

- Mary Eliska Girl Detective - The Millionaire Mystery – Book 54

© 2022

- Mary Eliska Girl Detective - The Mystery Whom God Hath Joined– Book 58 © 2022

- Mary Eliska Girl Detective - Book 59 – Mary Eliska Girl Detective and the Lorelei Rupert Mystery – © 2021 - Case 1-10582290111©2021 TXu 2-265-775 - [Republished as Book 8 Stave Two]

- Mary Eliska Girl Detective - The Mystery of a Coin of Edward VII - Book 63 © 2022 TXu 2-309-496 Case 1-11243958179 269pp

- Mary Eliska Girl Detective - The Mystery of the Yellow Holly – Book 64 © 2022 TXu 2-309-497 Case No. 1-11243958228 366pp

- Mary Eliska Girl Detective - The Mystery of The Girl From Malta– Book 65 –© 2022

- Mary Eliska Girl Detective - The Mystery of the Mandarin's Fan - Book 68 © 2022 TXu 2-309-498 Case 1-11243958130 282pp

- Mary Eliska Girl Detective - The Mystery of the Red Window – Book 69 © 2022 TXu 2-309-502 Case No. 1-11243958070 399pp

- Mary Eliska Girl Detective - The Mystery of Lady Jim of Curzon Street – Book 73 © 2022 TXu 2-315-157 Case 1-11337674021 526pp

- Mary Eliska Girl Detective - The Mystery of the Opal Serpent - Book 74 © 2022 TXu 2-313-114 Case No. 1-11277466081 298pp

- Mademoiselle Mary Eliska and The Phantom of the Opera - Book 76 © 2022 TXu 2-298-864 1-11110548251 326pp

- Mary Eliska Girl Detective - The Mystery of The Red-Headed Man - Book 81 © 2022 No. 1-11152531130 250pp

- Mary Eliska Girl Detective – The Mystery of the Sacred Herb – Book 84 © 2022 TXu 2-313-113 Case No. 1-11277515711 344pp

- Mary Eliska Girl Detective – The Mystery of the Sealed Message –Book 85 © 2022 TXu 2-313-112 Case No. 1-11277515950 296pp

- Mary Eliska Girl Detective – The Mystery of the Green Mummy – Book 88 © 2022 TXu 2-310-325 Case 1-11277549430 282pp

- Mary Eliska Girl Detective – The Mystery of the Disappearing Eye – Book 91 (1909) © 2022 329pp

- Mary Eliska Girl Detective – The Mystery of the Solitary Farm - Book 92 © 2022 112pp

- Mary Eliska Girl Detective – The Mystery of the Crowned Skull – Book 99 ©2022 TXu 2-309-552 1-11263042361

- Mary Eliska Girl Detective - The Mystery of Monsieur Judas– Book 104 © 2022

- Mary Eliska Girl Detective – The Mystery Queen – Book 106 (1912) © 2022 294pp

- Mary Eliska Girl Detective – The Mystery of Red Money – Book 107 © 2022 268pp

- Mary Eliska Girl Detective – The Mystery of the Lost Parchment - Book 115 © 2022

- Mary Eliska Girl Detective – The Mystery of Streets of Fear © 2022

- Mary Eliska Girl Detective - Fantômas Captured - Book 176 - © 2022

- Mary Eliska Girl Detective and the Mystery of the Harlequin Opal – Books 91, 92 and 93 © 2022 TXu 2-358-227 Case 1-11299311170

- Mary Eliska Girl Detective Professor Brankel's Secret Book 2 ©2023 TXu 2-358-212 ©2021 1-11299173361 98pp

- Mary Eliska Girl Detective - The Mystery of The Yellow Room – Book 70 © 2021 TXu 2-274-3701-10740460241 266pp

- Mary Eliska Girl Detective – The Mystery of the White Room – Book 71 © 2022 TXu 2-301-956 Case No. 1-11152531001

- Mademoiselle Rouletabille Mary Eliska Girl Detective - The Secret of the Night – Book 72 © 2021 TXu 2-295-430 294pp

- Mary Eliska Girl Detective – The Guarded Heights – Book 73 © 2022 TXu 2-201-503 Case No. 1-11144498241

- Mary Eliska Girl Detective – The Mystery of The Spider – Book 74 © 2022 TXu 2-301-934 Case No. 1-11152531030

- Mary Eliska Girl Detective - The Temple of Death – The Bride of the Sun King – Book 75 © 2021 TXu 2-296-617 Case 1-11077748851

- Mademoiselle Mary Eliska Girl Detective - The Phantom of the Opera – Book 76 © 2022 TXu 2-298-864 Case1-11110548251 326pp

- Mary Eliska Girl Detective - The Mystery of The Abandoned Room – Book 77 © 2022 TXu 2-299-769 No. 1-1119216531 559pp

- Mary Eliska Girl Detective - The Mystery of The Gray Mask – Book 78 © 2022 TXu 2-300-373 No. 1-11125258241 261pp

- Mary Eliska Girl Detective – The Mystery of the Scarlet Bat – Book 79 © 2022 TXu 2-301-961 Case No. 1-11152531059

- Mary Eliska Girl Detective – The Mystery of The Secret Passage – Book 80 © 2022 TXu 2-301-964 Case No. 1-11152498331 278

- Mary Eliska Girl Detective – The Mystery of the Red-Headed Man – Book 81 © 2022 TXu 2-301-967 Case No. 1-11152531130

- Mary Eliska Girl Detective - Book 82 – The Pagan's Cup and Silver Bullet - © 2021 - ISBN 978-1-09837-420-4 and 978-1-09837-717-5

- Mary Eliska Girl Detective - The Mystery of the Pagan's Cup - Book 82 © 2022 TXu 2-307-868 Case 1-11237102261 218pp

- Mary Eliska Girl Detective - Book 86 - The Mystery of the Disappearing Eye © 2021 -

- Mary Eliska Girl Detective - Book 88 - The Mystery of the Opal Serpent - © 2021 -

- Mary Eliska Girl Detective - Book 90 - The Mystery of the Yellow Holly - © 2021 - ISBN 978-1-09837-713-7

- Mary Eliska Girl Detective and the Mystery of the Harlequin Opal – Books 91, 92 and 93 © 2022 TXu 2-358-227 Case 1-11299311170

- Mary Eliska Girl Detective - Book 97 - The Mystery of the Sealed Message - © 2021

- Mary Eliska Girl Detective – The Mystery of the Society of Flies - Book 106 © 2022 TXu 2-314-501 Case1- 11326931241 299pp

- Mary Eliska Girl Detective - The Mystery of The Peacock of Jewels– Book 107 © 2022 1-10336308231 452pp

- Mary Eliska Girl Detective - Book 108 - The Mystery of a Hansom Cab - © 2021

- Mary Eliska Girl Detective - Book 134 – The Mystery of the Whispering Lane - © Case 1- 11354442141

- Mary Eliska Girl Detective - Book 135 – The Mystery of the Caravan Crime - © 2022 TXu 2-316-997 Case No 1-11354441431

- Mary Eliska Girl Detective - Book 423 - Vanishing Man © 2021 -

- Mary Eliska Girl Detective - Book 543 - The Gentleman Who Vanished © 2021

- Mary Eliska Girl Detective - Book 546 - The Lady From Nowhere - © 2021 – 1-10759399892

- Mary Eliska Girl Detective - The Mystery of the Purple Fern Book 553 ©2021 TXu 2-315-921 Case 1-11338176181

- Mary Eliska Girl Detective - Book 564 – The Mystery of the Wooden Hand - © Case 1- 11344674401

- Mary Eliska Girl Detective - Book 566 - The Mystery of the Sycamore - © 2021 -   [Republished as Book 8 Stave Two]

- Mary Eliska Girl Detective - Book 567 - The Mystery of the Red House - Fiction Case No. 1-10547943101 © 2021 TXu 2-264-820 - ISBN 968-1-09838-972-7

- Mary Eliska Girl Detective - Book 568 - The Little French Girl – by Anne Douglas Sedgwick - [Book 3 Stave 2]

- Mary Eliska Girl Detective - Book 569 - The Clue of the Gold Coin - ©2021 TXu 2-265-659-   [Republished Book 7 Stave 2]

- Mary Eliska Girl Detective - Book 570 - The Silver Ring Mystery - © 2021 - TXu 2-265-652 [Published Book 7 Stave 3]

- Mary Eliska Girl Detective - Book 571 - The Stowmarket Mystery - © 2021 Case 1-10595752961 ©2021 TXu 2-2662-430 - [Republished as Book 9 Stave 2]

- Mary Eliska Girl Detective –The Mystery at Dark Cedars Book 572 © 2021 TXu 2-308-721 Case 1-10602161171

- Mary Eliska Girl Detective - Book 572 – The Mystery at Dark Cedars - © Case 1- 10595752961 - © 2021   [Book 10 Stave 2]

- Mary Eliska Girl Detective - The Mystery of the Secret Band Book 573 ©2021 TXu 2-270-007 Case 1-10676090161

- Mary Eliska Girl Detective - Book 573 – The Mystery of the Secret Band - © Case 1- 10595752961 – [Republished Book 10 Stave 4]

- Mary Eliska Girl Detective and the Mystery of the Fires - Book 574 © 2021 TXu 2-269-991 Case 1-10676148519

- Mary Eliska Girl Detective - Book 574 – The Mystery of the Fires - © 2021 - Case 1- 10595752961 - [Published Book10 Stave 3]

- Mary Eliska Girl Detective - Book 575 - The Uttermost Parts of the Sea –- © 2021 - Case 1-10692479811 - ISBN 978-1-09839-778-4

- Mary Eliska Girl Detective - Book 576 - The Polly Page Yacht Club – Fiction by Izola Louise Forrester -   [Published Book 1 Stave 2]

- Mary Eliska Girl Detective - Book 577 - The Vanishing Comrade - © 2021 -   [Republished as Book 2 Stave Three]

- Mary Eliska Girl Detective - Book 578 - The Mystery Girl - Fiction -   [Republished as Book 4 Stave Two]

- Mary Eliska Girl Detective - Book 579 – The Phantom Friend - © 2021- [Published Book 11 Stave 2]

- Mary Eliska Girl Detective - Book 580 - The Puzzle in the Pond - ©2021 [Published Book11 Stave3]

- Mary Eliska Girl Detective - Book 584 - The Last Stroke - © 2021 – 1-10759399851

- Thrice Upon A Time - Horrific Stories Not for Bedtime © 2020

- Bedtime Stories for Bad Children – An Anthology of Ghost Stories – Volume 1 – © 2022 Case No. 1-11616027741

- Bedtime Stories for Bad Children – An Anthology of Creepy Stories – Volume 2 – © 2022 Case No. 1-11626445221

- Disconcerting Stories for Grownups - Not To Tell to Children in Darkness at Bedtime © 2022 TXu 2-336-941 Case No. 1-1170127589

- Mary Eliska Girl Detective Girl Aviatrix Series Sixty Adventure Stories © 2024 Case No. 1-14214796651

- Book 1 - Mary Eliska Girl Detective Girl Aviatrix - Wins Her Wings © 2022 Case No. 1-11371703511

- Book 2 - Mary Eliska Girl Detective Girl Aviatrix - The Mystery Plane © 2022 Case No. 1-11371703511

- Book 3 - Mary Eliska Girl Detective Girl Aviatrix -- Solves the Conway Case © 2022 Case No. 1-11371703511

- Book 4 - Mary Eliska Girl Detective Girl Aviatrix – The Double Cousins © 2022 Case No. 1-11371703511

- Book 5 - Mary Eliska Girl Detective Girl Aviatrix - The Air Pilot Mystery © 2022 Case No. 1-11371703511

- Book 6 - Mary Eliska Girl Detective Girl Aviatrix -- The Ocean Flight Mystery © 2022 Case No. 1-11371703511

- Book 7 - Mary Eliska Girl Detective Girl Aviatrix – Flying Girl © 2022 TXu 2-326-043 Case No. 1-11376521721

- Book 8 - Mary Eliska Girl Detective Girl Aviatrix - Flying Girl and Her Chum © 2022 TXu 2-326-043 No. 1-11376521721

- Book 9 - Mary Eliska Girl Detective Girl Aviatrix -- The Hollywood Flight © 2022 TXu 2-326-043 Case No. 1-11376521721

- Book 10 - Mary Eliska Girl Detective Girl Aviatrix – Gypsies of the Air © 2022 TXu 2-326-043 Case No. 1-11376521721

- Book 11 - Mary Eliska Girl Detective Girl Aviatrix - The Island Adventure © 2022 TXu 2-326-043 Case No. 1-11376521721

- Book 12 - Mary Eliska Girl Detective Girl Aviatrix – The Mystery of Seal Islands © 2022 TXu 2-326-043 NO. 1-11376521721

- Book 13 - Mary Eliska Girl Detective Girl Aviatrix - The Phantom Airship © 2022 TXu 2-326-043 Case No. 1-11376521721

- Book 14 - Mary Eliska Girl Detective Girl Aviatrix - Girl Pilots on Golden Wings – © 2022 TXu 2-326-043 Case 1-11376521721

- Book 15 - Mary Eliska Girl Detective Girl Aviatrix – The Sky Cruise © 2022 TXu 2-326-043 Case No. 1-11376521721

- Book 16 - Mary Eliska Girl Detective Girl Aviatrix– The Motor Butterfly © 2022 TXu 2-326-043 Case No. 1-11376521721

- Book 17 - Mary Eliska Girl Detective Girl Aviatrix - The Air Perilous Summer © 2022 TXu 2-326-043 Case No. 1-11376521721

- Book 18 - Mary Eliska Girl Detective Girl Aviatrix - On Adventure Island ©2022 TXu 2-326-043 No. 1-11376521721

- Appendix 1: Amelia Earhart Appendix 2: Women Aviators Appendix 3: Charles Lindbergh

- Preview Hawai'ian Bedtime Stories - Legends and Myths of Hawai'i ©2022 TXu 2-330-801

- Book 19 Mary Eliska Girl Detective Girl Aviatrix – The Double Cousins © 2022 Case No. 1-11371703511

- Book 20 Mary Eliska Girl Detective Girl Aviatrix - The Sky Detective - How She Got Her Man © 2023 No. 1-12136217511

- Book 21 Mary Eliska Girl Detective Girl Aviatrix - Eagle of the Sky - Along the Air Lanes © 2023 Case No. 1-12136217511

- Book 22 Mary Eliska Girl Detective Girl Aviatrix - Wings Over Rockies - Cloud Chaser © 2023 1-12136217511

- Book 23 Mary Eliska Girl Detective Girl Aviatrix - The Sky Pilot's Great Chase and Dead Stick Landing No. 1-12179904021

- Book 24 Mary Eliska Girl Detective Girl Aviatrix - Trackers of the Fog Pack Flying Blind No. 1-12179904021

- Book 25 Mary Eliska Girl Detective Girl Aviatrix -- Flying the Coast Skyways Swift Patrol No. 1-12179904021

- Book 26 Mary Eliska Girl Detective Girl Aviatrix - Over the Atlantic - The Longest Flight on Record © 2024 Case No. 1-14214796651

- Book 27 Mary Eliska Girl Detective Girl Aviatrix - Wizard Work in the Clouds © 2024 Case No. 1-14214796651

- Book 28 Mary Eliska Girl Detective Girl Aviatrix - A Cruise in the Sky © 2024 Case No. 1-14214796651

- Book 29 Mary Eliska Girl Detective Girl Aviatrix - Air Monster © 2024 Case No. 1-14214796651

- Book 30 Mary Eliska Girl Detective Girl Aviatrix - Flying for Victory Bombing the Last German Stronghold © 2024 Case No. 1-14214796651

- Book 31 Mary Eliska Girl Detective Girl Aviatrix - In the Big Battle Silencing the Big Guns © 2024 Case No. 1-14214796651

- Book 32 Mary Eliska Girl Detective Girl Aviatrix - In Southern Waters – The Search for Deserted Steam Yacht © 2024 Case No. 1-14214796651

- Book 33 Mary Eliska Girl Detective Girl Aviatrix - Over the Enemy's Lines - The German Spy's Secret © 2024 Case No. 1-14214796651

- Book 34 Mary Eliska Girl Detective Girl Aviatrix - Over the Rhine Fighting Above the Clouds © 2024 Case No. 1-14214796651

- Book 35 Mary Eliska Girl Detective Girl Aviatrix - Battling the Big Horn © 2024 Case No. 1-14214796651

- Book 36 Mary Eliska Girl Detective Girl Aviatrix = Daring Wings © 2024 Case No. 1-14214796651

- Book 37 Mary Eliska Girl Detective Girl Aviatrix - Her Giant Airship A Marvelous Trip Across the Atlantic © 2024 Case No. 1-14214796651

- Book 38 Mary Eliska Girl Detective Girl Aviatrix - Her Hydroplane Daring Adventures over the Great Lake © 2024 Case No. 1-14214796651

- Book 39 Mary Eliska Girl Detective Girl Aviatrix - Around the World A Young Aviatrix Among Many Nations ©2024 Case No. 1-14214796651

- Book 40 Mary Eliska Girl Detective Girl Aviatrix - In the Clouds for Fame and Fortune © 2024 Case No. 1-14214796651

- Book 41 Mary Eliska Girl Detective Girl Aviatrix - and the Cave of Mystery Adrift on the Pacific © 2024 Case No. 1-14214796651

- Book 42 Mary Eliska Girl Detective Girl Aviatrix - In the Clouds for Uncle Sam © 2024 Case No. 1-14214796651

- Book 43 Mary Eliska Girl Detective Girl Aviatrix - Treasure Hunt Daring Adventures in South America © 2024 Case No. 1-14214796651

- Book 44 Mary Eliska Girl Detective Girl Aviatrix - Lost on the Moon in Quest of the Field of Diamonds © 2024 Case No. 1-14214796651

- Book 45 Mary Eliska Girl Detective Girl Aviatrix - On a Torn-Away World Captives of the Great Earthquake © 2024 Case No. 1-14214796651

- Book 46 Mary Eliska Girl Detective Girl Aviatrix - Quest for Aztec Treasure © 2024 Case No. 1-14214796651

- Book 47 Mary Eliska Girl Detective Girl Aviatrix – Adrift © 2024 Case No. 1-14214796651

- Book 48 Mary Eliska Girl Detective Girl Aviatrix - Due North © 2024 Case No. 1-14214796651

- Book 49 Mary Eliska Girl Detective Girl Aviatrix - The Flight of the Flying Cow © 2024 Case No. 1-14214796651

- Book 50 Mary Eliska Girl Detective Girl Aviatrix - in the Barren North © 2024 Case No. 1-14214796651

- Book 51 Mary Eliska Girl Detective Girl Aviatrix - Ocean Flyer - New York to London in Twelve Hours © 2024 Case No. 1-14214796651

- Book 52 Mary Eliska Girl Detective Girl Aviatrix - On the Wing Seeking the Airship Treasure © 2024 Case No. 1-14214796651

- Book 53 Mary Eliska Girl Detective Girl Aviatrix - Over the Rockies A Mystery of the Air © 2024 Case No. 1-14214796651

- Book 54 Mary Eliska Girl Detective Girl Aviatrix - The Sky Trail © 2024 Case No. 1-14214796651

- Book 55 Mary Eliska Girl Detective Girl Aviatrix - A Run for the Golden Cup © 2024 Case No. 1-14214796651

- Book 56 Mary Eliska Girl Detective Girl Aviatrix - The Stolen Airplane © 2024 Case No. 1-14214796651

- Book 57 Mary Eliska Girl Detective Girl Aviatrix - Under the Ocean to the South Pole - Strange Cruise of Submarine Wonder © 2024 Case No. 1-14214796651

- Book 58 Mary Eliska Girl Detective Girl Aviatrix - Nobody's Girl © 2024 Case No. 1-14214796651

- Book 59 Mary Eliska Girl Detective Girl Aviatrix – Autobiography Six Months with Grandmother Christine © 2024 Case No. 1-14214796651

- Book 60 Mary Eliska Girl Detective Girl Aviatrix - Autobiography – My Final Stories © 2024 Case No. 1-14214796651

- Liam McAdams Boy Aviator Stories Series

- Fiction © 2023 TXu 2-379-009 Case No. 1-12213237491

- Volume 1 Liam McAdams Boy Aviator Stories

- Book 1: Liam McAdams In the Clouds for Uncle Sam; Liam McAdams of the Signal Corps

- Book 2: Liam McAdams and the Stolen Airplane; how Liam McAdams made good.

- Book 3: Liam McAdams and the Airplane Express; the Boy Aeronaut's Grit.

- Book 4: Liam McAdams and the Boy Aeronauts Club; Flying for Fun.

- Book 5: Liam McAdams' Cruise in the sky; the Legend of the Great Pink Pearl.

- Bonus Book 10: Liam McAdams The Quest of the Aztec Treasure

- Volume 2 Liam McAdams Boy Aviator Stories

- Book 6: Liam McAdams Battling the Bighorn; the Airplane in the Rockies.

- Book 7: Liam McAdams When Scout Meets Scout; The Airplane Spy.

- Book 8: Liam McAdams On the Edge of the Arctic: An Airplane in Snow Land.

- Book 9: Liam McAdams' Ocean Flyer – New York to London in

Twelve Hours

- Book 10: Liam McAdams The Quest of the Aztec Treasure In Passing **ã pa'sã** Four Score and Seven – © 2023 TXu 2-373-861 ISBN 979-8-35091-176-3

- Mariticide Club Wives Who Kill Husbands Nonfiction © 2023 TXu 2-378-397 © 2023 Case No 1-12662549461

- Uxoricide Club Husbands Who Kill Wives Nonfiction © 2023 TXu 2-380-728 © 2023 Case 1-12719760611

- American Madams Nonfiction © 2023 TXu 2-379-571 ISBN 979-8-35091-340-8

- Vice Presidents of the United States of America © 2023 TXu 2-386-635 Case No 1- 12812460821

- Earliest History of the United States of America © 2023 TXu 2-389-729 Case No 1- 12939010871 ISBN

- Political Scandals of the United States of America © 2023 TXu 2-406-358 Case No 1- 12938975211 ISBN

- First Ladies of the United States of America © 2023 TXu 2-396-220 Case No. 1-13025699681 ISBN

- 1001 Untold Bedtime Stories - Sixty-four Color Fairy Books of Bedtime Stories © 2023 No. 1-13156021681

- Book Club Epilogue - Book Club Members After Half A Century - © 2023 TXu 2-407-896 1-13337151851

- Mary Eliska Girl Detective Solves the DB Cooper Case © 2024 TXu 2-416-724 Case No. 1-13535657101

- Royal Samoan Hotel – My Unfulfilled Dream Nonfiction © 2024 TXu 2-428-896 Case No. 1-13626082011

- Living with Cats - My Life Shared with Zorro and Jupiter - Published 2024 In the Public Domain

- A Library of the World's Best Mystery and Detective Stories - Anthology Published 2024 In Public Domain Disappeared From Her Home Republished in 2024 by William A Stricklin USA In the Public Domain

- London Experiences of Mary Eliska Girl Detective © 2024 by

William A Stricklin Case No. 1-14116421951

- Mary Eliska Female Detective Volume 1 © 2024 by William A. Stricklin USA Case No 1-14135463281

- Mary Eliska Female Detective Volume 2 © 2024 by William A. Stricklin USA Case No 1-14135463281

- Mary Eliska Girl Detective Adventure Stories for Girls and Kona Kai Boy Detective Adventure Stories for Boys – Fiction Anthology Published 2024 © 2024 by William A. Stricklin USA Case No 1-14188205221

- Mary Eliska Girl Detective Girl Aviatrix Series © 2024 by William A. Stricklin USA

- Mary Eliska Girl Detective Girl Aviatrix Sixty Adventure Stories © 2024 Case No. 1-14214796651

- © Copyrighted and Published by William A. Stricklin

- In Passing **ã pa'sã** Four Score and Seven – © 2023 TXu 2-373-861 Case No. ISBN 979-8-35091-176-3

- She Pirates – © 2023 TXu 2-437-960 Case No. 1-14009915281

- Mariticide Club Wives Who Kill Husbands Nonfiction © 2023 TXu 2-378-397 © 2023 Case No 1-12662549461

- Uxoricide Club Husbands Who Kill Wives Nonfiction © 2023 TXu 2-380-728 © 2023 Case 1-12719760611

- American Madams Nonfiction © 2023 TXu 2-379-571 ISBN 979-8-35091-340-8

- Vice Presidents of the United States of America © 2023 TXu 2-386-635 Case No 1- 12812460821

- Earliest History of the United States of America © 2023 TXu 2-389-729 Case No 1- 12939010871 ISBN

- Political Scandals of the United States of America © 2023 TXu 2-406-358 Case No 1- 12938975211 ISBN

- First Ladies of the United States of America © 2023 TXu 2-396-220 Case No. 1-13025699681 ISBN

- 1001 Untold Bedtime Stories - Sixty-four Color Fairy Books of

Bedtime Stories © 2023 No. 1-13156021681

- Book Club Epilogue - Book Club Members After Half a Century - © 2023 TXu 2-407-896 1-13337151851

- Mary Eliska Girl Detective Solves the DB Cooper Case © 2024 TXu 2-416-724 Case No. 1-13535657101

- Mary Eliska Girl Detective Investigates the Mystery of the Missing Grand Duchess Anastasia Nikolaevna Romanova of Russia

- © 2024 TXu 2-465-268 Case No. 1-14473336681

- Royal Samoan Hotel – My Unfulfilled Dream - Nonfiction © 2024 TXu 2-428-896 Case No. 1-13626082011

- Living with Cats - My Life Shared with Zorro and Jupiter - Published 2024 In the Public Domain

- A Library of the World's Best Mystery and Detective Stories - Anthology Published 2024 In Public Domain Disappeared From Her Home Republished in 2024 by William A Stricklin USA In the Public Domain

- London Experiences of Mary Eliska Girl Detective © 2024 TXu 2-442-854 by William A Stricklin Case No. 1-14116421951

- Mary Eliska Female Detective Volume 1 © 2024 by William A. Stricklin USA Case No 1-14135463281

- Mary Eliska Girl Detective Adventure Stories for Girls and Kona Kai Boy Detective Adventure Stories for Boys – Fiction Anthology © 2024 TXu 2-446-304 by William A. Stricklin USA Case No 1-14188205221

- Father Goose's Bedtime Stories - © 2024 TXu 2-450-595 by William A. Stricklin Case No 1-14272011541

- Among The Cannibals -Non Fiction © 2024 by William A. Stricklin USA Case No. 1-14381997011

- Mary Eliska Girl Detective 18 Mystery Stories © 2025 TXu 2-488-160 by William A Stricklin Case No. 1-14699317551

- Family Secrets Third Edition Abridged © 2025 TXu 2-493-338 by William A Stricklin Case No. 1-14927825931

- I Married A Dead Man © 2025 Case No. 1-14950638141 by